Praise for *the Arizona room*:

"Part *Grey Gardens* and part *Crime and Punishment* if John Waters wrote them, Pam Jones's *The Arizona Room* is at once a fascinating character study and a rollicking road trip novel. You won't be able to get April Nimitz's voice out of your head."

—Leland Cheuk, author of *No Good Very Bad Asian*

"Darkly undergirded, but lithe and effervescent with comic notes, Pam Jones's novel *The Arizona Room* offers the reader that rare combination of beauty and riveting entertainment. For while Jones has created a compelling and three-dimensional female protagonist, and a motley crew of colorful supporting characters, all driven along a quick and at times rollicking plot line, the real motor (and achievement) of the novel is the nearly pitch-perfect prose style. Economical, precise, concrete, and rhythmical, Jones's insistent but unobtrusive prose wins the day for *The Arizona Room* and offers the promise of more from this delightful writer."

— Salvatore Difalco, author of five books, including *The Mountie at Niagara Falls* (Anvil Press), *Mean Season* (Mansfield Press), and *Black Rabbit* (Anvil Press)

"In her newest novel, *The Arizona Room*, Pam Jones keeps us tensely tangled in a ball of yarn that is the mind of main character, April. With a jaw-dropping beginning, Jones purposely takes us on an ugly journey and with alarming clarity, lets us know nothing is simple, nothing is right about the wrongs of the past. And just because the mind is going, we are simply not allowed to forget the very bad shit. A true page turner, *The Arizona Room* offers an outside look at the inside of someone dealing with dementia -- and so much more."

— Peppur Chambers, author of *Harlem's Awakening* and *Harlem's Last Dance*

"*The Arizona Room* remains with you long after its final pages. The madness, the depravity, and the tiny slices of joy amongst the horror crawl into your mind and lay down roots. In recounting a lifetime, *The Arizona Room* moves from an adolescence marred by internment during the Second World War, to the chaotic untangling of threads woven into a lifetime built on deceit. *The Arizona Room* is a reminder that although family is the tie that binds, it is also a prison whose victims are doomed to continue the tale."

— William M. Brandon III, author *of SILENCE & Selene, The Exile The Matriarch & The Flood*, and *Welcome to Spring Street*

"*The Arizona Room* is another volume in the increasingly impressive body of work from Pam Jones, one of America's truly great writers. Here Jones deftly handles time, memory, history, and family dynamics. In *The Arizona Room* a widowed mother and her daughters struggle against the weight of history and the hard truths of America. Jones' virtuosity brings compelling depth and humor to tragedy."

— Jordan A. Rothacker, author of *The Pit, and No Other Stories*

the Arizona room

pam Jones

Denver, Colorado

Published in the United States by:
Spaceboy Books LLC
1627 Vine Street
Denver, CO 80206
www.readspaceboy.com

First printed May 2023
ISBN: 978-1-951393-21-2

To Amy and Gen

"Every real American story begins in innocence and never stops mourning the loss of it: the banishment from Eden is our one great tale, lovingly told and retold, adapted, disguised and told again..."

— Joan Didion, 1962

Following the death of her husband, April Nimitz's two grown daughters determined that the best thing for their mother would be to come to Connecticut to live with one or the other of them. The plan of action (a phrase they'd all unknowingly inherited from Juan) was as follows: They would pack up the house in Himmel Creek as soon as the funeral was over. As the house was already sold, they would tie any loose ends with the buyer. They would have a small garden party, a last hurrah, with a few neighbors. They, April, Jenny, Paloma, would then make the three-thousand-mile drive from Texas to the Nutmeg State in the Astro that Jenny had rented for the trip.

April, having known that they had done three of these things (the packing, the loose ends, the last hurrah), felt herself emerging from a state of inertia, one that had numbed her faculties and left her muscles aching, now that she'd woken. She blinked. She swallowed. She rushed for the bathroom, relieved herself there as though she had been holding it in all this time; when she was through, she was lighter for it, saluting the waste as it flushed away.

She stepped onto the porch, facing with immediacy the neighbor across the way. The neighbor was a woman called Beverly, though her surname had changed from something to something else in all the years she had lived there. Like April, both women had inherited their houses from their parents, had grown up in them. Both had brought husbands in to live there. Beverly had never had children, April had.

Beverly had not so much as looked at April for going on fifty years. She had been too afraid.

April caught the other woman moving from her house to her car with the same guarded look, head edged to one side, tennis visor pulled down and crooked, shading her eyes. Beverly seemed to know when April Nimitz was on her porch and not on her porch, and seemed only to wear the tennis visor (or any other kind of brimmed hat) when April was indoors. Now that April Nimitz was leaving, she was taking no chances—though before ducking into her car, she allowed herself one little glance that way, eyes timid and darting under the visor.

April thought, How confident she looks. She thinks she's safe now.

The bitch had not even sent a card. It might have kept April from doing what she, quite spontaneously, felt like doing at this moment. April waved, fingers dainty, as Beverly's car backed out of the drive. She waited until it was out of sight before going across.

Her daughters knew where the bitch kept the key. Beverly had liked Jenny and Paloma. If she was out of town for a weekend and needed a cat-sitter, it was Jenny she called. If she was laid up with shingles and her daylilies were drooping, it was Paloma who came to water and mulch. April would listen to them, summers, Memorial Days, Thanksgivings (and with each tale the notch of envy went up and up), dropping little anecdotes of no real consequence, how Beverly's Bell's palsy had really improved, how Beverly had gifted two shopping bags of apricots in thanks for this or that. And she could not look at April.

As it happened, there were two shopping bags of apricots in April's house this very minute. She knew them clearly, a perverse memory, the kitchen shadowy, save for that place on the countertop where the two bags sat, like bulbous jellyfish, the fruit of their innards glimpsed through the membrane; there they were, spotlit by the skylight window. They trembled awhile, and then the girls tore into them. Paloma and Jenny had been munching on the apricots all day long; they grazed over the gutted bags, shooting the pits through the window into the backyard. They reminded their mother of lionesses, brooding over a heart, a kidney. April did not feel it would be her liberty to take any fruit, though her daughters offered the bags multiple times.

Under the mat. Under the flowerpot. In all Beverly's years as a neighbor, never had she thought to change the hiding places for her keys. Never had she thought that April Nimitz might overhear the whats and the hows and the wheres of entering another person's home. Jenny and Pal would read the written instructions aloud: "Key is under the porch mat. Key is under the flowerpot."

April lifted the mat, then, finding nothing, moved to the flowerpot. There were a few of them, actually, terra cotta all and rooting spots for her herbs. Beverly had labeled them, dill, parsley, mustard, chives, and April helped herself to leaves and fronds, nibbling this, spitting that, lifting pots until she thought she saw something flash under one of them, quicksilver and gone. At the same time, she had to remember where she was. She had to watch, her daughters might suspect, though they had no reason to presume anything. They had never seen their mother and Beverly speak, much less in the same room together. Surely, they by now had reconciled the notion that the two ladies occupied separate dimensions of being and nary the two would meet, beyond a deft hello.

She rose, wiping her hands on her thighs, eyed the street, then her own house across the way. Jenny and Pal had welcomed the property inspector, whose van was parked behind Jenny's in the drive, and April watched as they let him in for the final once-over. No one saw, no one thought to look. Didn't her girls wonder where their mother was?

And she thought, Did it matter? Wasn't life's latter half meant to be free of consequence? Juan was dead; what was the point? It was thrilling—there, it was said. For a moment, April Nimitz's brain crackled and glowed, the way it might if someone had told her that God was dead, the devil was dead. When you have only to answer to your own species, you have nothing to fear.

She knew, vaguely, that she might be arrested if her timing was wrong. Beverly was the kind of woman (at least, when April knew her better, back in the day) who would call the police on a cat. (At least, this was the image that persisted, and in April's mind it had never wavered.)

She heard the voices of two passing kids, a boy and a girl. The boy glided by on a scooter, the girl panted to keep up. The boy was saying, "—the only part I wouldn't want to eat of it is the big pit in the middle." The girl, between breaths, replied, "And the skin, cuz the skin's the poisonous part—" The boy went on, "—cuz there was this lady, who did eat that part and she died, and she was from France—"

She was patient until they passed, bent again. It was the pot of dill, April discovered, and she grabbed up the key, not bothering to right the planter. And then she thought, As long as no one's looking, knocking the cilantro with her heel, the parsley, the thyme. None of the planters cracked, though they did leave a marvelous spill of soil over the porch. The roots of the herbs had dislodged, and the whole thing gave April the impression of a wild hog following the hunt. Juan had brought one up to the house once, in a cart he'd hooked up to the back of the car. He gave Paloma a stick to prod it with, and she'd asked if those were the brains; she'd been a very little girl then, April thought, were it me, I would've screamed. And for the longest time after, April worried if she had done something in her second pregnancy to make her girls so matter-of-fact.

"You'd rather she screamed?" Juan asked her.

"What if she's a little psychopath? What if it turns out she's like that kid in *The Bad Seed*?"

"You're sure both of them are batshit and out to get you. What if it turns out Pal's a surgeon?"

Pal was not a surgeon, but something close enough. She was in her last year of medical school, poking sun-spoiled cadavers on what she called a body farm. The university collected the remains of those who had donated themselves to science and, in the name of forensic research, pitched them, whole and in parts, around a plot of scrub or woods or marsh for students like Pal to stumble upon in a creepy kind of treasure hunt. Her job was to determine how long the body had been out in the elements, the degree of decay, and if it had been nibbled at by animals.

Hadn't anyone ever looked at April and, in a mixture of horror and voyeurism, wondered about her? More days than not, she felt herself to be made of gauze, her organs visible, her meals inching along her intestine, which she felt to be protruding through her stomach.

There was more to it, and she did not know whether it made her feel small or liberated. Folks have notions and superstitions and fixations; they take root, they flourish. Her friends had liked astrology; her mother had water from Lourdes, which eased her arthritis, she said; April believed in ESP. Not the gilded kind as seen in New Age literature; nor the kind that was paranoia-tinted, the sour flavor that came when she thought of The Village in *The Prisoner*. What April meant was the current that telegraphed her sentiments to Juan. He knew when she was a liar, when she cursed, when she wanted to snarl at everyone and everything under creation. It was not oppressive. The was not to say that it was entirely pleasant; it is never comfortable being read, first slowly but capably, then with native fluency. You never appreciate what an intricate code your very gestures make, the meanest of them. You thought you had some measure of privacy in a smile, a shrug. Someone has learned your language, and nothing you say is neutral.

Was that proof of God, being read?

Now no one could read her.

Now no one could stop her.

So, she let herself in, once she found the key, once she fanned dirt widely around and around the porch with her sandaled foot, just as she might have when she was three years old, too doddery to quite know what she was doing, too feeble to be precise about it, too engaged to think of consequences. It was a fine mess. She stood to admire it at the threshold. Some of it had kicked up into the ratan patio furniture. She made a note to douse it all with the hose before she left.

It was a shock, moving from the white sun to its opposite. Summer, for all its long days, made the inside of every house brown and chilly and sad in your first moments of stepping through the door. The feeling made April want to bolt for the porch and shut the door behind it, because unlike before, the feeling stuck and she was possessed of the notion that she might be trapped in that brown chill eternally, now that she'd gone inside.

But it passed, less than thirty seconds, and she recognized ordinary shapes, a telephone, an oak hutch, pencils, pens, a television set, a loveseat and a recliner. The walls were yellow in the foyer, white in the TV room, yellow again in the kitchen, the bathroom papered in white hydrangeas on jade green. She recognized a toilet brush, a bowl of potpourri, Softsoap, everyday china and good china in a Dutch blue pattern, spoons, a coffeepot, bananas, one mug labeled HIS and its mate HERS, a fiesta bowl of tomatoes, a plaque over the stove that read, I COOK WITH WINE, SOMETIMES IT EVEN GOES INTO THE FOOD.

Ordinary shapes.

She had that same pair of mugs. April drank from HIS because it was the wider of the two and good for eating cereal out of before you poured the coffee. "You don't mind little bits of Wheaties in there?" Juan asked, as much here as there, as much here as gone, sipping steam over the rim of the HERS mug.

Ordinary shapes as ordinary shapes as ordinary shapes.

She began with those, HERS first, then HIS, and she recognized them as ordinary shapes when she reached the apparent surplus of mugs that filled all three shelves of one cabinet. HIS and HERS had been the only matching set among them. April appraised each one before casting it, as a pink and lackadaisical god might, to the floor. She stopped counting when she reached thirty, figuring there to be at least fifty, and decided that when she reached what looked to her like fifty, she would stop. She lost herself in the crashes, paused, looked. The floor was a mosaic, the mock brick vinyl to be caught in glimpses through the broken ceramic. She bent to take up the prettiest shards (a patterned bit of a rim, painted blue and flecked gold; a square from a glass cup, a variable emerald), secreted them inside her bra, moved to the plates and the bowls, taking again the pieces that caught her eye (mauve sea glass; from a plate rimmed in bunches of grapes), gritting them beneath her heel, thrilling at the crunch.

What gore this was already.

Anyone could have HIS and HERS mugs, no more outlandish than finding bananas in another person's kitchen.

Juan had asked her many times in life if she was going to kill Beverly Across-the-Way. He never knew her real name and, come to think of it, she never knew either. Beverly Across-the-Way smacked of old wounds and lore, implied by April's grunts and snorts and hisses emitted in reference to her and fed by Juan's naming of her. Their girls knew her as Mrs. Moore or Mrs. Dunne, not quite Smith or Jones. April's hatred of her remained a mystery to Juan, their girls, though they knew to say that April hated Beverly Across-the-Way would not have been wrong. Hatred was not too strong a word, they all understood. It was a word that fit; you could hate without reason when it came to a soul whose name you did not know. Beverly was an event—no, less than—an incident. Unsexed, insentient, in the way of a cartoon. You could allow yourself to unhinge. You could unleash.

Once, years and years and years ago, Beverly Across-the-Way, as amended from Beverly What's-Her-Face, said something to your mother.

Once, years and years and years ago, Beverly called me a Hun. Beverly called me a Hun and I kicked the shit out of her. I kicked the shit out of her years and years and years ago, and I've fantasized at least once a day about kicking the shit out of her since.

Understand: Beverly had not looked at April since.

What reason to hold a grudge as you might hold a gem? It was something that Juan had liked to say to her, among many things he liked to say to her, lifted from something he'd read or something he'd heard.

Her brassiere held a trove of gems, as it happened, emeralds in the bunch, pearls and aquamarines.

What reason to hold a grudge as you might hold a gem? It sounded like a parable or Merton. "I think it was in a gas station bathroom somewhere," she told him, now as then.

He told her, struck, "The Texaco station next to the chicken place. How'd you guess?"

No need to hold the gem. She was casting it now to the floor.

She noticed that she was limping when she reached the foyer. (Dim notions, almost visions: TP all over the bathroom, urinating, missing the toilet, how long she'd been holding it after all that coffee). Making it to the stairs (same as hers, only facing the other way), April toed off her shoe and shook out another little shard, from a mug, from a plate, who knew. It had made a fair cut, anyway, a little groove in the ball of her foot that looked spongy when she wiped at it, but did not bleed badly.

Then she saw, delighted, the track, a solid, dotty code, intermittently linked along the wood and tile and paisley runner by long streaks. It must be worse in the kitchen, and she was right. "Like a murder scene," the girls repeated April and Juan's reference to gore of any kind, from paper cuts to the variable scene of a massacre.

April said it aloud, just to hear it.

She was drowned out by someone's car, their radio, for while she could bring herself to say it, she could only bear to whisper. For a spell, she stilled and listened, and there were many noises that had easily eclipsed her own in volume. Joyful noises, yes, dogs, gnomes, angels in the garden, lizards, the kids coming around the block again and talking still about the poisonous thing that someone had eaten, the radio that mewed, *...cuz I love your smile* and burst into yellow light the rest of the song when April moved to the window, wincing when she tore the drape from the rungs. Bright yellow light that made her blind for a moment. She shut her eyes against it, the yellow light, groped toward the center of the foyer, away from the shock of it.

Cuz I love your smile

Was it one singer or a girl group? Was it a black gal or a white gal?

A few nights ago, Pal had said who it was, and now it slipped April's mind. A few nights ago, as part of the Last Hurrah, they hauled Jen's van, husband and boys at home to pack and order from the chicken place, Girls Only, out to the park near Elam to camp. It was April and Jen and Pal. They had brought their own order from the chicken place, along with a bunch of bananas, a paper sack of apples, and a jar of peanut butter, the runny kind without sugar. Pal sliced apples and spread peanut butter with her pocket knife. Jen unearthed three pairs of chopsticks, still in their plastic wrapping, among the items left in the rented van. They had ordered the taco plate, which came with tortillas and a large serving of beans and rice. At Pal's suggestion, they partook of magic mushrooms; the item was less than April had imagined, a lot of mummified twigs in a Ziploc bag, tasting of dirt. She'd featured the fantastic, the fat red fungi that were the dwellings of elves, the stuff of Smurfs, and told her daughters so. Instead, she'd vomited into the campfire. No visions followed, though the radio had never sounded so clear. She'd asked Pal who the singer or singers were. Pal told her. She'd gone to sleep.

And dreamed that she was at home, not the one she was leaving, the old one, when it was her parents' home, before anyone else lived there. She was on the screened porch, what her mother had liked to call the Arizona room, inferring a grand-ish salon. That was the funny part—her mother had made their sun porch, their screened room grand, rattan chairs with cushions in a monstera pattern, succulents like tiny royals on shelves and on the glass-topped tea table. This room (it had walls, call it a room) was bare. This room was unfinished, splinters in her feet. She, as her mother before her, had never left the screened porch bare. Or worse, as it was here, crowded with the refuse of the years of people having lived there, and now they didn't. Perhaps its opposite was the worst of all scenarios, of the place having been empty, now condensed, and the porch was the spillover. Acres of suitcases, though the porch room could not have been more than fourteen by sixteen, easy. There was an idea of commotion from the main house, not quite talking, not angered but aggressive, issued not from people but independent of any corporeality. It had give to it, though, and she woke when she understood the commotion to be about to burst into the Arizona room, for her ears had popped and something in her jaw had loosened.

She'd been surprised to wake and find Jen and Pal still up, still musing, largely sobered. They'd relit the campfire and were eating from the jar of peanut butter, as though they had always done it this way, with the chopsticks. Pal was talking about Daddy, then Jen was talking about Dad. They were quiet, there was the radio, then Jen was talking about her boys (Raffy was six, Gabe seven), her husband's job had taken the family to London for two years and Raffy and Gabe come back with English accents. Jen said that Raffy missed Cadbury and Lucozade, Gabe had gotten used to British home bathrooms and felt the lack of a bidet. They were talking about slang and curry and running into Sting at a Marks and Sparks. "I didn't talk to him," Jen was pointing up, "I just saw him. I didn't try to reach out and touch him or anything—"

"I did that once," Pal was saying.

"You what—you reached out and grabbed somebody—"

"Yeah."

"Weirdo. Who? Was it a famous person?"

"Yeah."

"Yeah."

"You can get away with that, if it's a famous person."

"Yeah. You just get maced."

"Well, that didn't happen, fortunately."

"Who was the famous person?"

"You mean celebrity."

"Fuck you. Who was it?"

"Big Bird. Or, the guy who plays him."

"I don't like to think about Muppets like that."

"What, as having Muppeteers?"

"Well, because it's like—"

April slept, then woke with a ketchup packet stuck to her face, and now all was still and the girls were in a state of gentle repose, breathing, eyes twitching, lashes long and starry. They'd put out the fire; it was not quite seven, by April's watch, and the light as yet was dark, though pearly. They shared a fleecy throw blanket, lying tops and tails in the van's closed hatch. Pal held Jen's foot the way she might a favorite bear, fingers and thumb wrapped around the big toe. Looking, April saw that Jen had Pal's foot in the same way, but cupped around the toes and ball, like a sock.

There had been some commotion, before, during, or after they thought April had gone to sleep, concerning what Pal and Jen were going to do about their mother. No real details, not even words, just a stiff back and forth. They seemed happy to drop the subject for Sting and Big Bird.

What they were going to do about April.

They had never called her Mom or Mama or Mother. She told Juan she did not think that she could stomach being called anything other than her own name. He'd never minded being called Dad, and it was a skin he slipped into and out of, almost indistinguishable, save for one or two things that April could still recognize in this new, gentled incarnation.

She wanted to tell the girls about how they got together. Would she just say it? Your daddy stuck his hands down my pants and played me like an accordion before we had a real conversation about it— and he didn't even ask? It was one of the stories that April and Juan had decided to include in the apocrypha of their conjoined soul. They had invoked it now and then, between the two of them in secret.

The official story was known enough, and subdued. The girls knew about places like Peralta Farm and Crystal City and Manzanar. They knew about the Axis Powers. They knew how many Japanese Americans were rounded up, they knew how many German Americans were rounded up. They knew that Omi and Opa Hesse had come to the States from Prussia, that Grandfather Nimitz came from Mexico by way of Erfurt before moving north into Texas, following the Great War. They knew that the Hesses and the Nimitzes were made to share a cabin, that

Bäbabba Nimitz was on his last legs and would die there, that to make space and sugar the pill, Opa decided to add a screened porch to their quarters and employed the young and the strong in the household to help him build it, being April and Juan.

It was a good story. It inspired. It told of optimism, of what can grow in the face of hardship from the sweat of one's brow and ingenuity. From the alchemy of chicken wire and concrete and two-by-fours came love, and that much was true. April and Juan could hardly believe it themselves. They would bring it out when they were alone to marvel at, turning its facets in the light for the gem it was.

Her father sang from Mozart, "Ein Madchen oder Weibchen". He was like a merry automaton, shifting from hammer to shovel, mixing concrete. Her mother exercised Protestant virtues, sewing silks for parachutes, typing and shorthand for the administrative office. They played bridge with the folks in the next cabin, just through the fence in the Japanese camp; the guards were actually quite lax, they didn't bother anyone. April and Juan still got cards at Christmastime from the Ogawas; in this last one, they wrote of their grandson marrying and their granddaughter teaching English in Mumbai.

Thus was the family scripture.

Her father said of that time, "It all worked out in the end."

Her mother said, "It's over. We're all right now."

Might as well have contended that nothing had happened.

And she thought, This was the approach you take, as time goes by. You move forward. You acknowledge the number of years that have passed, rather than the event itself. You clear your head of it, as you would a dream.

In Beverly Across-the-way's house, April found the shard in her bra and squeezed around it. She felt the skin give.

In the van, in the early morning a day ago, she had stood over her daughters and asked them, first thing, what they'd dreamed about.

She preferred this to Good Morning. The girls did, too. Juan listed it among the things that set the Nimitzes a bit apart from the rest of the neighborhood. They recounted dreams. They made prank calls on Halloween. They ate powdered lemonade from the can by the spoonful or (nasty habit) dipping their fingers into the grit and sucking it off. They used avocado instead of mayonnaise. The girls were the first in their class to have pierced ears, and they called their parents Juan and April. Juan preened over it; it was not exactly bohemian, though he knew folks thought of his nest as slightly exotic, the way one might view a sect of queer and cloistered devotees from the outside. People were curious, but considerate. There must be a reason the parents did not go by Mater and Pater. They must have a purpose for the avocado. There must be a ritual behind the powdered lemonade, and wasn't it written somewhere that it was good for your memory to talk about your dreams?

"We're like a little cult," Juan said.

"Then I'm the messiah," April said.

Juan: "You mean you're a monkey's uncle."

April: "No, Marie of Roumania, to quote Miss Dorothy Parker."

Oh, life is a glorious cycle of song
A medley of extemporanea;
And love is a thing that can never go wrong—

In the van, at first light, April tugged Jenny's hair and tickled Pal's bare foot and asked her grown girls what they'd dreamed about. Jenny blinked and smiled. Paloma went first, grabbing like a toddler for April's finger. April listened, among them, not above them. She never knew how to be above them, and it was rare that the girls allowed her among them.

Paloma told of a scenario in a city that might have been in France. Of dreams, Paloma remembered places; she could tell you of the scrolled pillars, watermarks and moss, stained glass, of smells, of the weather, of chatter and traffic. She had never been to France. She had never been to an Arab bazaar, either, or to a funeral held over a burning ghat. And yet, she could tell you what it tasted like to have someone's ashes waft into your mouth.

Jenny's dreams recalled places, too, though location was never specific. It was always an empty space, one that was built to be full and busy. A shopping mall, an apartment complex, an office, a cafeteria, an airport, a school, a hotel. Somehow, it was Jenny alone in these places, pacing brightly lit, tiled corridors or dining rooms made to seat three hundred. Sometimes she would run into someone she knew, real or imagined. They would walk with her and lean into her ear—

Pal rolled over and made a hoarse mooing noise into Jenny's ear.

—they would lean into her ear and whisper something to her, the words vague, the tone earnest, the message meant for no one but her. Then the space would change, into a neighborhood of large Victorian houses that she was sure she'd seen before.

"Maybe you're the Watseka Wonders," April said. "You're peeping into someone else's lives, it sounds like."

"Peeping Toms. Peeping Tinas—" Jenny and Pal babbled a bit, then Jenny asked, "Well, what'd you dream, April?"

Why, wouldn't you know. She eyed the ketchup packet and the memory of her second dream came at her. She dreamed that she was here in Beverly Across-the-way's house, after having speculated for many years what it might look like. And it only mildly disappointed, for it did not look so different from her own home. Her former home. She could not recall to whom she'd sold it.

Once, when she was in grammar school, she had wanted to dig a tunnel from her yard and into Beverly's, before Beverly and her people had moved in. She got the idea from *Meet Me in St. Louis*, seven-year-old Margaret O'Brien as Tootie Smith, who'd wanted to grab her unwary neighbor around the leg. Paloma, when she was seven, had actually started a tunnel, not to Beverly's, but into an old funfair, miles away and long rusted out, fueled by local legends of gold buried under the merry-go-round. April took Jenny there when it was still in operation, when the place had caramel apples and goats to pet and a pony to ride. The buried treasure rumor started when the funfair shut down, the land bought, the merry-go-round dismantled and the ground scraped clean, leaving a bare dirt circle. Pal's plan was to dig right into the center, where the gold was meant to be, but Jenny, then a high school senior, caught her making a hole with the spade in the backyard, and that was the end of it.

April hurt. The inside of her bra was damp. Her blouse was clean.

She drifted from the wreckage of the kitchen, stood a minute in the hall to look. She did not recall turning the table over, nor having broken any chairs. A vase of dried hydrangeas, long sapped of their color, was all shards and petals. And here were cocktail glasses, a pitcher, a grinning ceramic pig from Mexico now missing its bottom half. Had April thrown them or had she let them drop?

She hummed, going heel-toe-heel-toe into the foyer. Coming to the window and perching on the stairs' shallow landing, she had a full view of the street's opposite side. There was Jenny. There was Pal. Head to head, fingers laced. People used to think that Jenny was a young mother when she brought Pal places out of town. They used it to their advantage to get Pal into movies for free. Pal called Jenny Mama and Jenny would tell the pitying woman (always women) at the box office, the Dairy Queen, the arcade, of living in a group home with her little girl, and no sooner were those words out than any and all gatekeepers' eyes had moistened, and they were comped a showing of *Hello, Dolly*, soft-serve cones, tickets and tokens for the prize counter. Once, they let April in on the scheme and introduced her as their social worker. It was pathetic, her joy at their inclusion. In return, she taught them to fake seizures. Not that money had been an issue; it was fun in itself, these little misdemeanors.

It occurred to her that she might have lost her mind. Not losing, it was a matter of *having lost*, now that much time had passed.

And I am Marie of Roumania.

Actually, if you had asked, she might have told you that she felt rather like Marie Antoinette. Did she fear the usurpation of a throne? No. Did she fear a beheading? No—for she was sure that she had lost her mind, and a beheading amounted to much the same thing. Perhaps it was a simple as this: It was the act of getting into a car that was not hers. It was going to a place that she had never seen, where she would live, indefinitely.

Was it Jen's home? She had not seen this one, since they had gone to England and come back. They sold the old place, an expensive, two-bedroom rat-trap a few blocks from Yale University, where Jenny and her husband both worked. April's understanding was that they had found something farther out from the New Haven sprawl, not a suburb, but a village, not unlike where April lived now. Connecticut was a place where hamlets boasted their age and had signs on the main roads that declared the place SETTLED 1696, INCORPORATED 1830, and that the speed limit was now forty-five miles per hour where it could easily have been seventy. Jenny's new house (built 1750) was on the edge of a town called Increase Hill on a street called Coachman Pike. April had seen pictures. Four bedrooms, plus a made-over basement. The kitchen and bathrooms had been redone, with a jacuzzi in the master bed. The former residents had decided to leave some historical remnants of the house in the remodeling process: the original moldings (now painted cranberry), the cavernous fireplaces big enough to accommodate you on a stool, the water pump in the backyard, the creepy excess of doors that may lead to a closet or to a hidden staircase that plunged into the cellar. They lived in an area that had been farmland in the eighteenth century and was now overgrown, adding to the feeling that you were in a real cottage in the woods. April declared it haunted and talked about setting up a séance with the boys when they got there.

No, it wasn't Jen's house.

She heard Pal, going around and around outside, calling, "April—Ay-prill—" Never had April Hesse Nimitz been Mother, Mom, Mama, Mommy, Mumsy, Marmee or anything like it, never in private, never in public. She had insisted on it. It was a queer thing; never having been enamored with her own name before (wishing she had been named something grander or at least more summery, like June), it was suddenly golden to her, and she cleaved to the name APRIL as though it were the last in her hoard of jewels. It was pleasant to stand and listen to your own name, from your own child most of all. And Pal had a good voice for summoning, it was rich and high, not barking, and let the syllables ascend and descend luxuriously, aaaAAAprillll, aaaAAAprillll. Juan did that, too, when he was looking for her.

They don't know where I am or what I am doing. But then, neither do I know what I'm doing.

"I'm interested to see where this goes," Juan said, because he liked or had liked observing people when they were just about to really lose it. It was what he'd said when the Hesses got their house back at the end of the war and Beverly Across-the-way was still there, face tight, bloodless, when she saw that her neighbor was there to stay.

Fifty years, passing as moments, and Beverly Across-the-way lived in fear of the mad Hun across the street, never meeting April Nimitz's eyes, not quite speaking to her if a block party brought them into close proximity. At last year's Oktoberfest, bearing a tray of ribs, she had gone around the crowd chirping German niceties until she reached April, her head turned to the side, still polite, but now in English, "Pork rib?" April took one and, tearing into it with an eye that did not leave the cowardly little bitch, uttered, "*Danke, schatzi.*" It was part of what little German April actually knew, though she had a good ear and her accent was perfect. It was enough to send Beverly scurrying away.

Did Beverly have a scar? It had been fifty years since she had called April a Hun.

It was enough to make April want to shriek and tear at her own throat. It was wild and made her hot and cold, one after the other before they switched again, damp in the underarms and the well between her breasts, then freezing.

She'd had time aplenty to truly lose it. Juan had said as much. What he had said in actual fact was, "I predict one day, out of the blue, you're going to gun down a McDonald's." She wondered, only momentarily, Why now? She let it pass, along with any reservations, and noticed the hall table where the phone was. Next to it was a jar full of pens and a ceramic dish where keys and odds and ends washed up. It had a mermaid on it, reclining over boozy-looking words YOU CAN'T BEAT HONOLULU FOR THE FISHING.

It made April think of what Admiral Tadaichi had said of the attack on Pearl Harbor and its ultimate futility: "We won a great tactical victory and thereby lost the war."

She didn't think of anything else until she saw a large red Sharpie pen in her left hand and a fragment of the dish in the other. The pieces were around her feet and there was a deep pink smear on the heel of her hand. She looked up, covered her mouth.

HUNNY IM HOME HUNNY IM HOME HUNNY IM HOME HUNNY IM HOME, written like hexes across Beverly's wallpaper. The letters were blocky and stick-like, scrawled by a five-year-old or a bedlamite. She turned a corner and saw it continue up to the bathroom door.

Behind her, above her, Mother whispered, "Fool's names and fool's faces always appear in public places."

But it's not my name. Just my nature.

For all anyone could tell, certainly for all Beverly Across-the-way could tell, it was blue skies and green leaves. There was a U-Haul parked across the street, hitched to a van with the windows down, something like the Allman Brothers or Simon and Garfunkel coming through, the herald of summer in its mellow heeling-down, and so what reason should she have to suspect anything as she rolled her Taurus to a stop in the carport, pausing only a minute to look at her Land's End catalogue before going up the porch steps.

April either had not heard the other woman gasp or was too far away yet for the sound to register. It was the first, tiptoeing step into the foyer that made April dart around the corner and into the bathroom. She was, thankfully, unseen. The door, thankfully, whispered closed. She was sealed in, more or less, because she dared not turn the light on. There was potpourri, but it did little to cover the stink of something far more indelicate. April had an impression of needing to relieve herself and could not quite bring herself to do it in the middle of the kitchen. Feeling subhuman did not exclude you from the species. There were conventions. You shat where you were told. You cleaned yourself up. The trouble here was that she could not flush the toilet. Beverly would hear. Beverly would know.

So.

Was the joke, then, on her?

It had never occurred to her that she would be trapped. April Nimitz inhaled her own mess and made use of the light that came in cracks, shifting when Beverly crept up the hall. In the kitchen, Beverly did not quite shriek—it was closer to the sound you made when you sat on a yellow jacket, a clean, pinpointed "OH." It was a deceptive sound, for it made everyone around you think that whatever ailed you must not be that bad, was more of a surprise, really. April knew this because when she was twelve years old, she had taken a seat on a bench for the magic lantern show at the county fair. She'd thought she sat on glass. Her mother gave her the ice from her lemonade and told April not to made a scene. A few boys from school who had been sitting two benches down saw the whole thing. On Monday they hooted at her and bounced from their seats, squealing, "OH."

I thought I sat on glass.

Now it was all she could conjure up, every time Beverly made the sound, "OH." And she made it more than twice, though you would think the shock of the matter would have died by now. Was it really such a surprise to find your things out of place?

April found the shard in her bra and pressed. The edges of the room blurred and a certain heat filled her head from behind her eyes, making the color dim and the noise echo out of shot. It did what a lot of things could not. When you find yourself in situations that could be called "unfathomable", you are, more often than not, left without the buffer of a cocktail. You could shift your eye from the more abstract trials and sink into something much more immediate. She could feel this, not in short sharp shocks in the blood or the nerves, but here, here on the surface. It saw her through sobriety, the first through fourth times.

It was meant to keep her from doing what she had done and what she very well might do, if given the chance, if the time was right, if she knew there would be no consequence.

She bit into the ham of her hand and did not make a sound.

It wouldn't have mattered. With her eyes closed, April had not tracked the shifting light in the cracks. With her mind numb, she had not heard Beverly's pitty-pat draw nearer and nearer until the bathroom door swung open, too bright, and April was looking at her with her hand in her mouth.

What passed in the following minutes might have been described as a brief scuffle, a minor confusion of Beverly trying to get into the bathroom as April was trying to get out. This was what April would recall. Beverly had either grabbed for her or April had pushed her. April had been otherwise inert and was provoked or she had been hiding there for no purpose, save that of breaking Beverly's face.

"One minute you're sitting around like a lump of dough," April said to Jenny, following a detention, fourth or fifth grade, "—the next you try to bite that kid's ear off. Do they not feed you at lunchtime?"

"He was bothering me—"

"What was he doing, breathing?"

April never learned what it was the boy had done. Juan had, somehow, some way, and a certain young man turned up at school the next day, looking shaken. Jenny said the boy had a broken nose, but this was untrue; Juan had only threatened to give him one, and the boy's face was like a pug's to begin with.

Beverly Across-the-way was not a pug. Beverly Across-the-way was between her feet, unrecognizable.

What had happened?

Were you as a lump of dough, April Hesse? She imagined herself before a divine court, where God's voice was a caricature of her own, mocking. The angels snorted in the peanut gallery. *Was this the law of inertia, wherein you were unmoved until provoked by an outside force?*

Yes. Yes, I was.

Might you explain?

If she had not called me a Hun. If she had not called me a Hun. I am a citizen. I know no other nation.

What is a Hun?

You know. A kraut.

You think she thought you were a kraut?

Yes. Because she did.

Aren't you one?

No. Yes. Not a bad one. I know no German.

You know the word for sweetheart.

I am not a Nazi.

No one accused you. Ought we to?

The angels whooped at this, and it occurred to April that Paradise could become Pandemonium on a whim. Beverly's glasses were down the hall. There was a lot of spatter. It was especially thick around the crown of her head, blackening her bobbed haircut. Her nose was broken. Her jaw went one way, though she was able to look up at April with one blue eye, sagging open. In the fracas, April had pushed or Beverly had fallen back into the wall. April had kept her there, doing what she had done until she'd exhausted herself.

Her fingers were sour and red, and there was grit under her nails. April flexed her tongue and pulled a hair out from under it, not hers, tasting bitter and dripping spit.

I didn't know I had it in me.

And still her younger daughter called, "A-PRIL—"

And while April herself had not come to her senses, she allowed clarity to put things in their place. She had to flush the toilet, for one. She had to wash her face, for another. The mirror and the tiny overhead light were unkind, but she made good use of the bar soap and stack of clean hand towels by the sink. Opening the mirror let her discover the little supply behind it of lotions and potions, and soon she was dabbing cover-up to the worst parts (when had the bitch hit her?) and daubing lipstick. There was perfume, a cucumber-honeydew spray from Bed Bath and Beyond, but it camouflaged any trace of stale sweat. She brushed her hair, closer now to bronze than red, and, stepping lightly over Beverly Across-the-way, decided that it would be more prudent to leave through the back door, not looking behind, not thinking of it.

She stepped onto the back porch, screened like her own and facing a small pasture where a rancher had his alpacas graze. They were out now, dipping and bending over the grass, too delicate, too funny-looking to be real among the mules and dairy cattle.

When they saw her, they paused, and the bravest one, the largest, whose fur was blond and dreaded, tiptoed forward. When it flicked its ear, April noted a pink tag and a name: BIG BIRD, it read. The animal worked its jaw, made a flat humming noise which the flock echoed. Then, failing to recognize her, it turned and fled. The others followed, not galloping the way April had thought they would. Instead, they bounced, like ponies on the moon. The whole thing had a very snobbish quality to it, leaving April feeling small. The crowned head had spoken and the herd, about the way a passel of girls might, conceded, giving her their ass-ends.

"Well," she breathed, "fuck you, too."

"A-PRIL AAA-PRILL A-PRIL—"

It was not Pal this time, but a man's voice. Here was Buck Thune coming around the corner. Jenny and Pal had vowed to handle any dealings with the lawyer and April was happy to let them do it. Nothing wrong with Buck in particular, it was his demeanor was all, the sort of grey feeling that comes with official business, paperwork, the phrase "loose ends". Had he seen? Beverly's car pulling in? April going across? She ducked behind the generator and kept to the wall of Beverly's house, then the trees, inching, inching until she reached the curb.

Everything was very bright and placid, and for a moment she stood to catch whatever it was on the van's radio. Paul Simon, *"We both will be received in Graceland—"*

Jenny and Pal were ponytails, dirty blonde and deep brown. They wore blue jeans and t-shirts, little leather ankle boots. Jenny wore small gold hoops in her ears, Pal turquoise studs. (They had pearl earrings, both of them, that April had bought them several Christmases ago. She had yet to see either girl wear them.) They were head-to-head, not talking about much of anything. It was easy enough to creep up on them. It was easier to eavesdrop, not even a foot away.

Jenny was saying, "—the whole thing smelled like tuna fish—"

Paloma was saying, "—that stupid Sherpa jacket I thought I still had, turns out I put it in the bag of stuff that went to Goodwill—"

Jenny was saying, "—using this urine dissolvent to get it out, well, now someone else will get a rash from that thing—"

April leaned in with a burst, "Boo."

Now they turned, equal parts stern and rueful, maybe a little miffed.

You don't know what I did, do you?

Jenny's eyes grew that much sharper, but she smiled at her mother and said, "Well. What happened to you?"

Goodbye, house. Goodbye, Mrs. Fielding and Mrs. McCuistion and Mrs. Glau and Mrs. Polk. Goodbye, Buck Thune.

She told Jenny that she'd gone to pet the alpacas. When Buck Thune puffed across the street a minute or two after, he summed that he must have just missed her, and that the one called Big Bird spat at him.

"On you?" April asked. "Or just at you?"

Buck Thune huffed weakly, rubbed the corner of a tissue over his glasses. "Just at. They were too far out."

Goodbye, alpacas, the snotty bunch of you.

The Mesdames Fielding, McCuistion, Glau, and Polk hummed. They dipped and bent over the cut grass.

"Well, April," Buck Thune pronounced. "I guess you can call yourself a Yankee now."

"We've got roughly a thousand miles to go before I can say that," April said. "I guess I really don't live here anymore. Apparently, I'm going to a place called Incest Hollow."

"No, it's Incest Hill," Jenny put in.

"It's an incorporated village of Incest Hollow proper," Pal added.

"Got it," April concurred. "Same zip code, though?"

Acting alone, April knew that her humor made people shift. No one quite knew how to laugh or if they should until Jenny, then Pal came to buoy the joke. Suddenly, it was gauche, not oddball, and it gave their audience permission to laugh.

After that, and a flurry of embraces, April found herself in the way-back seat of the packed van, watching the neighborhood and everything in it grow smaller and smaller until the main road swallowed it up.

"Goodbye, house," Juan said.

One hour, then two, going north, then east. Pal poked her head out the passenger's window to point at a commercial airplane coasting overhead, to bet that it was the flight that Jenny's husband and boys were on right now, taking off from San Antonio.

"Can you see if its Delta?" Jenny asked.

Pal pretended to squint. "No. It's Air France."

Jenny, who was fluent in French, began to jabber, which made Pal mimic her, "Ah, *beaucoup du Jean-Luc Goddard, il y a beaucoup des gateaux, c'est beaucoup—*"

"*Beaucoup?*" Jenny asked. "*Combien?*"

"*Beaucoup, beaucoup, beaucoup,*" Pal chirped.

There was a Malcolm McLaren tape in the deck, "Paris, Paris", Catherine Deneuve purring, not singing, under the synths and piano. Pal and Jenny sang along, though more often than not, they repeated the chorus, "*Paris-Paris*", craning their heads like roosters.

They had wept at Juan's burial. They had read from the Scriptures. Because Jenny had renounced the Catholicism of her birth and was now a Jew (Reform), she recited the Kaddish, "*—may His salvation blossom and His anointed be near—*"

"I've got news for you," April had said to her eldest, twelve years old and teaching herself the aleph-bet. "The anointed already came. No need to set about waiting." She wondered what made her say anything, for her piety had never extended much beyond Sunday Mass.

"Yes," Jenny had allowed, noting that Jesus of Nazareth, according to the narrative, had also left. "A messiah shouldn't just pop in and then pop out, and then tell you he'll be right back. Once he's here, he's here." She scratched the letter Ayin, the tenth in a row of them, and added in blocky English at the top: SILENT.

"Is this a subtle way to tell me to shut up and fuck off?" April asked.

With great patience, Jenny told her that the letters Ayin and Aleph were silent in the Hebrew alphabet.

April pressed, "So. What was the trigger of this whole thing? You read Anne Frank's diary, then boom, you're enamored?"

Jenny answered, "I read the Five Books of Moses." To April's blank look, she named them: Genesis, Exodus, Leviticus, Numbers, Deuteronomy. She sighed, went on making Alephs and Ayims.

At thirteen, she begged rides into San Antonio to find a synagogue. At fourteen, she began Torah studies under Rabbi Elaine Kuntz, a spectral presence, as April and Juan had never met her, nor had Jenny ever got around to introducing them. At fifteen, she defended her stance before the Rabbi and two temple trustees. She was immersed in the mikvah (which, to April, sounded like a glorified swimming pool) and chose for herself a new name, so that when she was called to the Torah, she would be announced as Yael Hadas bat Avraham avinu ve-Sarah imeinu.

In the Bible, Yael drove a tent stake through the head of a Canaanite general while he slept.

Hadas became Esther, who rescued the Jews of ancient Persia by admitting to her husband the king that she was one herself.

April had asked why, upon reading her daughter's conversion papers, Jenny was known as the daughter of Abraham and Sarah, not Juan and April.

When Jenny was twenty and away at college, she met a fellow from France with, what April thought to be, an amusing name: Moishe ben Ami. Now her son-in-law, she called him Monsieur Mon Ami and it stuck.

From the middle seat of the packed van, she blew a kiss to the sky and the airplane. "*A bientot, Monsieur Mon Ami.*"

Jenny puckered her lips and smacked. "*A bientot, Messieurs Mes Amis.*"

Raffy and Gabe put on kippahs at the age of three. They got their first haircuts then, too, and learned the alphabet and the aleph-bet. There were home movies of these ceremonies, done in the synagogue's basement playroom, Mo holding the camera, Jenny and the rabbi flanking Gabe's, then Raffy's shoulders as the boys repeated the characters read to them from a printed sheet. After each recitation, Gabe, then Raffy, were given the token confection (M&Ms for Gabe, Skittles for Raffy) to illustrate the sweetness of learning.

Gabe grinned at the camera and picked his nose.

Raffy kept running his hand over his scalp, unused to the new buzzcut.

You could hear Pal off-camera, her applause. You could see her in fragments, accepting Gabe's, then Raffy's sticky hands to shake, now that they had come this far, now that they could read. "Muzza toff," they said.

"This is the best day of your life," Jenny told Gabe, then Raffy. "Not the first day of school or even your wedding day."

April predicted that her grandsons would be atheists by the time they were in high school. Jenny didn't speak to her mother for a few months after that, with Pal semaphoring in between.

Beverly Across-the-Way had been Jenny's chauffeur many times. Rabbi Kuntz mistook her, apparently, for Jenny's mother.

The land thinned a little way north, fewer trees, fewer undulations until the horizon was a line straight across. It was a shock when the inselberg rose, seemingly from the ether. Here was the only elevation for miles, eighteen hundred feet above sea level, veined with shrubs and deep, dusty pink. First, it had been a hideout spot for the Comanches, then a TB sanitarium, then a Catholic retreat, then a place of wartime detention, then a party site for hippies, and now it was known to biologists for stagnant pools containing fairy shrimp.

The consolation was supposed to be in the form of the obelisk that stood at the foot of the inselberg. April had only seen it from magazines, and knew it was inscribed on one side: TO THE INMATES AND SURVIVORS OF THE PERALTA FARM DETENTION CAMP, 1942-1945, WE DEDICATE THIS LAND. The other facets were filled with the names of those held there, one side for the Germans, one for the Italians, one for the Japanese.

Manzanar and Crystal City were on the National Register of Historic Places.

Stephen Spielberg shot scenes for *Schindler's List* at Auschwitz (so she'd heard).

April's mother said to her, precise, accented, "We were not starved. We were not worked to exhaustion. We were not tattooed or beaten or degraded like animals. Don't compare yourself to those poor people in Europe. We were at war. Who could we trust? Speak English. Go to church." The last she uttered toward the end, when the divide between the past and the present had blurred, and she confused April for Jenny. How Mother had wept when she'd heard that her granddaughter converted.

The royal we.

"We dedicate this land." Who is we? There had been a mayor there, and a congressman, both of whom had said a lot of wishy-washy things at the dedication about forgiveness and equality.

You wouldn't know to look at the place. You wouldn't know if you didn't read the obelisk. You wouldn't know unless you found the obelisk.

April rolled down the window and spat.

Krauts, wops, and Japs.

Now you couldn't even breathe those words without a reprimand from the younger generation.

Juan had called it Camp SAFU and, when they were both feeling especially flippant, Girl Scout camp. It was a time when it felt that the conventions once binding to one and all had been nothing more than formalities. It was a time when, to Juan and to April, the natural order had emerged in stark relief. As it turned out, nothing mattered. God's image, as it turned out, was all gut and groin. You had to eat. You had to maintain your strength. You had to be reckoned with. You had to do what you could. You had to get by.

Your daddy sold me to the fellows in the guard tower for penicillin. It's how I got my cherry popped, did you know that, not to your daddy, after all. Then I sold the prettiest, most pliable chicks to the fellows in the guard tower for bacon rations and cigarettes. On a good day, we could get ten dollars for a girl's pussy, seventeen, sixteen, fifteen.

Juan chuckled. "Remember that?"

No towers now, no barracks, no fences. You had to read the obelisk, and who would waste their time doing that?

Didn't matter now. No one need know. We got away with it.

Juan rippled his fingers at the inselberg. "Goodbye, Girl Scout camp."

They listened to Carole King and Tracy Chapman and Joni Mitchell, Castelnuovo-Tedesco's pieces for guitar and Mozart's horn concertos. They sang along to Broadway recordings of *Gigi* and *Kismet, Hello, Dolly* and *My Fair Lady,* to Bonnie Raitt's "Something to Talk About". They had *Interview with the Vampire* on cassette tapes. When the girls wanted something to keep them awake, they put on the Doors, the Beatles, the Police, Sting's *Ten Summoner's Tales* until April swore that she would crack the disc in two if she had to hear "Fields of Gold" one more time.

When they grew restless, they stopped to stretch. When they got hungry, they bought mixed nuts and turkey jerky and Cokes from roadside gas stations. In restrooms, they left their marks on the stalls, among the graffiti. April eschewed Pal's pen and scratched her initials with Beverly's chip from her bra. No one appeared to notice April's blouse and she did not press the issue.

When they were bored, they played guessing games, with two left guessing, more often than not, which number one of them was thinking of.

"Between one and one hundred," April said when it was her turn to drive.

"Ninety-nine," called Jenny from the back.

"I second that," Paloma sighed and pushed a green bubble of gum from her mouth on the long exhale. For this leg of the journey, she'd chosen to sit in the way-back, ostensibly because she wanted to nap. The way-back, up to now, had been filled with boxes that would not fit in the trunk. She'd stacked what she could on the floor and kneed the largest carton into the corner of the seat.

Meanwhile, April's purse road shotgun.

"You can't second that," she countered.

"Fine. Ninety-eight-point-five." Pal dropped the gum into a napkin and squeezed.

April snapped that it had to be a whole number, not a fraction. "That's not how the rules go."

Pal did not want to play. Ostensibly, she wanted to nap, and she demonstrated this by veiling her face with a t-shirt.

April pressed, as she was wont to do. Really, the more appropriate word to describe what she did was to dig. If it were a matter of physical combat, she would have used her nails, as girls do in fistfights. It was about as petty and nonsensical, steam-powered by nothing less than hormones. But where Jenny, in the old days, had been good for a fight, Pal grew mute, almost frozen. Though April could not see her face now, she knew her younger daughter's nose to have sharpened that much, her lips thin, and she would rest her eyes anywhere, save for her mother's gaze. Paloma was statuesque, a bust of a Roman senator. She was twenty-six and there was a distinct patch of grey that showed in her widow's peak, brightened by the rest of her hair. April had made light of it in the past, telling Pal that she ought to have her hair dyed. She'd told Pal that she ought to have her teeth fixed, nose reduced, breasts augmented because she had the body of a ten-year-old and people would wonder at this strange Quasimodo of a girl, sexless and straight as a pin.

April, feeling perverted, hoped against hope that these ugly words would one day ignite a fire in Pal that would reassure her—of what? Of Paloma's backbone? She observed decaying flesh with a keen eye; that took some spine, in addition to a strong stomach.

In the passenger's seat, Juan tittered. "You really are a nasty bitch," he said to April. "Anything to get a rise out of them. Anything to make them look at you. I used to think it was because you were jealous, but that's only half-true. You're afraid they'll leave you at some creepy gas station in the middle of nowhere without a word."

"Play the game," April demanded, "or I'll lose my sense of direction and flip this goddamned van over. If I can't concentrate, the onus is on you."

Don't you dismiss me. It's easier to hit back.

And then Jenny, brave Jenny on her white horse would come. Jenny had a smooth Madonna face that would flush hotly when she was angered, though she'd stopped the verbal combat some years ago. There followed a phase where she would drop her head and shake it, scoffing. Nowadays, she withheld any snappishness and her voice would take on the firm, lofty tones she used when admonishing her own small sons. She said, "That's enough" or "Let's have quiet" or, worst of all, would simply tell April to leave the room.

She told April, "You're tired."

April told Jenny that it was she who was tired.

Jenny sighed, "Pull over. You're tired, you can't drive. I'll drive."

"Is this the part where you tell me to leave the room? Will I get sent to bed without supper?" April obliged, peeling into a dusty shoulder. "Sticks and stones break your bones, and words assail your psyches. I'm astonished neither of you have imploded yet. You pair of pansies."

"You're usually not this charming sober," Juan said.

Jenny grabbed her arm when she tried to get in the back. "You're sitting up front with me."

"What the hell for?" April opened her mouth to tell Jenny that the passenger's seat was taken, choosing instead to say again, weakly, because she could think of nothing else, "You pair of pansies."

Jenny scoffed. Her eyes were red, moist. A small victory, April thought, to offload some of the burdensome ache. Jenny hurt, too, and now April was not alone in her suffering.

But in a moment, less than that, her older daughter's face cleared. She exhaled the way she would if she still smoked. Then she vowed that she was not doing this, whatever this was. "In fact," she mused, as though the idea had now been whispered to her from on high, "we're going to make a car rule. A special rule just for you. The seat up front is April's Seat, unless otherwise amended by myself or one Paloma Nimitz. This is not negotiable. I'd prefer we all made it east in one piece."

She actually marched her own mother to her seat and buckled her in. She would not grant April the dignity of slamming the door, doing it herself, nearly severing her mother's toes.

Was it because she hadn't cried yet?

She could tell her children what pain the physical act alone of weeping was, how her face swelled and her vision blurred and how she could not breathe. She feared that once she began, she would not be able to stop. There was nothing more exhausting. Better to turn the tears to acid. Better to let people see her and shake in their boots than pity her. Imagine, a little old widow being put away in her daughter's guest room, now that the dear husband had departed. April Nimitz, who was also April Hesse, was made of stronger stuff than that.

"And yet she had to buckle your seatbelt for you," Juan said.

A few hours of silence and everyone calmed; this was what they affirmed, airily, to each other when they felt that enough time had passed. This was their way.

Forgive and forget.

April could not have spoken for her girls, nor could she have spoken for Juan, though it had always seemed to her that when you claimed to forgive, you did not exactly forget. You kept your grievances in a cache, letting it build interest. To put it in a better way, letting it mutate, until the thing itself held a vague resemblance to the creature it had been. Or it withered, at least in your mind, and the other party did not recognize it as you did. It was no big deal. It was so long ago. I'm over it, why can't you be?

And where was April Nimitz's cache? She knew exactly where it was, deep in her gut, just where she'd buried it. Now and then, the thing inside would come out and wear her skin for a little while, when she felt too brittle to function on her own. And then she would be the one in the cache. That was the arrangement: If the thing stepped out, she would have to go in. She was helpless to watch while the thing performed her humanly duties, rough imitations of what she thought she normally did. It stumbled. It barked. It offended. It held an odor. It did not look, sound, or smell like April as she knew herself. But no one had reason to believe that it could be anything else.

The thing had found Juan. The thing understood him to have made a formal exit from this mortal coil, not a heart attack as April heard it tell her daughters, and heard her daughters repeat to everyone they knew. Buck Thune agreed that this was for the best: "They would feel differently about him." Juan had gone to bed with a drink as he did the night before. And April woke in the morning to find the bottle empty and his heart medication gone but for one or two pills. The girls would have wanted to know why, of course. Once they did, April knew, Juan would lose his title. When had Daddy ever sounded more golden than when his girls said it?

Before coming to Peralta Farm, Juan had already been in jail, somewhere in the Mexican state of Tamaulipas. She had asked what for once, when they were getting to know each other, and he would not tell her. Decades on, he still would not. And in death, it was just as unlikely. But April had an idea.

"What do you think I did?" Juan asked her.

She had to share the passenger's seat with him and was cramped into his lap. Jenny listened to NPR and concentrated on the road. Pal had read for a while, a book called *A World Lit Only by Fire*, then slept. She kept the t-shirt over her face.

"I have an idea," April said. "A pretty solid one."

"Pray tell."

"Same thing I did."

"And what did you do?"

She was seventeen and he was twenty-four and sitting in his lap, which was a green light for him to have done anything to her. He taught her how to grab and squeeze, not just himself but girls, too. Testing the meat, testing the merchandise. Again, the times were strange and everything was up in the air. They had been rounded up and that seemed to be reason enough to believe that there were no rules, now that they were enemies of the States. Why not become monsters?

Then she was old again and Jenny was asking her if she was hungry. "There's a Burger King coming up."

They had made it through the southernmost corner of Oklahoma and decided to stop for their first night in the Arkansas high country. The earth, slowly but surely, had begun to curve once more and the trees thicken. In time, you could hardly see the sky for the foliage. It gave April the creeps; she didn't know which frightened her more, a horizon that went on and on or no horizon at all. Not having been very many places (Santa Fe in spring, Mexico in winter), April imagined that this was what it must be to move through the Russian hinterlands; for a few minutes, she pretended that she was one of the last princesses of the Romanov dynasty, on the train to Yekaterinburg. The fantasy was tarnished by the fact that it was eighty-three degrees, though the sun was soon to set, as well as the presence of leftover campaign posters for Bob Dole and Bill Clinton. Someone had whitewashed one of the Clinton signboards so that the only letters remaining of the candidate's name spelled ILL CLIT.

They talked some about turning off and going to a movie, but none of them had a local newspaper on hand, and anyway, they had all seen anything that was worth seeing. Paloma found a Holiday Inn and they collapsed into their shared room for the night.

April had one of the two double beds to herself. Pal and Jenny shared the other, burrowed together in a bastion against the air conditioning. Jenny was the big spoon, Pal the little. They'd brushed their teeth and fallen into bed almost at once. Pal's toothbrush see-sawed between her fingers; April took it before it could fall and set it on the nightstand by her earrings.

When she herself fell asleep, there came no relief or release, perhaps not even true slumber. Its weight was fragile and there was no sense of having been anywhere else, save for this bed, this hotel. She hesitated to call them dreams, for if her brain had indeed relaxed to such an extent as to conjure images, they were of these perky furnishings, these sleek lines and blue air. There was the TV, there was the table by the window, the stiff armchair where her purse was. She had a suspicion that she had woken every hour, once an hour.

She puzzled over it until the next morning, but she was sure, at least confident, that at around two or three AM she had risen to use the bathroom and, on her way back, had looked and found the other bed empty. The sheets had been kicked to the end of the bed, the pillows mussed. The mattress bore impressions, faint ones, of its departed occupants, a sort of swirl to mark where they had spooned. April was too heavy yet with sleep to feel frightened. If anything, she might have said that she was miffed to find that her girls had abandoned her in the middle of the night in a strange hotel. But then she came to her senses. She was alert enough now to see that Jenny's duffel and Pal's rucksack were where they had left them, by the chair that held April's purse. Pal's turquoise earrings were aligned with the toothbrush, and here were the keys to the Astro. The only things missing were the girls' shoes.

She considered dressing and going to look for them, but thought the better of it. She thought she might watch television, but turned it off when it became clear that every channel at this hour was an ad. She swallowed, held her breath. She had a lighter and no cigarettes. Would it be worth it to explore Jenny's purse? Here, she found gum. If Pal smoked, April was certain that she would never have guessed it, not until she helped herself to the innermost pocket of her rucksack where, to her surprise, there was a pack of Newports. Not her preferred brand, but it would do. She lit up, using her own lighter, and cranked open the window, leaned out.

Did Pal smoke because that was what Jenny had done? And now that Jenny had quit, would she quit, too? April hoped so. When Jenny got her ears pierced, Pal, then three, begged to have hers pierced, too. When Jenny got glasses, Pal claimed that the blackboard at school was blurry—though, as it happened, myopia did run in the family, and the optometrist said he was amazed that the girl could see her hand in front of her face. But was it a coincidence that when, a few years back, Jenny had decided to get contact lenses, Pal went out and got them, too?

Superficialities, these were, April knew. Jenny converted, and Pal remained a staunch member of the atheist camp. Jenny went into archives; Pal observed cadavers. Jenny glowed in the warmth of marriage and motherhood; Pal was a confirmed bachelorette. She'd had boyfriends, a few girlfriends, too. April had once called her a confirmed loner, in response to her bachelorette declaration.

"She wants a bond," Juan said, "not a manacle." He asked for a puff of April's cigarette, and she ignored him.

She ignored him because she saw Jenny and Pal crossing the parking lot, emerging from just under her window and ambling, almost floating, toward the lot's far end, where one of the four street lamps were. Their arms were linked and they leaned into one another; sometimes Pal would put her weight into her shoulder and make Jenny stumble, and Jenny would do the same to Pal. They were not drunk, just pretending to be, an old game. Should anyone approach them, they would bellow that they could quit anytime they wanted. Most likely, they were stoned. They were singing a drinking song: "*Show me the way to the next whiskey bar—*"

April craned her head a bit further out, wanting to hear the rest of what Jenny was saying. What April had managed to catch was, "I want to show you something." They were hurrying away, toward the street lamp. Urgency, excitement. If it had been anyone else, Pal would have hung back, the suspicious one. Now, she tripped ahead, meeting Jenny until the yellow glare. To April, they had the look of two abductees, poised the moment before the UFO beamed them up.

Below, Jenny appeared to be demonstrating this or that to Pal. She had Pal right herself, then instructed, to bow her head, to cover her eyes, to sway in place. They were voices without words, save for one or two articulations: "Like this?" from Pal, "Just like that," from Jenny. Side to side or up and down. "Keep your eyes closed."

April recognized these as relics of the long-gone childhood, when you are primitive and atavistic. You are as a pagan, with strange rituals and gestures that you have apparently carried over from the life before. Having forgotten their significance, they remain a compulsion. And so, when you are tempest-tossed, you rock in place. You close your eyes. You hum. You expect that something wonderful will happen as a result of your compliance, that you will be transported or exalted or that you will vanish. At the end of it, all you are is calmed, and that was all you could hope for. Before Jenny had converted, or could even distinguish the difference between Jews and Gentiles, it was something she would do. It was something Pal had done, too, and April suspected, independently of her sister.

Before they left Texas, they had watched a documentary about Hasidim in Brooklyn, narrated by Leonard Nimoy and Sarah Jessica Parker. In it, men in white shawls and women in headscarves swayed in private corners. April had seen Catholics do this, too, and a few evangelical Protestants, the snake handling types. She had seen her husband do it, had caught herself doing it when they listened to music together. Beethoven's 9th, Sun Ra's "Enlightenment" and "India". It was likely why rock stars gyrated so much on stage.

But had it ever done this?

The light from the street lamp had flickered, once, twice, and went out. Then, the other three followed. The parking lot ought to have been completely dark. And yet, here were Jenny and Pal, weaving and waving, hands to their eyes, the eyes themselves squeezed shut, still spotlit, though the light was no longer flat and yellow. There was no moon, only a great crack across the heavens. Only a great crack. A fissure, a clean slice that emitted a beam as a stream of water. It had texture, not wet, an odor, almost sweet, like grilled fruit or wine, and it cascaded from its distance, without sound, to drip onto the crowns of

Jenny's and Pal's heads. Still, they swayed. Their hands remained solid over their faces, like vizors.

When they lifted, Pal first, then Jenny, April dropped her cigarette. They were a few inches or so from the ground at first; Pal's shoes scraped the grass in the blacktop. Soon, they were a foot, then two feet, taking off.

It was not the Sabbath, April knew. It was only Wednesday. There were no candles lit. According to Jenny, a woman on Shabbos could ask for anything she would like from God. And if this was God, it was not as April had expected it to be. For It was what she knew this phenomenon to be, a what, as opposed to a who, now that she had seen it. A what perpetuated by —well, what?

"Energy," Juan speculated. "Love. Spinoza's god. It looks like Einstein was right, as usual. The Beatles, too, come to think of it. All you need is love, bunch of hippies. Bunch of pansies. They were right."

So, there was no one who could be bribed or influenced. No one to judge at the end of days. You could open the heavens of your own steam or you could not. It made April grow warm, then chilled. If you could open the heavens, what else might be possible in such a minor being as a soul? Were we the ones, after all, who brought on the Great Flood? We exterminate species by the day, including our own. We fell civilizations and we send men to the moon. We eradicate polio with one potion, and mumps and measles and smallpox. Perhaps none of these things could be accomplished alone, which is why we are keen to call sights and wonders acts of God or, even more dismissively, impossible. It could not have anything to do with us.

Some called it prayer. Some meditation or, in more modern parlance, "re-charging". These things often fail to lift you from the earth. A Hail Mary could take a football team to victory, but it had never cracked open the heavens.

What does that mean for me?

"I don't know," Juan said. "For the moment, we're stuck."

Who's we?

"You," Juan said. "Me. Hey, look at that—"

But April could not look. She did not know what would follow, only that she was keenly aware of how much brighter the parking lot had become, almost noonday sun, even behind her eyelids. She understood there to be a quaking and rumbling, as though the earth itself had chosen this very spot, the site of this Holiday Inn, to split in two. Magma, flames, spitting embers. Not hell, nor a final judgment. It was the end of days without the opera.

"The bush is on fire," Juan told her. "Remember, you dropped your ciggie."

To that, April clapped her hands over her eyes. And so it was that she had caused this. And didn't she deserve it? Wouldn't the final destruction be as simple, idiotic, as dropping a cigarette into a dried-out azalea? You spent your time on planet Earth so dutifully? Why oughtn't your exit be as undignified?

"They're not coming back for us," Juan said.

She dug the hams of her hands into her head and rocked and howled—

━━━ and she turned on her shoulder with the sheet trapped between her thighs. She rose, breathed. The pillow was on the floor between the beds and the room was cold, and she was prompted to get up and play with the dials and knobs until the chill had gone. It was a quarter to eight and the sky was soft and solid, the blue of a hydrangea. The window was shut, the azalea bush below as dry as it had ever been, but unscorched. Paloma's bag had no cigarettes because if Paloma had ever smoked, April would never know. She went back to the window to watch guests come in and out of the hotel, not very many at this hour: a woman with two blue heelers (this was a dog-friendly establishment), two housekeepers sipping coffee from Styrofoam cups, two fellows hoisting a kayak onto the roof of a Jeep.

She oughtn't to look for signs where there were none. Two dogs, two women, two men. Three instances make it an omen. It smacked of Age of Aquarius drivel, though she'd been taught to find symbols in lowly places, the way you do in catechism, and it was a difficult process to shake it off.

In the other bed, where likely they had been all night, her daughters yawned. They were not ready for rousing yet, April could tell, and she would not wake them. They slept in their t-shirts and underwear. Jen preferred to rest on her side, Paloma on her belly with both arms tucked under her pillow. Jenny talked in her sleep, Pal twitched and drooled.

"Oranges," Jenny mumbled from the ether.

April bent over her. "What's that?"

"Get um ready or we won't have enough for the banquet—"

April nodded. "I'll get um ready. I hear you, the banquet."

Jen murmured an affirmation and snored.

Meanwhile, after brushing her teeth and hopping in and out of the shower, April tried to remember if there was a doughnut shop anywhere within walking distance. The idea of sitting across from the girls at a table in the hotel's so-called breakfast nook, toying with powdered eggs and over-sugared oatmeal, exposed to the two dogs, the two housekeepers, the two kayakers, was more than she could bear. She slipped into blue jeans and a t-shirt Jenny had picked up for her at a Sting concert. *The Soul Cages*, live at the Hartford Civic Center. It was roomy enough that she could skip wearing a bra.

Out of doors, she sucked in dewy air and imagined, upon release, the expulsion of bad dreams, bad thoughts.

Beverly might no longer be with us.

But I got away with it.

And she would not think of it anymore. No one would know and no one would care, not if she let it evaporate. Who was April Nimitz, an elderly character (let's be frank, now that she was over sixty-five and the feminine and masculine aspects of one's face tended to blur into ambiguity) with two grown daughters, two little grandsons, and two of everything that worked, eyes, ears, hands, feet, kidneys, lungs. She was in good health, but harmless. Some might call her kooky, the one with the fun earrings. That she could walk a few miles in search of a doughnut shop did not indicate her capacity for violence. She knitted. She did seniors' aquacise at the YMCA. She watched Julia Roberts movies. She volunteered at the animal shelter. She sat on the board at the library and raised funds for its expansion of the children's section. She went to church. She spoke English.

She stopped at a carwash to ask if there was a doughnut place anywhere nearby. The woman at the desk pointed with her pen and told April that there was a great place two doors down. "They got kolaches, too," she added.

The Doughboys was lit with Christmas lights and played Paul Simon, *"I've reason to believe/we all will be received in Graceland"*. Her dozen doughnuts came in a pink box topped with a bow, sticker-ended and opal colored, meant for birthday gifts. April thought it was a nice gesture and very pretty, and she told this to the teenaged girl at the counter.

When Paloma was in high school, she remembered, she'd had an after-school job at a market, working the registers. At this market, the bags were multicolored, kept in ROYGBIV order with pink at the end of the spectrum instead of violet. A fellow came to her register to check out, the kind of fellow who had a gun rack on his truck. Not that this was anything unusual, the Nimitzes had a gun rack of their own on their Ford pickup; Juan and Pal hunted and April and Jen liked target shooting. This fellow was the kind of fellow who refused a pink bag when Pal went to pack his groceries. He was also the kind of fellow who purchased toothpaste that assured the consumer that his choice was FOR MEN. He barred her when she took the pink bag, the one that happened to come after violet in the row. "Get me the blue one, or something," he said, "Folks'll think I'm swishy." This was at the start of the AIDS epidemic, when people thought the disease was unique to homosexuals. His tone was light, Pal's face straight and serious. Nodding, murmuring "Of course, of course", she picked up the telephone and announced over the intercom ("Attention all shoppers, attention all shoppers—") that the customer at register five would like to make it known that, despite his pink grocery bag, he was NOT GAY. "I repeat: The customer at register five is NOT GAY. God bless." She quit before her boss could fire her. Before leaving, she dressed the store's decorative scarecrow in her apron and hat.

April had roared; it was better than "Take this job and shove it."

Juan, already into his third Famous Grouse, surmised that the fellow's concerns were unrelated to AIDS. It was his theory that the more men asserted themselves as "real men", the weaker they truly were. It was not a case in which the fellow "doth protest too much". It was not about sexuality at all. Men made prey of themselves. In a world where everything was a pissing contest, everything a one-upmanship, men lived in fear of being eaten alive for an act as small as carrying a pink shopping bag. Was it any wonder that Nazism had come into fruition, the way men were encouraged to turn on one another? Kill or be killed. Dog eat dog, or *Homo homini lupus*, as the Romans said.

April had thought, Ouroboros. You will consume your own ass-end.

Juan Nimitz had eaten his. He had exited as his father had, and April's father, as had a generous handful of other fellows that she had known over the years. Famous Grouse, Johnnie Walker, Nyquil. Aspirin, Seconal, tricyclic antidepressants. This was what came of calling boys pussies when they cried. Tears distilled into rage. Rage became impotent and the sorrow that followed was alien territory. You start a fight. You make yourself bigger. You don't tell people you listen to Tammy Wynette or that you like strawberry daiquiris. Was it any wonder that these fellows, proud and strong, had decided to check out early?

April had read somewhere that, in the days of the Roman empire, suicide was not a moral offense but an economic one. Your reasons had to be sound ones, a military defeat or chronic illness. A girl could off herself due to the shame of having been raped. You could apply to the senate and, if your petition was accepted, you would receive a lethal dosage of hemlock without charge.

What if, at one point in your life, you walked into a room and everyone in it stood at attention, as did the hair on their arms? What if you were feared? What if there was reason for you to be feared?

When I was seventeen, I sold a girl younger than me to a National Guardsman for camp scrip and twenty dollars U.S. cash. Twenty dollars was a lot of money back then. The girl was there alone with her kid sister. I gave her a pittance, but they had extra milk rations, and the kid sister never knew where it was coming from. The Guardsman made use of every orifice he could find on her. When she hid her earnings from me, your daddy told me to slap her around until she ponied up, because he couldn't bring himself to do it. I put a cigarette out in her left ear and I told her I'd put the next one out in her right eye, and that got her scrambling quick enough—

More likely, when in Rome, the senate would banish her to a crumb of an island, one without trees, where she would never speak to another soul, save for the circling birds.

And wouldn't that be her just desserts?

On her way back, she stopped at the Kroger's and poked through their fruit selection. Their oranges were not all they could have been, swollen and tough-skinned, but they had Mandarins. They came in blue netting and smelled heavenly. She went to register five and the girl (MY NAME IS GEN) told her, absent, "Have a blessed day." April told the girl the same, her voice bright. Gen was already ringing up the old man behind her.

Attention, all shoppers. Attention, all shoppers. The customer at register five would like to make it known that she is COMPLETELY HARMLESS. I repeat, the customer at register five is COMPLETELY HARMLESS. God bless.

She marveled, crossing the road, negotiating the box of doughnuts on one arm and swinging the netted Mandarins with the other, at how gemlike her memory had kept itself. April Hesse Nimitz could tell you the day, hour, sometimes minute of when a conversation happened, what it had been about, what the parties involved were wearing, the occasion, what they had to drink, what music was playing. She could catch anyone in a lie. She could detect an exaggeration, a minimalization. And she was always keen to point it out. "That's not what you told Val Fielding at the McCuistions' New Year's party. You said you'd have nothing to do with it. I remember it as plainly as that hacky little brooch you had on and the glass of punch in your hand. Two minutes before midnight." And she was so reliable, having corroborated with other witnesses about the brooch (a swan covered in rhinestones, if you were wondering) and the punch. Bing Crosby singing two minutes before midnight, 1970. *"Just a jackknife has MacHeath, dear—"*

And yet she could not recall what she had been trying to prove. Who had said about what that which they would have nothing to do? And had April seen them do it, whatever it was?

What she wanted to know was if anyone had caught her at anything. And if they had, would they have had the spine (the courtesy) to get in her face about it?

Juan was gone. Correction: He was more or less gone. He was in her periphery. In death, it seemed, he had nothing better to do.

He was the one who had the nerve to rub her face in her own mess. He did not know to be afraid of her, as she did not know to be afraid of him. When they met, just off the buses at Peralta Farm, photographed, numbered and deloused, assigned to the same cottage, they circled one another for the first few days. They had recognized a scent in the other, and it was difficult to know who was the predator and who was the prey. He was out of jail and his father had embraced him, lifting him, a bear of a man. Both father and son used the same cologne; it was nothing April had ever smelled before and the brand was still unknown to her. It was a soft smell, almost candied, and disarming. Juan's eyes were narrow and black, and he was very still when he looked at her. Not an animal, closer to what the Puritans must have pictured when they heard tales of witches' sabbaths and pledges to the devil by way of the osculum infame. If the devil looked at you the way Juan had, it was easy to imagine yourself eating his ass, because before long, you'd be doing just that. April, now as then, burbled and smoked, Vesuvius before the eruption. Juan told her she had the look of a volcano.

April told him he looked like someone who belonged on a registry.

"You and me both," he reminded her.

By contrast, everyone else walked on pussyfeet. April had once cornered her younger daughter, then ten. She had blocked Pal and grabbed for her when the girl tried to leave. April had been trying to get her younger daughter to say what she knew to be true. Cajoling, begging, threatening. Just say it. Just say it. Say I hate you. Tell me you hate me. You know you hate me. Everybody knows. Say you hate me. Paloma, determined to show that she was made of stone, shook her head. Her lip twitched, she blinked rapidly, her nose was red. The tendons on her neck stood out, for the words must have been churning there like vomit. But she had swallowed. She insisted that she did not hate April, though she looked sick. Would she have been sicker if she had just gagged it up? Jenny was away at college. Jenny would be gone for good. In retrospect, April thought that Pal was playing it wisely. She would be alone with her parents. You don't bite the hand that feeds you, do you? But before all the words could be said, Daddy had come home. Pal had run to him and he'd bundled her off to the backyard with the Rottweiler they'd had then. Nothing to be heard for miles around, save for barking and laughter, suburb sounds.

Juan never lost his cool.

And April, the one with the short fuse, had survived. Edit that: So far. She had survived so far. For as often as she'd said she'd do it, the idea of offing herself terrified her. Juan's afterlife seemed boring, and while April loathed having nothing to do, it was not eternity that scared her. Hell was a lot of unbiblical nonsense, and Heaven did not distinguish itself much from the purgatorial state that Juan now occupied. Words occurred to her: *separation, isolation, elimination.* The fear of being left out. Having to scream and croaking instead. To confess a murder to someone, only to have them wave you away.

Or say, "Well, what happened to you?"

After a while, you'd find that you'd prefer to be boiled in oil.

She'd forgotten her room key and had to bang on the door for a good two minutes. There was a bit of hustle and bustle as someone rolled out of bed and pawed around for clothes. Then it was Jen who came, yawning, rubbing her eyes. Pal moaned and turned in their shared bed.

April held out her offerings. "Out of the eater came something to eat—" it was an old riddle they had — "Out of the strong came something sweet."

Jen giggled. She snorted, too, a happy little grunt that was completely involuntary and absolutely genuine. Juan had called her Pigpen. She lifted the lid of the pink box and let her jaw drop. "I didn't know they did kolaches this far out," she said, taking one that was filled with raspberry jam.

April hadn't ordered any kolaches.

"There's two I guess they threw in," Jen told her, using the corner of her pastry to point. She went to grab Pal's toes. The youngest of their party jerked awake. "Doughnuts. And a kolache."

April let Pal have the second one, apricot. "Hey, there's oranges, too. So's we don't get scurvy on this voyage."

Pal split the netting with her pocket knife, took a Mandarin.

"Why oranges?" Jenny asked.

"At your request," April said. "For the banquet."

Now Pal brightened, and she wagged her finger as if to jog her memory. "Right, right. Remember?"

And Jen nodded. "Right. We had to make sure everyone at the banquet got one because they were made out of gold."

Her daughters were not twins, though in recent years, as they evened out in height, as they matured into these straight-up-and-down, ponytailed figures in blue jeans and leather boots, people were now more inclined to see them for the sisters they were. Pal had that grey patch and Jenny had good skin, and they had brown eyes and large, bunny-ish front teeth, the same dip in their upper lips. In Himmel Creek, out-of-towners would say it flat-out, "Y'all must be twins." And they were shocked to hear of the age difference: "Stop it. Y'all stop it. Really?" The days of the teen mom and fatherless mite were in the past. Now it was entertaining enough to tell people the truth.

They made a picnic on the bed and littered the mattress with peels and crumbs. April told Jenny that the girl who rang her up at Kroger's was also named Gen. "But spelled with a G," she noted. "What's that supposed to be short for, I wonder. Like Gennavere? Or Gendolyn?"

"Genevieve," Pal pronounced through a mouthful of blueberry cake doughnut.

"The hell kind of name is that?" April scoffed.

"From *Madeleine*," Jenny put in. "Those *Madeleine* books, the old house in Paris, twelve little girls. There's a dog in it who loved biscuits, milk and beef—"

"And so, they called her Genevieve," Pal finished.

April had named her first daughter Jennifer because everyone was calling their girls Jennifer. She had named her second daughter Paloma because she and Juan had tried a cocktail of the same name, and when they were throwing around last minute ideas, Paloma was the one that stuck. To think they could just as easily have called her Brandy Daisy.

Jenny had named her boys Gabriel Elijah and Rafael Akiva. Their first names were for angels. Their second names were for men who had seen the heavens and who had lived to tell the tale.

In the midst of the hubbub (sorting, packing, hauling, cleaning), the boys had raced around the Himmel Creek house. They did not know where they were. They did not know who Opa was, only that he was dead, and they had not gone to the funeral; they'd been at Beverly Across-the-way's all afternoon, brushing her cats, feeding the alpacas, playing Mouse Trap, helping the bitch make peanut butter cookies for the reception. They did not know who Oma was either. A curiosity? A witch? Had they figured that because Juan was dead, April would be next? When they were not racing around the Himmel Creek house, they trailed April's footfalls, freezing when she turned around, creeping up when she thought she was rid of them. She went to the bathroom and ten minutes later, guess who was waiting when she opened the door? They'd scattered when she asked them if they had nothing better to do than listen to someone take a shit. Jenny summoned them, using their full names. And then they trailed her; they called, "Mum Mum Mum, Mummy Mummy Mummy" before shouting "JEN-NAY". Here she would spin around, hands to her cheeks, mock surprise. And the boys would chirp, suddenly coy, "Hi, Mum." They stuck to her and Mo and Pal until it was time to split. Pal took them to the general store and bought them squirt guns. April asked the boys if she could play with them (unclear of what the game was, something along the lines of Cops and Robbers meets Star Wars). They'd told her No, because Gabe was Han Solo and Raffy was a Jedi cop (or something). They only needed two people.

She let her eye fall on the clothes horse outside the bathroom. Among the girls' socks and underthings was April's blouse, still stained, large as life, looking damp to the touch on the breast pocket. It was made of linen, this was how you took care of linen things, sponging them if you didn't happen to have a washer handy, hanging them up to dry. Jenny or Pal had done it for her, she supposed. Anyone else would have made a remark about the stain. Anyone else might have offered something to get it out. Or said something to the effect of, "Who shot you?" But in Texas, no one had. And in Arkansas, no one had. She took it as read that when they got into Tennessee, Kentucky, West Virginia, Pennsylvania, and up into New England that no one would notice either. The girls had not even touched it with water, just hung it up.

I got away with it.

"I guess you did," Juan said.

The room was quiet. They, April, Jenny, Paloma, sat in a minor coma, digesting, and Pal turned on the TV. They made coffee in the hotel's tiny pot, drank from Styrofoam cups. They caught the end of Maury Povich before rousing to tidy up. ("So, he's NOT the father. Shouldn't he be happy he's NOT the father?")

Pal suggested they leave the doughnuts they hadn't eaten in the lobby's breakfast nook; there were six left.

April pointed to the clothes horse and asked if the things there were clean.

Jen craned her head. "They should be, yeah." She peeled underpants and bras from the rungs, crammed them into the bags.

April's bra was fouled, too, and chilly, not having dried in the cold, cold room. It was a flesh-colored garment, bought from Land's End. As it happened, it was her only bra, the others too itchy or too tight for comfort, and she had thrown those away before leaving Himmel Creek. One of the cups, the one bearing the stain, held a muggy fetor, beyond the regular odors of healthy sweat. A human was not meant to smell of meat; a human did not like to be reminded of that fact. And only some of this odor was April's. The shard of porcelain was still there, she could feel it rolling from one end of the cup to the other.

She was pleased to see that she had not soiled Jenny's t-shirt. She had not looked in the shower, and locked herself in the bathroom, claiming a final pee before checkout.

"We have your key," Jenny called. "We'll meet you in the parking lot."

April's wound did not pain her, though she was disgusted by it. A real puncture, puckered red in the flesh of her breast, the skin warm all around it. It did not pain her, though she recalled reading something about how the rising temperature of skin around a wound was a sign of infection.

"Maybe it's plague," Juan mused.

While everyone at Peralta Farm caught lice or ringworm or whooping cough, we (you, me, the girls we picked up, a handful of guilty camp police) got the clap. You said it was all right for us girls, we would be asymptomatic. But wouldn't you know, we were red and flaked all over. It burned trying to pee, and that ought to have been retribution enough. You were the ones who went around scot-free. Asymptomatic. Everyone knew. We might as well have had signs around our necks. GONORRHEAL. RAVISH AT YOUR OWN RISK. You thought that was funny, so that was how I warned fellows about who had what. You worked things out with a crooked doctor at the medical block (he had a rash, too), and the Red Cross was suddenly very generous with their penicillin.

When she caught sight of Juan, it was in glimpses. He was a composite of what he had been and what he had become. As Frankenstein's monster was built from the filched pieces of criminals, Juan shifted, twenty-four, now fifty, now thirty, now seventy, smooth hands and yellowed teeth, thick hair and a reedy voice. She'd recently thought of her memory as a gem and it was, in its facets, not its clarity. She could take him to task and, while there was nowhere for him to go (where could he go?), he would have to let her blow off steam.

No scoffing and sauntering out the door for you, my fine, feathered friend. That's right, old buster, old pal. No going and doing God knows what. Now you have to stay put. Now you have to listen to me screech at you.

"I guess I had that coming," Juan agreed.

Now you'll have to suffer an eternity of bitching. I hope you're ready.

"As ready as I'll ever be." Sometimes he spoke with his old accent, sometimes he didn't.

So, no going and reincarnating as a grasshopper, or anything like that.

"I wish. But I have to listen to you bitch first. Neither of us deserve to come back as grasshoppers. I don't think we're going to come back at all."

What's this We jazz?

"I was tired. I am tired. Aren't you?"

Yes. April did not hesitate, for it was the truth. Yes, she was tired.

Separation. Isolation. Elimination. So, that was what happened. There was not a judgment, after all, no one waiting to bring her home or to cast her out or to reshape her. It elated her and saddened her. The heavens could not crack, not for her, nor for anybody. There was Sheol. C.S. Lewis had said of the nether place that souls did not burn there, only their remains; Hell was not made for humans. But this was not Hell. What, then, did you call this borrowed space within another person's grey matter? It was not a nether place because you were still very much IN the world, if no longer OF it. Correction: you were in the world, until you were not.

She shook the porcelain piece out of her bra and put it down her underpants. The ones she had on were standard issue "granny panties", as Jenny and Pal called all high-waisted briefs. The porcelain rested flat against her ass cheek, then shifted when she stepped back into her jeans. She found that when she sat down, the sharpest corner bit her flesh, and she was satisfied. She pocketed the tiny bottles of shampoo and body wash. A compensation for punishment? Or a reward for being thick-skinned?

"They have shampoo at other hotels," Juan told her, but she pushed past him.

She passed the payphones by the ice machine in the hall, catching a man say in one of the open booths, "Are they pretty? Do they party?"

In the lobby, she lifted breath mints and miniature tubes of Crest from the concession. No one saw. Or if they did, they let her. A little old white lady could get away with transgressions like these. A little old white lady could fill her pockets with this and that and explode in a fit of outrage when anyone tried taking her to task. Better to let her be. Shut her up. Get her out of the way. Covenants were broken. Laws did not apply. Delinquent white grannies ran themselves out of steam quick enough. So, she pinched orange Tic Tacs while she could.

The two blue heelers she'd seen earlier that morning lolled by their mistress's feet as she picked at one of the Doughboy doughnuts at a table in the breakfast nook. She was talking on a cellular phone and squinting out the window. Both dogs watched April as she stuffed a box of dental floss into her back pocket. One yawned, huffed. The other eyed her, equally unimpressed, and put its head down on its paws. Then they traded a glance, as if to say, "We must forgive them, for they know not what they do."

Human behavior was the least cut-and-dry. People got dogs because humans had to be looked after. April remembered how hesitant she was to step out of line when her Rottweiler was watching. He was ninety pounds and beefy and had a jaw that cracked bones. Juan named him Mars for the Roman god of war. In truth, he was such a sweet-tempered dog that the girls amended to calling him Mars Bar or Marzipan. He guarded them at night, walked with them to the general store off-leash. He puked in the lap of one of Jenny's early beaux and left a turd in a pair of Juan's oxfords. Following the latter, it became the norm for April to say, whenever someone was looking glum, "Who shat in your shoes?"

She wasn't hungry, but she took a doughnut from the box, the last one, doused in powdered sugar. Her face was sticky when she reached the car.

She remembered to ask the girls about their dreams when they were on the highway.

At this, barely inclining their heads, Jenny and Pal looked sideways at one another. April doubted if anyone else, even Juan, would have detected as much.

Jenny, then Pal smiled; April noted how their cheekbones lifted just that much.

"Well, you all had a banquet," she goaded. "With oranges. That sounds pretty colorful."

The girls allowed that it was, indeed, colorful.

April asked them if that banquet took place in the hotel parking lot the other night.

Pal snorted. Jenny glimpsed through the rearview mirror. "As a matter of fact, it was in a supermarket," she said.

Pal added that a supermarket was the best place to host a banquet. "You don't need to go out and shop for anything. And no one has to bring anything."

"You know what I mean, miss," April chided. "You're not supposed to be smoking crazy things like that."

"Would that we had crazy things to smoke," huffed Jenny. "Anyway, I don't know how you got to sleep at all."

April asserted that she slept as babies and logs do, save for the interval of unmarked time late in the night. "Wherein I heard you two living it up down in the parking lot. Singing and everything."

Pal, ensconced in the passenger's seat, snorted again. She bent around *A World Lit Only By Fire*, though her cheekbones twitched.

"You want to tell me what Little Miss over there is laughing at?" April snapped.

"Maybe she read something funny," Jenny countered.

April peered over Pal's shoulder, the book open to a passage about Ostrogoths and Visigoths.

"Maybe you dreamed it," Jenny said of the other night, the parking lot, the weaving, the crack, the flames.

"The fire alarm went off at around three," Pal put in. "We had to evacuate, but it was only for a few minutes."

Here was April, quieted. She listened.

"They had us get together in the front," Jenny added. "Outside the lobby. Not where you could've seen anyone."

Pal said, "It was only for a few minutes."

In the event of a hotel fire, it had not been their first priority to wake their mother? April could picture it clearly enough: warm smoke smell, the haze in the hall, the fire itself in a room two doors down, the biting alarm, the girls thick with sleep, hobbling among the Holiday Inn undead, remembering keys, handbags, shoes. Of their mother: "Never mind. She can get herself out."

Jenny placated, and April caught a trace of Juan in her voice. It was a gentle condescension. "It wasn't serious."

April gawped, countered that a hotel fire was normally considered disastrous.

"Someone tossed a cigarette in the bushes," Pal sighed. "The front desk people put it out with a bottle of water. They didn't call the fire department or anything like that."

And still the girls grinned. There was a joke between them, and April did not like finding herself as the butt of it. She accused them, affecting gaiety, her voice breezy, of neglect, calling them a pair of abandoneers. She declared that she would write them out of her will. She invoked their dead father, claiming that he would come back to haunt them for that.

"I'm not haunting them," Juan said, "I'm haunting you. You're infinitely more provokable."

He'd taken to gripping the back of her shirt in the way that her girls had done when they were small. April had not liked to hold their hands; Pal's were sticky and Jenny's were always wet. He tripped her up, yanked her left then right so that she might lose her balance. Going out to the van that morning, he laxed his hold on her, and just as she let herself ease into her stride, he summoned such strength that she found herself landing on her bottom, the kayakers peering over her. One fellow guessed vertigo, the other dehydration. April assured them that it was her own ditziness ("That's what I get for not looking where I'm going.") and puffed ahead to the van where her daughters waited, ponytails swaying. Now Pal was the one to come out with, "Well. What happened to you?"

The porcelain had fixed itself into her flesh. Then it came loose and was rolling again freely around her underpants.

In another era, April had thrilled at this kind of thing. Juan would pop, seemingly out of nowhere, and grab her up. He'd intuited this about her, that to April Hesse, violation was the height of fantasy. She gravitated toward demons. They consumed her and they did not sugarcoat it with sweets and flowers and holding open the door for her. Men like that, the chivalrous ones, thought that in these courtesies, they had paid for her already. The chivalrous men would drop the act upon rejection and demand what they were owed. These kinds of men wanted to pay at the end, not half now, half later, or up front, the way Juan liked it. Because of their status as fellow inmates, they thought themselves entitled to certain privileges. Certain procedures could be waived. When Juan organized dates with these kinds of men, he trailed them. He was in plain sight, but you had to really look for him. At the first hint of trouble (grabbing her wrist, calling her a cunt, threatening to tell her parents), he stepped from the shadows to drag her away. "If she don't like you, she don't like you," he would tell them, German and Spanish warring his English.

Joke was on them. My parents knew. Everybody knew. My mother did not want to touch me after that, let alone hold my hand.

"We weren't Nazis until we went to Girl Scout Camp," Juan had said to her in the past, as he said it to her now. "But. We got away with it, didn't we?"

The myth of Juan and April was a necessity. It was a romance. The girls held it up as a shining example of what could grow in captivity. Think of it, nothing was more American, nothing more fit to star people like Paul Newman as Juan and Eva Marie Saint as April. Even in the midst of Uncle Sam's gravest mistakes, love could find a way.

Jenny knew about Manzanar, and Pal had done a project on it in junior high school. Juan came into her class to give a lecture and answer questions. Times were hard. Rations were small. Space was limited. Everyone had to band together. Juan and his father had to share quarters with another family. Because there was not enough room in the small cabin, he, his father, and the patriarch of the other family, Mr. Hesse, built a screened porch for him to sleep on. In those days, people called enclosed porches Arizona rooms. In the Arizona room, the families gathered to play cards, to wave at their detained comrades and invite them in. Where else would you have seen folks from separate corners of the world telling tales, both myth and mundane? Juan had learned the story of Kaguya Hime, the bamboo princess, from his Japanese neighbors, and Juan's father and Mr. Hesse taught them "A Mighty Fortress is Our God" in German.

And romance, too. Of course, love was in the air. As it happened, Mr. Hesse had a daughter, a girl with hair as rubies and eyes as emeralds. Confinement allowed for conversation, then affection, then contact.

In the Arizona room, Juan and his bride-to-be welcomed the dawn and knew that they would have no other.

And it was true. April would have no other. And neither would Juan. As far as April could tell (and she could), he had never been unfaithful. Likewise, neither had she.

"Well, how would you have told it?" Juan asked. "You have something better, I presume?"

Not better.

N ot better, but April had put the experience through countless drafts. She trimmed this and added that. She scrapped and went back for that which she'd rejected, finding that it would be a useful detail after all. Things blindsided her, an odor, a phrase. It took no more than that, and April would picture herself not in the produce aisle of a supermarket, but in the camp mess hall, not doing much of anything other than scouting a place to sit with her orange and her half pint of milk. Virginia Woolf or someone had called it the continuous present, these lapses into a time you thought was over and done with. It was not so much that the past crept up on April; it simply tapped her on the shoulder.

It was never the worst parts. It was never the glamorous horror that boys coming home from warzones or survivors of Auschwitz were said to become engulfed by, likely because the hell that they had experienced was not of their making. April did not remember what she had done. Well, she did remember, but it was without dimension. They emerged as cold, hard facts, clear, enough to indict her if they were written on paper. When she pondered them (now, with countless hours and hundreds of miles, she had no choice), they had a stiffness to them, for she'd gotten to a point where sentiment had gone and she could confront them as words, no more or less. She could pretend that they were the narrative of someone else, also called April.

What if it had been April herself who had given the lecture and answered questions? Would Pal's eighth grade social studies class have been so keen as to view the whole thing through the lens of enchantment? Would any of these youngsters have approached the obelisk with reverence (affected or not) on their field trip?

On or around that spot, April would have told them, I made a girl my age dig her own grave. There was a fellow who paid to watch her do it, hiding on the rock. I told her he had a gun, though he was just another inmate. But she believed me. She kept digging. After a while, she stopped crying and threw down her shovel and said, Go ahead. I could have told her at any time that there was no gun, that the fellow was only jacking off; he liked weeping, apparently. I decided against it. Which would you rather hear? That there was a man somewhere waiting to gun you down? Or simply that your terror was exciting to him?

They came on school buses, the way that prisoners are transported, carrying with them what they could, as they did not expect to stay for very long. Like its Californian counterpart, Peralta Farm had been built to inter the Japanese, though it seemed that recent speculation had extended to include all possible sympathizers to the Axis Powers, Rome-Berlin-Tokyo. As per the Third Geneva Convention: *"The Detaining Power shall assemble prisoners of war in camps or camp compounds according to their nationality, language and customs."*

Manzanar had been named for the apple orchards of its ranching past.

Peralta Farm had been named for its view of the dome that rose up out of the earth, a great, pink hump against the flat horizon. The Germans who saw it from behind the fence called it an inselberg, meaning "island rock". Before long, the majority of detainees were German nationals, first generation, second generation, or dual citizens.

April was among the first generation.

Juan, though having grown up on just this side of the United States border, was nevertheless counted among the first generation through his mother (God rest her) and the second generation through his father.

In Himmel Creek, April Hesse made use of the space left in her vanity case by rolling her pajamas into tight bundles. Her suitcase was full, as were her Scout knapsack and overnight duffle. Her parents waited in the foyer. The police waited in the yard. The neighbors waited in the street.

In Tamaulipas, Juan Nimitz was given his civilian clothes back and told to board a repurposed cargo truck. Through the legal thoroughfares, a letter had come to the attention of the warden of a jail in Reynosa. Thus Juan Nimitz, also known as Hans Anton Linus Nimitz, learned that his father's health had declined. An old man before his time, Anton Gerhard Florian Nimitz now reaped the hindrances of a life colorfully lived. A bad heart, a bad kidney, a bad lung, the letter elaborated. He had what people then called the horrors; in the letter to Juan, it read more officially as delirium tremens. The younger Nimitz's sentence had been commuted to Peralta Farm where his father now waited.

In Himmel Creek, April wanted to feel as though she had done something to deserve her going, and so it came as a matter of course when a girl from across the way thought she might get away with calling the Hesse family "a lot of Huns" as they were being loaded into the truck. She saw that April had seen her and turned away to hide. But April was on her, too red, too angry, too propelled by those things for anyone to stop her. She made a quick work of the girl in the time it took for anyone to recognize what was happening. Imagine how it might have been if it were a regular day. Would the girl look as she did now, unrecognizable, a tooth gone, nose flattened? Or would nothing have happened at all? The first hands on her made April limp as a doll, and she went away willingly, having freed the demon in her, having taken for it blood and let the punishment fit the crime.

It was her father's hands on her, and with them he threw her against her mother before lumbering into the truck himself.

Miles away, Juan wept and did not care who saw. His father, who had alternately held titles of confidence trickster, enforcer, brothel owner, procurer, fixer, and smuggler, was to his son Bärbabba, or roughly Papa Bear. Likewise, Juan to his father was Bärchen, or Little Bear.

April's own father would not speak, not just to her, though that was but a small part of it. He would not speak to her mother, either. It was dark in the truck, the three of them, plus another family with a pair of twins a few years behind April. They were not girls that she knew, not from school or around Himmel Creek. It was dark in the truck, and yet they went stiff upon seeing Mr. Hesse. They did not speak, nor did they look at him again. Her father stifled a belch and studied his hands, fingers steepled, the wedding band wide against the knuckle. Her mother hissed, "If they didn't have reason for taking us off, you gave it to them. Animal. Animal." April thought at the time that her mother had aimed this denouncement at her.

"It was easier to snap at you," her mother would say many years later. "You never fought back. You were a sneak, but you never fought back."

April counted these words, and they seemed inadequate for the circumstances. At seventeen, as at sixty-something, she understood that this was what you did in order to live with yourself. The circumstances were not your fault (true or not) and so you used smaller words to scale down the chaos, make it manageable. April, being a sneak, was not guilty of anything other than naughtiness. Her father had the onus of subscribing to the German language newspapers, of submitting a letter to the editor long before the war expressing sympathetic tones toward the then fledgling Hitlerist brand of national socialism. He did not know what they were up to in Europe, he said when the camps in Europe were liberated. How could he, when he was here and they were there?

He would find himself in a very small minority of those at Peralta Farm who had ever harbored feelings of affinity for the Nazi Party. He was one of maybe two or three. And they would learn to shut up about it quick enough.

She would see her father among Juan's customers. They had an understanding, that she did not know him, as he did not know her.

Her mother withdrew. She had not liked to hold April's hands before, as they were prone to dampness and stickiness. She had never been one for embraces, for close contact made her freeze and she found herself unable to breathe. As her husband's affections were infrequent, April's mother learned not to trust them when they were doled out. She would come to ask, of father and daughter, "What is it now? What have you done?"

They, April and Juan, journeyed first by truck to municipal parking lots, miles from any town, where converted school buses waited. They were many like them, all burdened with bags, heads sweeping to the sound of a bullhorn that honked over the tarmac, which buses were full, which had open seats. Very little was articulate over the bullhorn, but the necessities jumped out. "PERALTA FARM. PERALTA FARM. SINGLE FILE. PERALTA FARM."

Juan, in later years, would come across a concept of Eastern folklore known as the red thread of fate. The thread served as the connection between two soulmates, each following the line of inclination or intuition that would lead to one another. In the cases of a male and female union, one end of the thread was tied to the man's thumb, the other end to the woman's pinky. It made for an absurd mental picture: two fools crossing the length of the globe, stooping to pick the yarn (April had always imagined red yarn instead of red thread) that had wheeled itself around trees and fences and parking meters, looping it from thumb or pinky to elbow until it amassed into ropy braids thrown over their shoulders. Meanwhile, the distance between them lessened, inch by inch.

They were soulmates. This was true.

April did not ride with the Hesses. She would later say, as they would, that in the confusion, she had gotten on the wrong bus. How awful it had been, they would all agree, that poor April had had to make that ride, hours and miles as one, alone. In truth, they were glad to have been rid of her for the five-hour drive south, into the hills and out again, as she was of them. They needed time apart from what they had seen her do. April needed time to sit in her own mess. She reveled in it, sneering at anyone who tried to talk to her, "How old are you, sweetheart? Where's your folks? Are you coming from Fort Worth? Smithville?", farting audibly and inhaling the stink, taking up more space than needed for her size. She steeped herself in loathsome thoughts. What could she have done if there had been a Coke bottle at her disposal? Would she have broken it, used its edge to cut out an eye? Give the woman a Glasgow smile, the way gangsters did in the movies? Or (and April laughed at this, drawing sleepy attention from the people in front of her). Or. She would not have had to break it at all, not yet. She could have left it in one piece, for it was big enough around with which to violate this opening or that, wedge it in until whichever hole she chose looked horribly overfilled, the strain to accommodate, so far up the canal that the only thing to see would be the blue-green glass bottom. And then April would break it.

Juan had seen her before she could see him. He maintained that she'd pushed people; she had no recollection of having touched anyone. People approached her, then stepped away. Before long, she was the only passenger with a seat to herself. "People know to be afraid of you," he would tell her. "No one's scared of me. No one believes I'm scary."

"I was never afraid of you," April would say.

"You didn't know to be. I don't think you would've talked to me otherwise." He was Bärchen. No one could be afraid of him. "You, now. You don't care if you look mean. These girls—" he would gesture the flock they'd procured from Peralta Farm's branch of the Federal High School—"—they think they can play me. And I don't complain, I can be played. And something else: they just want to be sweet. Gals live in fear of being anything less than sweet. Nice, polite. All that."

"The Not Like the Other Girls play," Juan would say on the night of their thirtieth wedding anniversary. "It got you to do your end of the job, didn't it? And it all worked out in the end, didn't it?"

We got away with it.

There were stops in the hills as the day went on. Now and then, more people would get on, a head count in a parking lot, owl-eyes and suitcases. And then they would roll on, into green pastures, creek beds, cypresses. The officers organized picnic lunches in order to make the trip jolly. And it did make it bearable. There were blankets put down, there were roadside stands selling chicken and corn on the cob, watermelon, lemonade. The buses had been segregated, whites on this one, Japanese on that one. But the mood was made high, if forcibly, and folks mixed, shared blankets, talked turkey; Mrs. Ogawa was delighted to learn that Mrs. Kirchhoff had been looking for a bridge partner ("If I can get my Jay and your Frank in on it, we'll have a proper setup."). Kids spat melon seeds and tumbled in the grass. You could overlook having been escorted to a toilet or into tall grass, pistols drawn in plain sight but held limply like toys. Everyone here followed the law.

April did not sit with her parents on these stops, and they did not look for her. She shared a blanket with a family from Erzengel, Mr. and Mrs. Engels and their children. April counted, six of them. Like the Hesses, Paul and Kristina Engels were in that murky place, not quite naturalized, no longer German, though they had lived in Erzengel longer than April's parents had lived in Himmel Creek, and came from the same part of Prussia. Their children were Peter, Emmi, Nikki, Rossi.

"Oh. Oh, he's not ours." Mrs. Engels patted the shoulder of the boy beside her, some years older than April, rightfully a man, red-headed and red-eyed, long-limbed, tight-lipped and protective of his rucksack and guitar case. Mrs. Engels introduced him as Hans. "Our neighbor on the ride up here." He was stiff, though his gaze was loose, flitting from one

Engels child to another until he landed, nimbly, on April.

"The mean one," he would say later on. At the time, he offered, "It's Juan, these days", and he expanded his survey to include the picnickers around them. His appendages were still, his head turning and lifting and craning.

At the time, April had thought of him as feral, a feral fellow, vulpine yet indelicate, who moved only when he must, and all the while he looked this way and that. It was mostly at the girls, April noted, and tracked where his gaze fell. He'd made an assessment of those in his immediate environs, at Emmi, then Rossi, whom April put to be about her age. (They were fifteen and seventeen, she would learn, pretty, malleable, as eager to embrace a new wickedness as she was.) Nikki, no more than four and greasy with chicken, was dismissed as a nonperson. It was clear that any female below a certain age (about fifteen or so) was a nonperson.

April continued to follow where Juan looked, and she found herself measuring up, cutting down, appraising, belittling. This was not a new habit, for she had never liked other girls and did not trust them. Was it really something so silly as jealousy? No, no it wasn't that. Competition was closer to it but for what? For a boy? It made April scoff. Boys, for all their folderol of the easiness of women, were beasts that could be duped, anytime, anywhere, for anything. Her mother told her that her body was a leaky vessel; the only ones who took any notice of the crack were the good old gals. The gals would snipe and sneer at anything that made you look loose, and they turned around and did the same things. You both kept score, how many boys wanted you, how many boys you'd gone so far with, and how far. If a boy was forceful, if he took what you'd hinted he'd get, the onus was on her. Didn't she know how stupid boys were? If anything happened that she didn't like, she had herself to blame.

That's what her mother said, anyway.

April summed: Too heavy, too busty, too cowy, too tall, too short. Too pasty, too gawky, too skinny, too oily. Her zits were an abhorrence, her nails were grimy, her hair was stringy, her lips like an anus.

"Fuck off, like you're Brigitte Bardot," Juan would say.

She paused when she saw the twins from the truck. They were sixteen, April would learn. Their parents came from the Nagasaki prefecture as infants and did not remember it. When Fat Man dropped a year later, they did not weep because it was not home. The twins themselves had twangy accents, outing themselves as country people, farming people, not from town. It explained why April had never seen them around. They were not identical, she observed. One was too prim, too pink, too prissy, too flat in the chest. The other was too perky, too plain, too posy, too duck-footed.

Juan caught her eye, smirked. "You ever seen a pair of twins before?"

April jumped. She'd thought she was being fairly subtle. Finally, she allowed that, Yes, she had seen twins before. "Just not in real life." She nodded at the guitar case. "What've you got there?"

She was truly astonished when he, indeed, produced a guitar, not a Tommy gun, as she'd envisioned. "I'm a creep, not a gangster," he would tell her. "What did you think?"

Of course, he'd had his belongings picked through before he got on the bus. And, of course, there were other inmates who brought instruments of their own, in trunks and wrappings of varying shapes. Guitars, mostly, but there were violins, trumpets, a flute, a trombone. Juan wandered off, taking the guitar with him from its case. The strings were nylon and warped a bit in the heat, but the song came through, again and again. He played and did not sing. But folks picked up on it and hummed along. A brave baritone came forward: *"Und MacHeath, der hat ein Messer/Doch das Messer sieht man nicht."* Then came whistling, and it flitted as a butterfly under the baritone. It was one of the officers, meant to be standing at the edge of the picnicking prisoners. But he lounged among them, shared their chicken. He'd unhooked his pistol and placed it by a Dixie cup of lemonade. Those who could snap their fingers did, and it became a regular little concert.

At the time, it was a funny ditty from the Weimar Republic.

In time, no one would resist "Mack the Knife".

Louis Armstrong would sing it. Bobby Darin and Frank Sinatra and the rest of the Rat Pack would sing it. Ella Fitzgerald would perform it in Berlin, forget some of the lyrics, and make up new ones on the spot. Bing Crosby would sing it on a stereo, two minutes before midnight at a New Year's Eve party in 1970. Sting would play MacHeath on Broadway. April would be hard-pressed to avoid hearing it, as anyone would be. It was so snappy, you could forget that it was about a killer and a rapist. It had a way of clinging, a favorite at parties, diners, on lounge lizard radio stations.

It had a way of luring, too, or Juan did. From the grass rose girls. To April, they materialized, emerging like nymphs from the ether. They stepped over chicken bones and melon rinds and reclining pairs of legs. There were too many to count, as it had seemed at the time to April. The ones who were too plain or too pasty stood near Juan and his guitar and absorbed from him a glow that made their eyelashes thick and their lips red.

This ought not to have been a problem, save the fact that April had already claimed Juan for her own. She hovered on the fringes and hungered. Her mother had called her a leaky vessel, and April knew it now to be true. How her mind had filled with fantasy. A lot of frenzied notions crossed her mind, and it took very little time for them to combine themselves into a single, concrete reverie: That she, a demon, would possess a willing host, being Juan. How or where she might penetrate him, she did not know, only that she might burrow into him and cling to his outer core, a proper parasite. Alternately, she fed off his spunk and his blood.

Love was in the air.

Love must have been in the air, or else Juan would not have looked at her the way he did, over the scads of simpering bitches sleepwalking his way. He looked at her. She looked at his fingers, his wrists, his indented upper lip, and imagined grafting herself to him as a second skin.

She followed, but did not allow herself to get too close. That one tenet of her mother's concerning young men stuck very much in place, to let the young men come to her in their own good time. To make the first move was to suggest her own desperation. And April Hesse was not desperate, not like this shuffling bunch, these woozy-eyed gals that were so easy as to fall for a fellow with a guitar.

"Not you," Juan said. "Not old April. Nothing gets by her."

And so, she did not sit with him or near him when the buses reloaded. She did, however, make sure that they were on the same bus. She calculated a place where he might see her. Of course, she wanted to see him, too, but Mother's law adhered, and she let Mrs. Engels take the seat next to her. They were toward the front for this leg of the ride, with Juan five seats behind across the aisle.

If April let her head rest just so against the window, she caught a hazy image of him, though in pieces, his fingers, his wrist, the curve of his lip. A scavenger, she fed on fragments. To feast one's eyes was charged with new meaning, for with her eyes she consumed so that her groin might be full. She might have stayed this way, exalting, not moving, for the rest of the trip, but the heat made her drowsy, and in another minute, she was in the thick of a horrible dream. She was in the Himmel Creek house. She was sitting at the kitchen table with her mother, but it was not her mother, it was a creature who wore her mother's skin like a veil and who spoke in a voice that was loud and deep enough to make April's fingers twitch. The creature said that it would pull out all her mother's teeth, and it would pull out her mother's eyes, and then it would take April and—

"Babe." Mrs. Engels patted her awake. "Babe. No more bad dreams. No more bad dreams."

Kneeling on the seat in front of them, Juan said, "Some bad dream. You're soaked right through." He'd rolled up his shirtsleeves and his bare arms draped in a pretzel over the edge. April wondered what he'd do if she decided to lurch forward, right there, to take the skin of his elbow between her teeth. He was lean, foxy, but fey. His arms were almost hairless.

Her dress stuck to her. She smelled damp.

She submerged when Jenny read the "Welcome to Kentucky" sign. The state motto was UNITED WE STAND, DIVIDED WE FALL. "Isn't that a Pink Floyd song?" Pal asked, and sang the line according to whatever song she thought it was. She had a good ear for mimicry, if not music.

"I think it's Sunny and Cher," Jenny mused.

They yawned and sighed and forgot about it and listened to a radio interview with an astronomer or an astrophysicist about the advent of human extinction. She was an academic from a university in California, with a lot of degrees following her name. A lot of the terminology was over April's head, as well as the girls', theorems and so on. Jenny might have changed the station were it not for the scientist's maneuver back into plain language, by way of stating that the first stages of man's fall could be expected by around 2040. There would be many factors responsible, disease, pollution, infertility, perhaps an asteroid. The scientist, also an ethicist, hazarded that whatever befell her doomed species would be through man's own folly. In the event of disease, there would be a portion of the population that would refuse to comply with mandates, thus making the idea of herd immunity obsolete. Pollution came from the general mentality of putting profit before preservation, through oil companies and other corporations. We would become infertile likely due to the growing pollution. The hole in the ozone. The felling of rainforests. The pointless endeavor of war. It made an asteroid sound like a blessing, she concluded.

It was at this point that Pal asked Jenny how all of that jived with her faith.

Pal never would have asked if she thought April was awake, and Jenny would not have answered. April kept her eyes closed, and she heard them shift in their seats to peer at her. When they judged her to be out, Jenny said, "I think what'll actually go extinct is the idea of life as we know it, not the species." Disease, pollution, and infertility had happened on grand scales in human history before, there was no reason why it shouldn't happen again.

"You think we'll go through another Dark Age?" Pal asked. She sounded intrigued, rather than frightened. Jenny affirmed that something like that would come to pass. She sounded certain, almost hopeful. They speculated and mused a bit more, and then concurred that maybe this time, "We'll get it right." In that, limited resources would force the species to reconcile all differences and, by abandoning the lust for immediate gratification that had fueled the twentieth century, man would finally understand the importance of putting the needs of the group before those of the individual. There would be no more billionaires or millionaires. There would be no more celebrities, no more pop stars, no more models with whom to compare oneself. There would be no more body-image issues, because food would be assigned its rightful importance, as fuel that was necessary to keep yourself going. Organized religion would be obsolete. Private property would be obsolete. Racism and sexism would be things of the past, as racism and sexism would be recognized for their divisiveness, ultimately their absurdity. There would be no mass-production, probably no electricity outside of solar power.

A world lit only by fire.

"Well, I can't wait," Pal crowed.

April calculated that she would be dead by the time this brave new world came about. She was not sure that she wanted to be alive to see it. In this world lit only by fire, would its indwellers see her as obsolete and throw her away? Or would she be an absurdity, wherein they would keep her as a relic, the way they put iron lungs in museum exhibitions? Or would she be a warning, to personify the message of, HERE'S WHAT WE USED TO BE LIKE, SEE HOW EASY IT IS TO SLIP INTO BAD HABITS? But her epitaph wouldn't be quite so sloppy. Very likely, in this bright and beautiful future that she would peer at from her zoo's cage, they would fix a proper slogan, something that would stick in the minds of anyone observing her. UNITED WE STAND, DIVIDED WE FALL wasn't bad.

She was seized by the need to ask Jenny why her daughter had not included April's and Juan's names at her conversion. She knew the answer. Officially, and in truth, it was because she was not a Jew and neither was Juan. A convert, when choosing a Hebrew name, always declared herself the child of Abraham and

Sarah; Jenny told her that more than once. And it would not be the first time that April would ask her about it.

Just say it. Just say it. Say you hate me.

Jenny never would, of course.

A pit stop: 87 gas, bathroom breaks, bottles of water and chips from Subway. They sat at a picnic table and fed tuna fish to the cat colony by the dumpsters from April's sandwich. She'd wanted to go back into the restaurant to complain; she'd found a shard of something, then another one. Whether it was glass or plastic, she couldn't tell. The girls inspected it on a napkin when they came back from the restroom. Pal offered to take the sandwich apart and promptly did so without waiting for an answer. She laid it out with the roll splayed wide and poked at the filling with a toothpick. The mayonnaise by now had settled into the bread and was turning it into a sponge. There were flecks of tuna fish spattering the napkin. To April, it made her feel like an observer at an autopsy. She snatched up her miniature bag of chips and said that she'd make do with them, as they were, at least, pre-packaged. Pal, finding nothing, shrugged and took a bite before tearing up a portion of the roll for the grackles that strutted around the tables.

"Big risk to take," April said.

"Not really." Pal flicked a crumb to a grackle that was brave enough to peck at her purse. "I think you got the only little bits of whatever it was. I got a scab in a sushi roll once." This last was meant for Jenny, who squirmed. It was one of their things: Pal would try Jenny's level of disgust, and Jenny would play up to it.

"Why do you tell me things like that?" she mewed, then asked, "Did you eat it?"

"The scab?"

"Creep. The sushi roll—"

They wandered back to the parked van, checked the tires, shooed bugs. They decided that the windshield and rear window needed scrubbing and were soon dunking wipers and tearing paper towels.

It was at this point that April judged them busy enough to forget her. She wanted them to forget her because she wanted to get a closer look at this fragment of glass or plastic or whatever it was. She paused, breathed. It was a common thing to find a scale in a can of tuna. You came across so many pulverized bits and bobs in the making of a salad that you'd be hard-pressed not to roll around in your mouth something that didn't belong. Juan had once found a bone in a tuna noodle casserole, and a worm in his mashed potatoes, and a larva in his carrot cake.

He'd once accused her of putting them there herself.

She said he must have scooped up the only creepy-crawly in the pot. She told him to eat his dinner.

Of course, because she hadn't done it was no indication that she had not wished it. What people called the wages of sin were now blithely referred to as karma. Juan got nasty and belittling with her, and so it was only just for a worm to appear in his dessert. April expected the same. She got nasty and belittling with Juan, and a fingernail might turn up in her omelet. It was only just. She'd long since given up on any suspicions of someone else tainting her food, for how many times since Juan died had she bitten into a cookie, an orange, a doughnut and made a discovery of this or that kind of vermin?

Jenny scrubbed the windshield; Pal scrubbed the back. They were talking about Daddy, that time they shot bottle rockets, that time they went berry picking, that time the tire blew out and they screeched offroad, that time they killed a snake with a shovel. "I still have the tail," Jenny was saying.

"Did we do all that stuff in one day?" Juan asked.

April told him to get out of her way and reached across the table for Pal's bottle of water, half-full, and tipped some of it over the thing from her sandwich. It had not quite felt like glass, it was too pliable. Catching it on her tongue, she remembered that it had a curve, a curve that came to a point. She patted it dry with the edge of her shirt and squinted.

Juan whistled. "I don't think we ever found one of those." He laughed, looked over at the cat colony. "I wonder if they let all the kitties into the kitchen on wet days. Remember when we used to do that? Leave tuna out for all the kitties?"

April had hated Juan calling cats kitties, and told him there was no need to keep it up now. While a cat's claw was unusual, she would admit, it was just. It was a loose claw, one of those that flake off when a cat kneads its paws. She could hardly make it out, clear as it was, akin to a human fingernail, save for the point. She decided to laugh about it, too, and asked Juan if he remembered that poem about the fellow who found a mouse in his food.

> *Said the waiter, "Don't shout,*
> *And wave it about,*
> *Or the rest will be wanting one, too!"*

Juan nodded.

Peralta Farm welcomed its inmates with a rendition of "The Liberty Bell March", performed by an already remanded troop of Eagle Scouts. It made one and all think of Fourth of July festivities and they did not make a fuss when suitcases were opened, underwear rifled, army knives and sewing kits and corkscrews and bottle openers and handguns (and their accompanying registrations) pocketed. There were Rottweilers, which could be made cuddly upon demand; kids ran to them and officers told them to let the dogs sniff their small hands first. "Want to see this one do a trick?" One of the officers gathered a crowd and clapped his hands for the dog to stand at attention. The kids did, too. "Old Alfalfa here, he can count." The officer held up six fingers, and to the children's delight, old Alfalfa barked one-two-three-four-five-six, snapping up a treat when the officer put his hands down. But there was only time for one trick, for the bullhorn appeared again, a godly crackling from a high tower in the corner of the sky, and the command was handed down and everyone split, Huns, Japs, Wops.

At Peralta Farm, it was mostly Huns. Was that why they got a chicken lunch?

April hid behind the Engels clan. She wondered if anyone would guess that Mrs. Engels was not her mother. She followed them, who followed an armed quartet of National Guardsmen into a place that had at one point been a barn and was now decked out with long tables and benches. More than ever, it smelled of body. It was not the sharp, animal funk of cows or horses; people, by and large, had a flat, stagnant odor, one that crept up, disappeared, and crept back. You were always looking for the source of the smell, you shifted your head right and left, you scowled at anyone whose eyes you met, to say, "Was it you?" But what did you do when everyone reeked? April found that she could not smell herself, and remembered her mother saying something to the effect that it was a sure sign a person was in need of a bath if they could no longer detect their own stink.

A few folks fainted and space had to be made on some of the tables for them to be laid out. Juan Nimitz, she saw, helped bring around Rossi Engels and one of the farming twins, the plainer one. His eyes were soft with concern, as were his hands to their foreheads when they woke. How grateful they looked when they saw it was him. He bent and whispered something into Rossi's ear, then Mildred (the name visible on the girl's luggage when Juan brought her suitcase). While he played the gentleman, he managed to catch April's eye, and he grinned.

He would later say, "It was like you knew what I was up to. Not just that, but like you knew you'd be missing out on something."

She could not do what Juan could do, and she did not want to. She was no good at subtlety and to play up to anyone, simpering, made her physically ill. You catch more flies with honey, as the saying went, but what was the point if the ones you caught came to hate you for your trickery? Better to be hated, she decided. The emperor Caligula had said, "Let them hate me, as long as they fear me." As long as they knew what April was about.

She lumped, suitcase and vanity banging either hip, as directed to the end of a long table. Across from her sat a Red Cross woman and between them, a clipboard, a pen, a pitcher of ice water. The woman called her Miss Hussy and it was difficult for April to answer her, for the woman was asking the same questions as the other fifty-odd Red Cross women and they all overlapped.

"What—" April shook her head. "What was that again?"

Her Red Cross woman sighed and enunciated. How old was April Hussy? Was April Hussy still in school? How many more semesters did she have left before graduating? Did April Hussy have any secretarial skills?

"Like what?" April Hussy sniffed.

The Red Cross woman patted her hairline with a bandana. "Do you type?"

"Sure."

The Red Cross woman glared. "It's Yes or No. Do you type?"

"Oh. Then, no."

Moving on: Had April Hussy ever had measles or mumps?

"Every chance I get."

The Red Cross woman made a gesture of surrender, a grand flap of both hands, and told her to take this ticket (she held it between fore and middle fingers) and to join those assembling as Group 4. "They'll be your neighbors while you're here. So, be considerate."

April rose.

The Red Cross woman thumped on the table with her fingernails. "We're not done yet," she barked and motioned for April to sit. She then waved for a guardsman, who told April that she would have to be fingerprinted.

April showed them her greyed hands. The Hesses had been fingerprinted already, at the post office, before the police brought them home to pack. There had been a hold up when the time came for April to have hers done. Unbeknownst to her and to her parents, April Hesse had no fingerprints, at least none that could be inked and reprinted. The police officer had shunted her hand from the ink pad to page after page of identification sheets. Her hand beyond her fingers and thumb was grimy with the stuff, her mother hissed and her father swore. April snapped at them that she wasn't doing it on purpose. The police officer had tried to make a joke of it, saying that April had a bright future as a thief, and her father shouted. She wasn't sure if it was at his daughter or at the officer, she didn't speak German. Finally, the officer relented and chose out of all the sheafs of wasted paper the prints that were the least smeary.

"No harm in trying one more time," the Red Cross woman said, and April splayed her hands for her, the way she would in a salon. Indeed, her nails were black, darkest at the tips and purpling toward the cuticle. Again, the ink. Again, the ID sheet. First, her thumbs, then each of her fingers, then all of them together.

The guardsman frowned, asked if she had done anything to remove her prints. To her stony eye, he elaborated, "Some folks try and burn them off or cut them off."

"Like who?" April asked, despite herself.

"Mob guys," the guardsman said. "Pickpockets, people like that. John Dillinger tried it, but they grew back." He mashed her thumb into the ink pad again and smeared it onto a second ID sheet. The whorls and hills were more prominent in this one, and the guardsman said it would be easier to find her than she thought. The Red Cross woman sat deaf to this exchange. He wiggled his eyebrows and April told him to go and finger himself. She tried to sweep coolly away under the weight of her luggage; she tripped and the guardsman laughed. The floor was moist on her rump, where of course she had to land, and it was a struggle to get up without showing her underwear. But she did it, luggage and all.

Her parents tried to be innocuous and kept toward the middle as Group 4 trudged ahead. April kept to the edge of the herd; she was certain that everyone had seen her failed rebuttal, her fall on her bottom. Her mother held her hat to her head with her free hand. April thought she looked very stoic, but then Kathe Hesse was not one to crack a smile or shed a tear. Max Hesse adopted the same stance, though while his wife kept her head down, he did not appear to register much of anything, save for the inclination to move forward. He lumbered under the burden of his and his wife's suitcases, while she had her handbag and his rucksack and a footlocker. She, greying and pin-straight, anchoring that crocheted cloche with the bow in the back, ankles bleeding and blistered from her shoes, her breasts drooping. He, wide-eyed and limping from his bad knee, sweating through his white shirt so that you could see the knobs of his spine, his nipples.

Along the way, April learned that the camp's third or fourth incarnation had been that of a desert retreat for the Secular Order of Discalced Carmelites. The Red Cross woman, a friendlier one, walked backward so that she could face Group 4, as though this were a guided tour. The guardsmen perked up, feigned interest. The sorority put its name to the test and would go barefoot for the duration of their stay. They were bested when, in the late-thirties, a plague of fire ants rose up and chased the nuns toward greener fields (and sturdy sneakers).

April heard whistling, saw Juan before he saw her, and tried to keep up with him, *And did those feet in ancient time...*

"Excuse me—" The group came to a halt as the Red Cross woman waved toward the back. She bleated, "Could there be quiet, please? This is an orientation."

April wolf-whistled and she was embarrassed at her pride, having made Juan laugh.

The original cottages remained, tiny replicas of Swiss chalets, painted pink and green and white. This was where the Engels and the Ogawas would live. The camp, as determined too late, was too small to be completely split by Axis affiliation, and so families were doubled up, some tripled up to a single house. Some, the luckier folks, were given the new prefab cottages that backed up against the old chalets. Perhaps it was because Max Hesse had been a part of the Chamber of Commerce. Who knew? Here was where April would find them, Mr. and Mrs. Hussy, as she let herself call them, who were shaking out their clothes, accepting that this was where they now lived.

Her mother looked up. "Well. What happened to you?"

She directed April to a cot, two of them altogether, lined up as in a hospital. Numbly, April put her vanity case at the end of the mattress, her suitcase and rucksack under the bedframe. She righted herself to speak to one or the other of her parents (maybe she had wanted to be held by her mother), but they had already gone, out into the little yard they were allotted, talking in close, quiet words. She didn't know what she was so surprised about; the Hesses kept to themselves, each of them in a retreat from the other two. They were three people who happened to live in the same house, and the present circumstances were no different. She came to a conclusion and it stuck: In the time between being called Huns and their arrival, April had been subtracted. Had the Hesses talked about it on the bus? At the picnics? A cold shoulder, a foggy recognition, and then invisibility?

She was seventeen and certain things settle and become fixed.

Caligula or Tiberius had said, "Let them hate me, as long as they fear me."

She recognized how small the cottage was, how much space the four cots took up. She stepped into the smaller, second room. Another two cots in here, lined up, too. One of them was occupied by an old fellow who looked to have been a Titan in his youth;

his feet hung over the end of the bed, and his hands were enormous, folded over his chest. He emitted light snores through his teeth, making a *zzzuh-zzzuh* sound. He reminded April of a man out of a legend, Goliath or Jove. But he had a beard, and his hugeness was minimized by the fact that he might wake up, as Rip van Winkle did, confused and bumbling, and it made April feel sorry for him.

She tiptoed away from the cot to get an impression of this room as a whole, who else the Hesses would be living with. Here were boots, a trunk opened and lived out of at the end of the old man's bed. But the second cot, closer to the window, whose white tennis shoes were these, whose rucksack? She jumped, for there was a closet, slatted door swung open to deep darkness, humming from within, and she was reminded of the dream she'd had coming out here. April shut her eyes, remembered, *I'll pull out all her teeth, I'll pull out her eyes, and then I'll take you and—*

"You ought to wash up." A voice behind her, a hand in her hair, squeezing. "You're looking a little rough." And there was Juan. He smirked and rolled the dust from April's hair in his fingers.

How was it that she could tell a guardsman to fuck himself, and at the same time want nothing more than for Juan Nimitz to touch her again? She told herself that it was simple, the guardsman did not have Juan Nimitz's voice, his hands, his wrists, his teeth. Chemistry was one half the battle, anatomy the other. The guardsman and men like him were not made of the same stuff, though they said and did the same things. It was what made it easy for April to join Juan Nimitz in the tiny galley kitchen, to accept a damp cloth.

When she'd scrubbed her face and neck and ears, she took a seat opposite him at the table, in the room that would serve as a dining area, a lounge, and partial bedroom for the Hesses. There was running water, but it was warm and tasted of sulfur. There was electricity, but it went out half the time. April watched flies buzz about the room and Juan watched her.

At last, she thought to ask who the big fellow was in the other room.

"Bärbabba."

"Say again?"

"Papa Bear."

"Who's Papa Bear?"

"Him." Juan pointed.

April rolled her eyes. "No, I mean. Who is he to you?"

"My father." Juan nodded out the window, at April's mother and father, still wandering, not talking. "Who're those people?"

"They are Mr. and Mrs. Hussy."

"Who are Mr. and Mrs. Hussy?"

"Them."

Juan probed, "Does that make you April Hussy?"

Not knowing what else to say, she fell back on the questions the Red Cross woman had asked her. How old was Juan Nimitz? Was he in school? Did he have any secretarial skills?

"Twenty-four. Not in school. I can't type, but I can build, do plumbing, light electrical, cut down cedars. This and that."

Did Juan Nimitz have measles or mumps?

"I had the clap once."

"What's that?"

He told her.

She nodded. Under the table, she swung her right foot, her left tucked under her. She dug her thumbnail into the ham of her hand, well aware of the gap in conversation. She had never spoken to a man, a man like this, before. In the time it took for the light in the galley kitchen to go off and then on, she racked her memory for the cues and stances that actresses had. In the movie *Camille*, Greta Garbo played the part of a courtesan, at once cool, but without any chill. Greta Garbo's whore understood that talking to a man required some strategy, the right tone, the right words—

It was at this point that Juan asked April, "So, did I hear right? Did you tell a member of the military police to go fuck himself?"

"I told him to finger himself. Which is the same thing, I suppose."

Juan Nimitz put his palms together in light applause. His hands were black, too, his fingertips the darkest and April showed him hers, her very faint prints. "I don't have any either," she said. But she noted something about the pads of his fingers, how their texture appeared slightly pillowy. He turned them over for her to examine. The palms themselves were run with calluses, yellow, some picked at like scabs. The fingertips had a shine to them, a rawness that indicated the middling stages of healing.

She said, "John Dillinger did that."

"I used a cigarette. He cut the top layer of his skin off, then burned his fingers, I think, with acid."

"Do cedar choppers not need fingerprints?"

Juan shook his head. "It's for the this and that part. I figure, we're already here, behind the fence. I oughtn't be ashamed."

"Are you a thief?"

"Sometimes."

"You're not in the mob, are you?"

"Not exactly, no."

"Is this and that your full-time thing?"

"When I'm not doing this and that, I play the guitar—" He broke the word up, pronouncing it "ghee-tar"—"—I paint, I write poetry—"

"No, you don't," April cut in flatly.

Juan chuckled. "No, no I don't. And you? Do you paint or write poetry?"

April panicked for a moment, debating the right answer. It was something she used to worry about, and she despaired at all the time wasted on pointless calculations, divining what it was her mother and father wanted. It was easier, she found, to be plain about herself. She did not have the energy for much else. She told him, "I can make a sailboat out of a napkin."

"Show me."

She showed him.

Again, she made him laugh. The pleasure of it was inordinate, since nothing she'd said or done had been particularly funny. What she'd produced was maybe slightly more competent than what a child could've done, and she'd managed to stain the napkin with her soiled hands. He took the paper boat from her and glided it across the table, whistling "Anchors Aweigh".

What made her think of it, she didn't know, but she blurted, "Have you ever been in jail?"

Juan laughed again, and he folded and refolded the little sailboat. "How'd you guess?"

"It wasn't a guess. Just a conversation piece."

"It's one hell of a way to make conversation."

"To be honest, you have the look of a mobster."

"To be honest, I'm not a mobster."

April swung her foot, dragging the toe of her shoe. Her other leg was brimming with pins and needles. "You said you weren't exactly."

"I've only ever seen the hide of them," Juan told her, "A bunch of wops in a pissing contest. They're all paunchy. They're all short; their guns are taller than some of them. The krauts have one, too, because they bitch and moan if they're left out of anything. And those guys all smell like ham. You'd be disappointed."

She was about to ask what he'd been locked up for when a stirring came from the bed in the other room.

The giant had woken. At the first grunt, Juan sprung from his chair and was at the old man's side. He murmured something into a great conch of an ear, and April picked what German words she knew from the exchange, something-something-something *kopf,* something-something *kopfschmerzmittel,* something-something *wasser,* something-something.

The old man hacked and spat and uttered a phrase she'd heard both of her parents throw around: "*Wer rastet, der rostet.*" They'd never translated it for her, though she had an idea that it was close to "The early bird catches the worm." That said, and to prove his vitality, the old man arranged himself upright, ran one hand through his hair, the other through his beard. He had his son's wide mouth, the same dip in his lip. He lifted his arms in a grand stretch, and his fingers graced the whitewashed ceiling. April observed two runners of pale, purplish streaks there, where his hands had touched. She was curious to see if Bärbabba hadn't any fingerprints either.

His height caused April to rise from her chair. Her leg had fallen asleep. She made a picture, resting all her weight on one foot like a flamingo, clinging to the table's edge; it was all she could do to keep from falling on her rump a second time. What she could do, she reasoned, was to keep her voice low and straight. (Did she look seventeen? Could anything be done at this moment to appear a minute older?)

Juan's father had an appraiser's eye. Like his son, he took a moment to weigh her up and down before any words were said. April understood it, it was something that men did when a girl reached a certain age. Here, your worth was counted. Your lips, legs, bust, waist, neck, navel, feet, hands were dissected, analyzed, and reconstructed to form a general impression. This was not to say that every man she met had done this, but it was a common enough practice of which she knew by now to submit. She knew, also, that it was wise to play up to it. Her mother called her loose when her father's friends on card nights made furtive glances at her, but it was these same men who gave her dollar bills, in their words, "just for looking pretty".

No woman had ever given her a dollar bill for looking pretty.

She did not know if she was pretty. April Hesse, as a female specimen, had always known herself to fall on the plainer end of beauty's scale. Her natural expression, the one that emerges when you find yourself or think yourself to be alone, was one of sullenness. And her nose was snubby, besides, and her hair too bright, her feet too big, her teeth too yellow—

"Bärchen," the old man croaked, then in sudden English, "will you introduce me? Will you introduce me to this lovely lady?"

Stunned, she sifted through what she could remember of Greta Garbo's heroine in *Camille*. It crossed her mind to curtsy, and thankfully, she did not. *Camille* took place in 1850s gay Paree. There were no ball gowns or hoop skirts here. But she could extend her hand, palm down, for him to take—a ladylike gesture, and one that would conceal her the worst of her inky fingers.

Juan introduced her as April Hussy.

His father kissed her knuckles. She let out a yelp of surprise, the same "OH" that came the day the yellowjacket stung her thigh. His mustache pricked her skin, and he left a wet stamp where his lips had been. And his fingers, the tips scabby where his son's had pillowed over into scar tissue, linked, ring by ring, around her wrist. (If he'd wanted, he could have broken it.) A bit of purpled ash flaked from his hand to hers.

She really ought to be grateful. It beat subtraction.

"*Shatzi,*" Bärbabba pronounced. Then he craned his head back. He said to his son, "*Sehr schön,* April Hasi." For April's benefit, he added, "Hasi is, it means little rabbit. Eh? April Hussy, April Hasi?" He repeated, "*Sehr schön.*"

Juan nodded.

They pulled over in Memphis to walk around. The house at Graceland was closed for renovations, but the grounds were open to the public. They paid respects in the meditation garden, at the graves of Elvis and his parents and his stillborn twin Jessie. Pal etched her initials into the brick wall around the estate and Jen stooped and gathered pebbles to place at the graves, three for each headstone. When she could not find pebbles small enough, she settled for nicely shaped bits of broken glass, from green beer bottles, mostly. The gravesite was gated and so she had to throw them just so. Many of them got lost in the deluge of flowers and bouquets and wreaths.

Pal asked, "Didn't Lisa Marie marry Michael Jackson?"

Jen said, "Yeah, but now they're divorced."

Pal: "Isn't he supposed to be a eunuch?"

Jen: "He's gross is what he is."

Pal: "Why's he gross?"

Jen: "Don't you watch the news?"

April considered leaving the porcelain shard and the cat claw to mark her visit, but thought the better of it. A rash had flared on her breast, and when it did not itch like the devil, it burned. It was the most sensitive toward her nipple; she yelped when she scratched it.

"Get rid of that crap," Juan told her. "You're scaring the girls."

April informed him that they saw nothing, therefore, they knew nothing.

"You'll get, you'll get whatever it is folks get from dirty cats. Trichomoniasis, or whatever it is."

"Toxoplasmosis," April corrected.

"What about it?" Pal at her elbow. She had Juan's nose.

"We've all probably got it now," April sniffed at her, "From those nasty strays at the gas station. I hope you both washed up good, loving on them like you did."

Following Graceland, they were reluctant to get back in the car just yet, and extended their Memphis tarriance by going to the local cineplex to see *For Love of the Game*. Because it was midafternoon on a weekday, they had the theater to themselves. It was a rather pleasant time for the three of them, as it turned out; Kevin Costner and Kelly Preston hadn't any chemistry to speak of, with Kevin so clueless and Kelly who seemed to cry at the drop of a hat. The Nimitz women played the peanut gallery, hollering at the screen when they were not saying snarky things about the plot, the dialogue, the goofs.

"Here she goes," Pal crowed when Kelly Preston burst into tears for the umpteenth time. "Every time Kelly cries, you have to cry with her." And they would ham it up, boo-hoos and drawn-out whines. "Don't let that bitch cry alone. She's in love with a moron."

"Just DROP him," they shouted at the screen.

"Go for the guy at the airport bar, with the pretzels," Jen suggested.

"She's revving up now." April sipped at their shared Dr. Pepper in a king-sized cup. "Old Kevin did it again. Here comes the flood—"

They were as a trio of cats.

Jenny had cried and Pal had cried, and it seemed that they would cry again here, for real. It had happened before on this trip, out-of-the-blue wellings that would mysteriously come, inspired as they were by hidden, almost secreted things. Blink and you might miss them. A portion of a song could do it for Jenny. Since having children, weeping came easier for her. Since her father passed, her eyes would acquire a glazed, overfilled look, so that she had to pinch her nose to keep from leaking. Pal's tears came from a more remote place. You could not tell if it was the song playing, or a color, or an odor, or a taste. Pal was the one least likely to let herself collapse, and yet here she was, fake blubbering become true in this theater, before this awful movie.

April was astonished, too much so to say anything useful. She managed, "You give Miss Preston a run for her money."

She was sitting in the middle of the middle row, flanked by Pal on her left and Jenny on her right. Jenny reached, napkin in hand, to blot at Pal's nose and eyes. Her arm blocked April's view of the screen. The movie had taken a more exciting turn. Kevin Costner had injured his hand so badly he doubted he would ever play baseball again. April ducked and craned, seething. She knew, of course, that Kevin Costner would play baseball again (as he did in all his pictures), and if he didn't, he would get Kelly Preston as consolation. Knowing what would happen, however, was not the same as seeing it happen, and April moaned aloud when her daughters leaned across their mother to embrace each other. ("For GOD'S sakes—") She could feast her eyes on their tattooed forearms. Jenny had been inked first, a thirtieth birthday present to herself, a copy of a little rabbit a la Beatrix Potter on her left. Because anything Jenny did, Pal had to do, too, the youngest Nimitz got a series of tats, lines and dots in a Morse code that wrapped around her arm from elbow to wrist.

Their conjoined heat made April sweat. Her blouse was damp, slightly oily over her breast, in which the shard and the claw both settled comfortably. Had they both worked themselves into the flesh completely, or had they simply rendered it?

Once upon a time, tattoos were for the loose and unsavory. Now, everyone was getting them.

If tears were a sign of one's ability to change, what was the reason for the stuff of blood and pus? Wages of sin? Another avenue for release when tears would not come? In school, she'd learned to say the Confiteor and to beat her breast three times, uttering with each strike, "Through my fault, though my fault, through my most grievous fault."

Don't they know I'm here?

"You pansies—" April could not breathe and slapped her daughter's arms apart. "Couldn't you do this in a more private place? Like the bathroom or somewhere? Instead of making a public thing—" She stopped when she remembered that the theater was empty, save for the three of them. Without looking at them, she pushed past Jenny on her right and stalked up the aisle. "I mean, GOD. Have some poise."

Behind her, Jenny's cracking voice, asking her where she was going.

"To the bathroom."

"To do what?"

"To do what is considered appropriate to do in a bathroom."

April locked herself in a stall and peeled off her blouse. She'd lost count of how many shirts she had ruined. She was down to one unsoiled bra, and that was the one she had on. The sourness of her clothes caught in her throat, and it roused a momentary passion in her that caused her to tear it from her body. A strap snapped and kissed her cheek, leaving a mark. One cup was spotted, though wet by another substance than blood. April retched; she could stomach pus less than blood.

That breast was swollen. The implements looked to have been absorbed by her bosom, rather than driven into it. She put the flat of her hand to the spot, tapped it three times, for it hurt just as much as if she'd brought down her fist. Through my fault, through my fault, through my most grievous fault. She sank onto the toilet seat.

You got away with it.

Because there was no one else around, she asked Juan if he'd ever done anything to the girls.

They'd had this conversation before.

Again, Juan was steadfast. "Never."

"You swear on—" April fumbled. He could not swear on his life because it had ended. And he could not swear on the Bible because he was against that kind of thing. Anyway, the Good Book had its share of heroes getting up to vile acts. "I don't know—swear on this." She offered him her filthy bra.

He put his palm to it and swore. "What would you do if I'd said Yes?"

"Resurrected you and beheaded you."

"Is that a euphemism or do you really mean my actual head?"

"Why not both?"

He looked the way he did when they met, his hair thick and auburn, his teeth white and straight, his eyes clear. It was his hands that repulsed her, for they were as they had been in his last days. She could see the mechanics beneath the skin, how the sinews and bones connected, and how readily they moved when Juan rippled his fingers. His epidermis might have been made of paper by that point. He'd been ashamed in those last days of the keratoses that marred the backs of his hands, black scabs and other rough spots that he'd been convinced were cancerous, despite his doctor's and Pal's reassurances that they merely looked hideous.

"Jesus God, help me," he'd sobbed that last day, "it's the plague."

In this toilet, April asked him now, "No one else? Not their friends?"

"I was tempted. There were one or two. You could've picked them out."

April puzzled. The girls had always seemed to prefer to visit with friends at their houses, rather than bring them home. Pal had had that one birthday party, and people were hesitant to come back, as though the place were cursed. And Juan's tastes tended to be all over the map. He'd liked the meek and the short-fused equally well. She considered Jenny's circle of gal pals growing up. Had it been Eileen McCuistion's girl, that mealy-mouthed thing whose presence (and name) you quickly forgot? Or had it been Val Fielding's Esther, who would've bitten your hand as soon as shaken it?

It was a new low, to find herself jealous of girls she had made peanut butter and marshmallow sandwiches for.

"I made you watch your step," April told him.

"Yes. You did."

"If I'd suspected anything other than temptation, you know what I would've done to you."

"I would've had it coming."

"Yes. You would've."

"Hell hath no fury, as they say."

"Lucky for the both of us that you're a pussy."

"You probably would've gotten away with it," Juan said, "if it ever came to that."

Paloma had once asked April about God. This was back when Jenny was a fairly new convert, still, and had lot of positions on things, some superficial (no pork, no shellfish, no Jell-O), some more profound (not to take the Lord's name in vain, though this seemed to be a green light for her to use the F-word in all its bounty). April and Juan had stopped going to Mass and kept the Sabbath in their own way, which usually took the form of lazing around and adding something fun to their orange juice at breakfast and to their coffee throughout the day. April had been dozing on the backyard grass and opened her eyes to her second child peering over her.

"So," Pal said, as though she were picking up where they'd left off on a talk they'd never had. "God punishes people when they do wicked things. Right?"

April had laughed at her daughter's use of the word *wicked*; it made her think of green-faced witches. "That's how it works, yes."

Then Pal's face darkened, and looked craggy. It was possible to imagine her in an Old Testament court, the glowering eye of a rabbinical judge. "Aren't you afraid?"

April asked her to repeat herself.

"Doesn't that scare you?"

April had insisted that whatever transgressions she'd committed in life would be forgiven in death. In this instance, despite her lukewarm approach to what lay beyond human comprehension, she became possessive of the rituals done in her name, the baptism, the communion, the confirmation, the (albeit diluted) confessions. She had the paperwork. She passed the classes. She was told, time and again, that her conscience was clear because she had accepted that the messiah had come, had died, had risen, had ascended, and would one day return. *Credo in unum Deum.* She wore a medal of the Sacred Heart around her neck.

To all that, Pal listened, weighed it, pronounced, "I don't think that's how it works." She then turned and went indoors, Mars in tow. April thought at the time that surely Jenny's influence was at hand. "A messiah shouldn't just pop in and then pop out, and then tell you he'll be right back," as she'd said.

"Pal asked me that, too, you know," Juan said. "If I was scared."

"How old was she then? Not even ten?"

"Aren't you?"

"What?"

"Aren't you scared?"

April flushed the toilet. "I ought to be asking you that."

But Juan did not mean eternal torment. "What you did, is what I'm talking about now."

Beverly Across-the-way could be dead. She could be alive. She could be on either side of that word, none the worse for a bad knock, or blissfully brain-damaged. It would be April's word against hers, whichever way. And until April was found out (if she was found out), there was no point in bringing it up. You could say that she got away with it. Go and sin no more.

At any rate, Juan did not appear to be suffering, for all he'd done. "I don't know what you're complaining about," April spat.

"I'm not complaining."

"You're like a bad smell. You cling to everything."

It was here that Jenny and Pal came into the ladies' room. They called and peeked through the cracks in the stalls until they found hers, knocked.

She wrestled into her blouse, abandoning the bra on the hook behind the door. "Is listening to your mother take a shit more interesting to you than making Miss Preston cry?" She unlocked the stall.

Jenny's face crumpled. Not that she had seen April's blouse, her bra hanging limp as a fish behind her. "Aw, Mom—" She dove for her mother, such as she had never been inclined to do before. Pal followed. Their arms had her snared, and she might have let herself succumb to this measure of softness. It would have been easy: to fall under an embrace that wanted for nothing. It filled her head and made her drowsy. Indeed, this is what people did. After a lifetime of keeping affection at arm's length, you knew that you could not stave it off forever. Everyone needs a hug, don't they? That was how affection tripped you up. It conquered so sweetly, it got you pliable, then it got you talking.

So far, I got away with it.

April writhed and wriggled and when a girl from the candy counter came into the restroom on her break, they let her go.

"Jesus wept—" April wiped at her face. "You're like a straitjacket, the pair of you. Do you cling like this to everybody?"

"Mom—"

She reminded her girls that her name was April. "Since when do you call me Mom?"

Jenny traded a glance with Pal. April had always harbored an irrational fear that her daughters used a hidden language to convey their plans for her. It might be a code, transmitted through the blinks of their eyes. Or it could be plain English, but now the driest of conversations had taken on a new significance, talk of celebrities meant talk of captivity, to reminisce of the good old days was to cipher future torments.

Well. I won't have that.

Jenny put her hand to Pal's elbow to lead her out. She called over her shoulder for her mother to wash her face, that they would meet her at the car. "Your nose is running."

In the mirror, so it was, and her eyes swollen and her face pulped by tears that April Nimitz could not recall having shed. But they had come. And by the time the girls found her, they had already worked their way, cancerous, into her chest. They must have heard her, April thought, from all the way in the theater. She blew her nose on toilet paper ripped from the roll, as Miss Preston had done at the beginning of the film.

She was about to secret the roll itself in her purse when she noticed that the candy counter girl had emerged from her stall and was at the sink next to her, doing her eye makeup. Her tag read, I'M TRASH, the name picked off and the letters rearranged.

April asked the girl if that's what her parents called her.

The girl affirmed, toneless, that it was her baptismal name and went to work on her lips.

"Well," April murmured, backing into the lobby's powdery chill. "I'll see you on *The Maury Show.*"

She passed the candy counter and took note of the tags pinned to the vests of the three yawning teenagers behind the rows of Swedish Fish. They were marked FLACCID, CIRCUMCISED, and RABID. They straightened up when she approached them to ask if they happened to really be any of those things.

The boys, Flaccid and Circumcised, blushed. The girl, Rabid, allowed that it was part of a dare, "To see if anyone would notice." They were Uri, Mitch, and Ariel. The one called Trash was Layla. Mitch added that April was the first who had spotted the change their whole shift, and that not even their supervisor had taken another look.

Mitch said, "He's just happy we're wearing tags."

April asked, "So, do I win anything?"

This stumped the three of them, and stumped Trash, too, when she moseyed behind the counter. April supposed they found themselves met with an ultimatum: they come up with a prize or the old white lady calls for the manager. But April decided to play the good sport and put on her perky face, to the quartet's relief. Uri ducked under the counter and surfaced with a roll of scratch-and-sniff stickers. They were meant to be for the arcade opposite the concession, consolation for the kids who used all their tokens and hadn't won anything.

"My girls will love these," April vowed, and bid Trash, Flaccid, Circumcised, and Rabid farewell.

Meanwhile, she wondered why it was easier to be sweet to people she would never meet again.

April was Hasi. Emmi was Mausi. Rossi was Spatzi. Mildred was Schnecke. Flora, Mildred's prettier twin, was Blumi. A rabbit, a mouse, a sparrow, a snail, and a blossom.

It was how Juan and Bärbabba introduced them, and soon enough, it was how a certain kind of man at Peralta Farm came to know them. This kind of man had few qualms about dividing himself in two.

The first half was that known to his neighbors as the one who kept a traceable routine. He was nothing special. He rose at five with his fellow inmates to prepare for a day's labor, in carpentry, general maintenance, machine shop work, and to prove to his captors that he was a citizen, home-grown and God-fearing. He attended religious services, usually Christian. Often, he was a family man. He could be college educated or blue collar. He, behind the fence though he was, contributed to the war effort; his vegetables came from a Victory Garden. Asked the things he loved most, he would tell you in this order: the Lord, the nation, and his bride.

Through their mutual devotion to this trinity, the second half could reconcile his differences with the first. The first half, the citizen, granted him, the stranger, absolution. Thus, the citizen could sleep at night while his impious double prowled. The second half had an appetite nigh unknown to the first, only that it was there and that it must be satisfied. The stranger was driven by groin and gut. He was a bounder, a gambler, a rapist, a hedonist. He banked on the sanctity of his forgiveness, knowing that what he did in the night would be of no consequence by morning. He sniffed every orifice and tasted each one before penetrating them. He used his tongue, his fingers, his member. He did not take his time, for this was how you did it when your wants were laid before you; you gobbled up them in quick succession. What of his wife? What of his wife when he could gorge himself on a small harem for a modest fee? Of course, she would want to know where her husband's camp scrip was going and what had happened to the supply of cash they'd brought. The stranger told her not to worry about it, leaving the reasoning to the citizen, for daylight.

No one would believe the split. The men themselves hardly felt it.

At that time, April had become very studious at the accordion. She'd been made to play it, starting from age nine, and had largely forgotten about it until the Hesses' recent captivity. It was a heavy thing, pulling the player forward by the shoulder straps by the weight of the bellows alone. Its buttonboard scaled the length of April's body, so that she had to spread her legs to accommodate it. Its bottom end rested against her crotch, and any vibrations yielded by the instrument could be felt there. She'd had little appreciation for that, growing up, practicing arpeggios and barely articulate versions of "Battle Hymn of the Republic". To think that all the while, she could have burned her concentration down to a single point, the potential for eruption. And an added bonus, not thought of since her days at Mrs. Autry's studio: There was the bliss to be derived from the bellows themselves. Before, they had been lethal, sharp, biting at her chest and sometimes under her chin. Now, she knew the value of her nerves and knew that any minor agony could be transformed, through the right positioning, the tightness of the straps, the right fingering of the buttons, even the right song, into something delicious. She could catch her nipple just so, play fast and hard, then catch a bit of her breast, her navel, absorb the breath of the instrument and everyone around her would mistake her throes of pleasure for musical passion. Now that she hadn't her own room anymore, and could not easily find a private nook in which she could touch herself, she thought she might as well get away with what she could out in the open.

And she got to be pretty good at the squeezebox, too.

She did not have the memory for reading music, but she could play by ear. Her fingers clasped and clutched and pumped and stroked, from breast to groin. She learned "Rock of Ages" and "Salve Regina", "O Haupt voll Blut und Wunden" and "Ein feste Burg ist unser Gott". The leather shoulder strap would sometimes get her around the throat at the moment of climax, and she would mash her lips together to keep from howling in ecstasy.

Juan applauded, and April noted how his eyes were aglow in his head, deep amber and green and gold surfacing in the black. He smoked when he watched her, the good kind, laced with Mary Jane, and shared with April when he had them. He explained: Tobacco and grass rolled together made a spliff, and a ciggie rolled with grass alone made a reefer. They went to the small garden, in their own haze.

"Well." April gestured grandly, the guard towers, the dust, the inselberg. "How do you like it so far?"

"Okay." Juan shrugged. "I expected more cowboys, to tell you the truth."

"What do you call that?" April pointed, an officer in the tower picking off jackrabbits with a .22. His M1 was propped in the tower's corner, next to an umbrella.

"Fair enough."

The guards skinned and sold the rabbits in exchange for cigarette rations. The Hesses made a stew of them, the Ogawas and the Engels across the way barbecued them. It was a step from their yard into the other, as it was for every cottage. Because of proximity, folks often ate supper together, as they had at the picnic. The Ogawas had bridge parties and then, because Mrs. Engels had a mahjong set but never learned how to play, mahjong nights. As it turned out, no one at Peralta Farm knew how to play mahjong, and so rules were improvised and the game became a hybrid of dominoes and boo-ray. Now and then, a guard would join, share his cigarettes, spare a little of his dried fruit and booze rations. There was Annette Hanshaw and Billie Holiday, for someone had a Victrola. Once, Juan sold his reefers and they had a ham in time for Oktoberfest.

"If this were anywhere else—" Mrs. Engels would start.

"—you'd think it was some kind of never-ending block party," Mrs. Ogawa would finish in her broad accent, displaced Minnesotan.

And they would laugh.

Another one was, "If you were here—"

"—you'd be in hell now."

And they would cackle.

People forgot (at least, it sounded to April) that they'd had anything beyond Peralta Farm. If the outside were brought up, it was in reference to the other camp the big one in Crystal City. Her mother said, "At the big camp, I hear, they've got a German school, a German paper. They've got a swim pool—" To which Mrs. Ogawa would say, "And if your name is Ogawa, you might get running water." That shut everyone up until April's mother noted, "At the big camp, they've got a tennis court."

Meantime, Juan recruited a few of the senior boys from Federal High School to made hooch. From dried fruit and sugar rations, orange peel, sandwich bread and water left to brew in a mixing bowl came something that could be a proper cocktail if you closed your eyes and held your nose. If the day, the dust, the fences were too much, April smuggled it to school in a canteen, sipping during lectures on the Boston Tea Party. Juan called it moxie. Federal High School was in a quad of trailers. The air in them was close and, as there was little room for desks, the kids sat at long folding tables. And if there was no room at the tables, you sat at the windowsill, you stood at the back. The teachers had their own canteens, too, secreted in their desks, from which they would take furtive sips, then all-out mouthfuls as the hours wore on.

Moxie proceeds bought sugar rations, and with them April baked a carrot cake for Juan's birthday.

April asked Juan where his mother was.

"Gone."

"Gone where?"

"Gone dead." A walk up a hill, a misstep, head over heels until Willie Nimitz, of the stuff inside, Berlin and birdwatching and everything else, was gone. Here was her body, here was her blood, her plywood vertebrae.

At night, they would meet in the little yard, the air like gauze, and tell ghost stories. There was a nine o'clock curfew, only enforced if you left your allotment, and so they were left to sit in the dry grass, the air thick and close around them, cocooned.

Juan was telling her about the Chupacabra. "It's part wolf, part lizard."

"That sounds like a taxidermy gone wrong. What's it do?"

"What's it do? What do you mean, what's it do?"

"Does it eat bad little kids that stay up past their bedtime, or what? Even Santy Claus does something." She'd told him about Saint Nicholas, or the incarnation brought by her parents from the old country. Instead of coal for the naughty, he brought a birch rod and used it to beat wicked children into black-and-blue obedience. It had always left April with the feeling of a nightmare on Christmas Eve, and she would lock her bedroom door.

Juan chewed a blade of grass, winced when the grit caught in his teeth. "It's a goat-sucker."

April laughed, a big HA that came from her belly. Then Juan moved to clap a hand over her mouth and she slapped him away. "A goat-WHAT?"

"Goat-sucker. What did you think I said? Goat-fucker?"

April put her head in her hands, red, swollen, shaking, laughter bottled. "I don't know what's better. Sucking or fucking." She sniffed, rubbed her eyes, exhaling, "Ohhh, my stars, my stars. That poor goat."

"I was thinking suck, as in suck like a vampire. You took this story for a ride down into Yuck City."

"—where no goat walks safe at night."

Juan called her an idiot. Then, after what seemed like a bit of deliberation, he asked her if she believed in ghosts.

"No." April told him that she did believe in demons. "Not the devil," she specified. "Demons." She described to him her dream, which she had had again twice since arriving at Peralta Farm. Following the sleepless first night in the cottage, the demon appeared as her father. The second time it was Juan himself. "That's what scares the hell out of me," she went on. She knew her mother. She knew her father. She did not know Juan Nimitz.

"So, I must be a demon?" Juan asked.

Juan, for all his charm, was filled with vibrations that left April exhausted and slightly sick. They came and went, ethereal. In those moments, you held your breath until he was out of sight. The fear was not provocation, for he was not one to start fights nor finish them; he seemed content to egg two opponents on until they were rolling and bloodied on the floor, Juan himself but a passive spectator. He was empty. He fed off chaos until he'd had his fill. In those moments, you just wanted him to go away, to go away before the room filled with his melancholic stink and you succumbed to it, voiding, becoming like him.

"It would be better if I did cry," Juan agreed. "Or beat the hell out of some old lady."

"You haven't cried." April had that first night. Her mother had. Even her father, in the midst of boo-ray and swill, had collapsed when someone started to sing "Fur Danzig". The amber shore, the blue seas.

"Sure, I did."

She kissed Juan. As far as she knew, there was no one watching.

The next day, when the weather turned, and her father was struck by the idea for a screened-in sun porch, and Bärbabba was asleep, April practiced her accordion. She wore no underthings. Juan (sensing it? or just lucky?) came up behind her and drove his hand down her skirt. Outside, space was being cleared in the garden. There were shouts from her father and from a few of the boys from the Federal High School, hauling rolls of chicken wire and lumber.

"Keep playing," Juan panted. "Whatever it is, keep playing. They can't see."

It was "Lili Marlene". Lale Anderson sang it; her father had ordered the record the year after its release in Germany. Bing Crosby would sing it, and Connie Francis and Vera Lynn. Marlene Dietrich would sing it, in German and in English. She and Spencer Tracy would talk about how the German lyrics were much sadder than the English in *Judgement at Nuremberg*.

Und sollte mir ein Leids gescheh'n
Wer wird bei der Laterne stehen
Mit dir Lili Marlene, mit dir Lili Marlene

In the future, the song would excite her, regardless of where it was played. The sight of an accordion would excite her, too, more than any pornographic rendering of human anatomy. The musician's gender would not matter, nor, when April really thought about it, would the presence of any musician matter. If you only knew, she wanted to tell people. It was like fondling yourself through a breathing, moaning corset. Juan's fingers articulated what her own could not. He rocked against her. He probed. He rubbed, he fluttered, mimicking her own hands in their groping of the keys. April rested her head against the side with the buttonboard. She held her breath. The bellows got her belly, her breast—

She whimpered when she came. The climax took her and shook her and left her sore in the fork of her legs. She would never achieve such heights again.

While she returned to earth, Juan got up and wet a hand towel, unhooked her hand from the bass buttons and pressed it there. He told her to collect herself. Dazed, she wiped the towel across her face. She emitted funny, squelching noises when she rose, and there was a damp spot on the cushion of the stool she'd been sitting on. The accordion clung to her, and when she freed her blouse from the bellows, she observed a gathering of red dots, spotty around the embroidery, concentrated around the breast pocket into a single, sodden bullseye.

Footfalls. She clapped her arms across her chest, dropped them when she knew it to be Juan, moving in between the kitchen and his shared bedroom with his father. April listened. Whispers, German. Now and then, a word she knew would materialize. She waited until she heard it, not her name, but her euphemism. In no time at all, she came to recognize April Hesse and Hasi as separate entities. And so, it was Hasi's ears that twitched when Bärbabba said it. And he said it more than once, and she thrilled when she heard Juan say it, too.

Whispers, German. Coughing, hawking, mucous hitting the bottom of a bowl. And her name: "Hasi."

Juan reappeared, palming a soapy cloth. A shirt was draped in the crook of his arm and he threw it to her. It was one of his own, April knew it by the smell. She ducked into the kitchen and buttoned it up, tucked it into her skirt. The blouse she ran under lukewarm water (the temperatures from the taps was tepid or scalding), began scrubbing. "Out, damned spot," as Lady Macbeth would say.

Juan behind her. Such moments were crystallized forever in their placement of where and when and who. In later years, they came to April in shards. Juan behind her. Juan's lips on her ear. Juan asking her if she wanted to do something like that again, and Hasi breathing an answer in the affirmative, not really a word.

She fancied herself not quite devouring him—she would attach herself to him, she decided, by fixing herself into the hollow of his throat, as a tick might, and feed on him indefinitely. His blood would be more potent than moxie, she knew, and moxie did its job in removing her from the earth.

What had her fantasies been, before now? Were there any? She could not have claimed an attraction to anyone in her old life. She'd glued cut-outs of James Cagney and John Wayne to her bedroom wall when her mother fretted at her daughter's lack of interest in boys. And it was true. She did not much care for boys. It was perfectly acceptable to profess an undying love for James Cagney and John Wayne, so long as they remained graven images on her bedroom wall. There was more to a man than a boy, she wanted to say. She would feel like a child molester if she went with someone her own age.

Of course, what did that make a man who wanted a girl not yet eligible to wed?

She hadn't an answer to that and she did not want one. Instead, she followed Juan's instructions to meet him at the camp's nondenominational chapel later that night, thirty minutes before curfew. He told her not to worry about making it back to the cottage in time, to make herself pretty and to do as she had done that afternoon, to forgo underwear.

She kept the rendezvous. She arrived twenty minutes early, despite fears of appearing overzealous. The chapel was dark and because of her punctuality, she was alone. There were revolving searchlights from the guard towers, porchlights from the cottages and the barracks, but the chapel itself was tucked into a corner of the common yard, by the machine shops, and she had a rare intrusion of bright yellow through the windows that filled the sanctuary for an instant and passed, leaving April in the heavy blue shadows to wait for it to come again.

Instead of pews, there were folding chairs. Instead of an altar, there was a podium draped in ratty velvet. The tabernacle was an old Hav-a-Tampa cigar chest; the Baptist pastor who visited Peralta Farm had painted over the lady on the inside of the lid and pasted a print of Eric Enstrom's *Grace*. April noted that the communion wafers tasted different after the change, a little saltier, and wondered if it came from having to look at an old bearded fellow hunched at a table rather than a gal dressed like a Grecian temptress every time you went up to receive the Host.

Whispers, English. Here, at last, at last, was Juan, and April strained to catch his voice. Again, no words, none that she could make out. Very inarticulate because it had to be very discreet.

She used the time before he came in to arrange herself. Like the lady in the Hav-a-Tampa box, she tried resting her arms on the backs of two folding chairs, and quickly barred that when she thought it made her look too eager. She decided, in the second before the chapel door opened, that she would sit in one of the chairs, her back to the entrance, the chair facing forward and her arms draped over the rest. That way, she would be ready for him. No need to play at nonchalance. She curled her toes to keep her knee from jigging.

She wanted to turn, but he would not let her. The chair tipped and creaked as he pulled at her clothes, and she felt her breasts mash against the back rest. He maneuvered her in such a way that he now had the seat, and she was atop him and folded over the top of the chair. Her fingertips graced the floor, collecting grit. It was, indeed, possible for him to crack her in two, if he'd wanted.

And that was it.

And that was it.

The leaky vessel had burst.

She'd expected the act of copulation, the real, full-on discipline of intercourse, to have been a grand occasion. This was not to say that April Hesse had illusions. It was how you were fruitful, how you multiplied. People did it. Men seemed to like it more than women. Women seemed to know its worth as a bartering tool, and sometimes they could get a kick out of it, too. April was a virgin and now she was not. She was doing it now with a man (not a boy) whom she loved. Wasn't that right? What else would you call it, when you wanted nothing more than to smell him on you again, when you wanted him to fill every orifice you had? Obsession? Nymphomania? Did it make her a fiend—or, by common consensus, a hussy?

She wanted to see Juan's face. She wanted to smell him.

Her eye was on her own gritty fingertips and the concrete floor. Or it was straight ahead, where the tabernacle had been left open after the last Sunday service, the Catholic Mass at two o'clock. The Baptists went first, then the Methodists, then the Adventists, then the Catholics because their liturgy went the longest. They pulled from the same cigar box when the time came for the Lord's Supper. Someone had left it open. Someone had neglected to lock the tabernacle. And now she was made to look at the inside of the lid, where the little old man bent over his table of bread and soup. She was thinking that, in another light, if he did not look so humble and if his beard were trimmed a bit neater, the little old man had a more than passing resemblance to Bärbabba.

She squeezed her eyes shut. Behind her, he worked and repositioned her, sitting up instead of bent over the chair. She knew this to be buggery, what he was doing to her now, first his fingers then himself, and she had only ever understood this to be something done between men. But she was not unwilling. Yes, it hurt. Agreed, it was not unlike having a cucumber as the penetrating implement. And yes, she could get used to it. It was possible, even, that she could like it. She gritted her teeth because she could take it. If she could take this, she figured she could take anything.

Anything for Juan.

But then she touched his hands. They were larger, blocky, coarse. The fingers were stubs, the palms were ape's paws. There was a blood blister under one nail, and the rest were yellow, like calluses. Impetiginous, unclean.

She wrested herself from the chair, and the searchlight filled the chapel.

She did not know who this was. She could not have told you the color of his eyes or the shape of his mouth. His identity was irrelevant, pared down to the cold, hard fact that he was Not Juan. Too big, too hairy, too beefy, too smelly.

I'll pull out all his teeth, I'll pull out his eyes, and then I'll take you and—

She burst into open air, a fraction before the revolving light fell upon her. Standing numbly, she let it, and there was no consequence, as Juan had promised there would not be. In the guard tower, the fellow on watch had been peering from his perch until April caught him, and he ducked his head, turned away. A shuffling from the chapel, a scuttle of buttoning up and righting clothes and hair. A sniff, a cough. The light fell on him, too, his barnacled hands, then his hang-dog face. April knew him, a fellow called John or Jim who worked in the machine shop and played boo-ray with the Ogawa and Engels clans. A kraut, American born, one wife, three boys. He retreated when she took a step toward him, bleated something about how Juan said he'd settle up with her after. And he, John or Jim, gave her his back, and he scurried into the dark.

She could smell him off her.

Walking, tottering, swapping her weight from one leg to the other, April considered the mythology of men. They never lived up to it. Their true nature was preceded by Herculean tales of forthrightness, of brawn and brass, and here was a man standing at six foot two who could not look her in the eye, who turned tail when she got too close. And here was man whose absence alone sparked at her numbness. Juan, she knew, was nowhere around. Too, she considered, rather re-considered, the word *faggot*. The usual definition was aimed at homosexual men, though she'd never made the connection. It took a fair amount of time for her mind to fire up and her gait to quicken, and she thought that the word was aptly applied to fellows, burly straight boys, like the one who had recently helped himself to her. They were the sort who claimed fearlessness and prowess and anything else that burly straight boys were made of, going about thinking that whatever caught their fancy was theirs for the taking—and who would absolutely buckle if you just knew to knee him in the groin. You told people to grow a pair when they were being wishy-washy; see how wishy-washy you really were once you'd grown them, once someone brought their foot down on them, one-two.

Straight men. Her father, Juan. Faggots, the lot of them. Not half the men their queer and female counterparts were.

She reached the Nimitz-Hesse cottage soaking under her arms, between her breasts and legs and the cheeks of her buttocks. No porchlight here because there was no porch. The Arizona room project, having lagged in recent days, amounted to a raised platform of wooden planks. The chicken wire lay in scrolls in the corner of the yard, among handyman flotsam, hammers that hadn't made it back to their kits, bits of balsa wood, pry-bars, shovels. She did not feel able to sit and shifted toward the Victory Garden, which was a thicket of carrot and turnip tops.

Had she not moved, she would not have seen him. The revolving searchlight cast itself just enough for the detritus on the platform to reveal itself. She might have mistaken him for an old suitcase, a pile of space blankets. Him, Juan, there on the platform with a coat bunched under his head and resting atop a hill of quilts pulled from the clothes line. It was hot, too hot to sleep indoors. His head was in his arms, his belly to the quilts, his trousers a bit looser on him now than in the summertime. He wore no belt. April waited until the light passed over him again to see the crack of his ass, the bifurcated line marking the east and west of his flat-as-pancake cheeks. The curve of him rose and fell, even undulations, the beautiful dreamer.

This is what a pervert feels. This is how a pervert thinks. April's lust returned and became articulate. It began in her groin and rose to her belly and a hunger there was initiated beyond anything her imagination could summon.

I want him. I can have him. And I will.

Now that she knew herself to be a pervert, she operated like one. There was a plan to all of this; it called only for stealth. She scanned the yard for the right tool. It was very factual, a compulsion recognized and one that must be followed through. A hammer handle was seductive, but wrong. Balsa she spurned, too. It had to be fleshy enough, and she nearly laughed aloud when she brushed the ferny Victory Garden greens. A little rabbit, indeed. She knelt and dug and found a prize, as big around as the real thing, furred with whiskery roots. When the searchlight came around again, she stuck the carrot between her legs and marveled at her shadow against the cottage clapboard. Had it been the real thing, it could've made anyone on the receiving end scream, wherever she chose to put it. She bucked her hips in the spotlight.

Juan turned, murmured, turned again.

April knelt when he turned, murmured, turned again.

He stirred. He blinked. He looked over his shoulder.

Perversion must be instinct, April thought. An incubus knows what to do. You pin your prize down. You tell them not to say a word or make a sound. You work fast, not so much out of the worry that you'll be caught. You want to keep your prize and hold it motionless, one hand on the back of the neck, the other twisting the arm around by the wrist. You had to hear joints snap. You had to know when to take up your implement because the time it took for you to get a free hand and drive it home was not on your side.

Juan cussed and got free of her, hands and knees, halfway across the porch when he realized that his trousers were hooked around his ankles.

April pounced. April bit his ear, then the bend of flesh between his neck and shoulder. April was fast and laid him flat. The carrot found Juan's hole and Juan hissed. April worked it and herself, stuck her thumb in his eye when he tried to roll onto his back. She fixed her teeth to that bend of flesh and drooled.

He watched her crest. Mid-spasm, and she was still in another place when their positions reversed, and now she was the one under him. Now it was as it should be, *his* hand over *her* mouth, *him*self conjoined with *her*self.

Had anyone come upon them from behind, they would have surprised themselves at an initial impulse to laugh. Imagine: a burly straight boy pounding away with carrot greens swinging like a long pony's tail.

They shared the pile of quilts that night and rose at first light, when the whistle sounded for the working men. The yard had grown small and grey and full of mist. Juan threw a bottle cap at a rabbit nibbling at the turnips.

April looked around. "What happened to the carrot?"

Juan pointed to a mound by the outhouse. He had not quite made it. April must have been asleep, of course she had been. She would have wanted to see him squeeze a whole fat carrot from his person. She could smell it from here. She could see it, too, bright orange, shit-streaked.

Juan assessed that they were even.

April didn't know about that. Let it be known, however, that some measure of justice had been served. That's what she thought, at the time.

Juan asked if she might do something like that again.

April accepted her share of the profits, more than she expected. It occurred to her that whatever she made, in camp scrip or dollars, was irrelevant. She likened it to pressing her finger into an infected cut: you get curious as to how much of it you can take before the hurt finally, finally, transcended to yield one prismed drop of elation.

"You'd be me, this time," Juan said.

He told her to go to school the next day (she'd been skipping lately), to put on a friendly face and survey the lay of the land. He would fill her canteen with moxie; he told her to share it. He filled her pocket, too, with cigarettes, the normal ones, and told her to offer one if a girl seemed like the type who smoked or wanted to smoke.

April asked, "Just like that?"

Juan said, "Put on a happy face. Just like that."

So, she put on clean white socks, a pressed blouse and skirt. She pressed her heretofore unused textbooks to her chest. Bobby pins and Bass Weejuns.

No one had ever accused her of being a nice girl, and here was no indication that she was about to start. Yet, it was astonishing what an iron and a lick of soap could do. You'd never guess what she had in her pockets, what she had up her sleeve.

The clothesline bounced. There, among the men's black socks and white shirts and her mother's calico apron, there was her blouse. And there were Juan's trousers. They'd spent the wee hours of that morning scrubbing and, for their efforts, their transgressions had faded to pale yellow. Bärbabba told Juan where to find bleach, for women's hair, as it turned out, and the results amounted to what looked like old baby spit-up on April's top and a voiding of bowels on the seat of Juan's pants.

The thing that turned her to stone was when Juan told her, after they'd married, "You think that was the first time someone did something like that to me before?"

April's mind locked, bolted, no further questions.

I suppose we're even.

She watched Emmi and Rossi and Milly and Flory go to school. Nice girls, all of them. There was that lust again, now unsexual, nevertheless perverted. Have you ever looked at a porcelain doll and felt the impulse to swing it by the ankles, how you would a baseball bat, so that you could watch the pretty, passive head shatter? It was in that ballpark, you might say.

April did not want to be alone in her foulness.

Well, she never touched an accordion again. And Juan, for reasons of his own, never touched a guitar. So much for a Jack-and-Jill vaudeville.

Here was where her memory grew hazy. No, correction. Hazy was inaccurate. Here was where her memory rocked shut, the way it would for a guilty party. Following the war, Germans across the pond insisted they knew nothing. Another favorite, one that was so harebrained as to render it a catchphrase: We were just following orders. Indeed. Were you struck deaf, dumb, and blind? Did an act of God turn you into a passel of wind-up soldiers? Or was there no God at all, and now that your ugliest fragmented notions were being spoken aloud, you had permission to slough off any semblance of decency?

Alive in her, little April Hussy spat, "Faggots."

Her father saw the films of camps on their liberation days and sat like a stone through the whole thing. He shook his head, and for a while voiced his doubts that so many people had been eliminated. Hollywood, he declared, until he removed himself from the earthly equation.

Her mother, meanwhile, had plighted her troth to her new home. GIs took on Herculean proportions. The president had the same infallibility as the pope in Rome.

How about this, Käthe.

Where do you think the krauts got their ideas from? Was there anywhere else so eloquent in their step-by-step process of separating US from THEM? They gave it a name, you know. *Eb'ry time I weel about I jump Jim Crow.* Heinrich Krieger is not a figure who comes up, but perhaps the Führer would never have come up with the Nuremberg Laws, forbidding the sexual and marital unions of Jews and Gentiles, had Mr. Krieger not come to the University of Arkansas to study American racial legislature. We could be blaming South Africa. But America fascinated Mr. Krieger.

And let us not forget that other incision, once the blacks were separated from the whites, and the Jews from the Gentiles. In America, we had a clear definition of what categorized an individual as FIT or UNFIT. Consider the origin of the IQ test. Lucky for you and Dad that you had a firm grasp on the English language. Otherwise, who knows what would've happened to you. You might have been labeled retarded, a word you can't say now without some stern young person correcting you. Sterilization was a popular method of dealing with the UNFIT. We even toyed with the idea of the gas chamber. We argued that it would be the kindest thing for the surplus population: Thus, the Euthanasia Society of America was born.

How proud you were when you entered me in the Better Baby contest at the county fair. You had the blue ribbon and my picture on your night table at Peralta Farm.

There were people and there were imbeciles.

There were the FIT and the UNFIT.

There was US and THEM.

Consider, now, the old neighborhood, the one April had left.

Mrs. Glau's mother-in-law lived to the age of one hundred and two. She occupied the spare room at the top of the house and was moved to a cot in the study when she became poorly. She had been around in the plantation days, which was where her maiden name came from. She, Jessamine Hatfield, had been born upstate, and sold to the owner of Hatfield Prospect, where, until Juneteenth, she worked in the kitchen for Mr. Hatfield and the six Hatfield children. Following her emancipation, Jessamine, due to her unspoken parentage through her previous owner (an Irish called McCuistion, of all things) understood that she need only fix her hair, apply a little powder to her face and hands, and she could pass; her eyes were green and her nose was small. April saw the papers in Mrs. Glau's library, she'd come to sort through mementos after the old woman passed. A legal document, lofty script on crisp paper: *Jessamine, a Negro female, aged four years. Teeth: Good. Temperament: Good. I hereby grant, sell, and convey unto Mr. Asa Jacob Hatfield.* It might have been a deed for a horse. She asked Mrs. Glau why her mother-in-law had it framed; the papers had been cut to fit inside a small inverted fillet of hammered rose gold, and had hung for decades over her secretary. She then asked Mrs. Glau why her mother-in-law had it at all. Mrs. Glau had said, "Because it happened."

Lest we forget. Or else tell God when we stand before Him or Her or It that we did not know.

J uan poked her.

April cracked an eye. "I can't rid myself of you for a nap, can I?"

"No."

She sighed. "What do you want?"

Juan was blunt. "You're supposed to come with me."

April told him that she could do what she liked, and at her own pace.

Juan pressed, "I can't do this alone. You promised."

April told him that she had made no promises of any shape or form. She told him that the dignified exit (his words, not hers) made no guarantees. Who was he to blame when everyone knew that April not only, in life, drank him under the table, but swallowed twice as much of anything and complained of a mere hangover in the morning?

"If you really wanted me to go with you," April said, "we would've loaded one of your guns."

"Two of them."

"Whatever." She paused. "You know what I think?"

"What's that, Hasi?"

"I think you had cold feet, just a split second too late. Now you're there and I'm here. And you don't like it, and now this whole thing is going to turn into a great big back-and-forth. And then you'll weasel me into doing what you want anyway."

"I don't know what else to do."

"Well. Find out. Let me sleep."

Could a person be marked a suicide, even if they'd survived? Or, more to the point, if they'd been half-assed about it?

Juan had swallowed his medication and Seconal and let them brew with firewater.

They had not talked about what Juan was going to do, though April knew. Juan had spent a lot of time in those last days looking at her out of the corner of his eye, or else perking his head up and saying "Hm?" to a completely silent room. Did he want her to stop him? And April had, at present, to laugh at herself, because she knew it to be true, that he did want her to stop him. Did he want her to stop him? What a question.

People talked about couples who could finish each other's sentences. People bragged about knowing what their spouses were thinking.

April would gladly tell them, it's no picnic. If you really could grow so attached to someone as to read his thoughts, and he read yours, you wouldn't be at all keen to tell everyone. More than that, you had grown so used to having that two-way frequency, over the decades, that you did not know how you could ever live without it.

So, when Juan went to sleep that night, April came up. He had not hidden the Seconal or the firewater, he was likely too groggy to do much more than get under the covers, put out the light, as though it were the end of another day. He had left no note. There were no phone calls. There were only instructions for April to call the girls and to call their lawyer, scratched onto the legal pad he kept on his bedside table.

But there was one message for her, outside of the plan of action.

It was, "Come along, if you want. I didn't take all of it."

Call it panic.

I can't do it alone.

April had the Seconal. She had the firewater. She'd fallen asleep, knowing that she would wake. She would call her daughters and Buck Thune, informing them of a heart attack that was, under her own eyes, which were as good as the eyes of God, absolute fiction. No, there need not be an autopsy, for Juan's heart had been poorly, as were the rest of his organs. He'd had trouble with his bowels, his bladder; twice he'd shat himself in public, once at the chicken place, once in the pet food aisle at HEB. They had dinner with the Fieldings and he rose from his chair to find a puddle on the cushion—newly re-upholstered, too, in the buckskin of a white tail that Simon Fielding had shot.

Somehow, that had been the point of no return. He'd shat himself twice and pissed himself once.

Beverly Across-the-way called April a Hun once, and that was enough to warrant the beating of her life. You don't call people names. No, be honest. You don't kill people who call you names.

What was I supposed to do, otherwise? Take it? I could take everything else, allow me some leniency. Justification for leniency: Mr. and Mrs. Hussy ought to be enough, his foulness and her silence. Wrongful incarceration. A husband lost to a heart attack. And if you can't talk, you do, as was the natural order of communication. Evil will out, either way.

Did I kill her?

Juan said, "If you'd come with me, you wouldn't be in this mess. With regards to everything else, you'd have gotten away with that, too."

A multitude of misdoings, reduced to "everything else".

April turned. "Let me sleep."

Pal's voice was low. "Is she asleep?"

April shut her eyes and let her mouth go slack.

She'd been in and out and surfaced when the van came to a sudden stop for a horse that was crossing the otherwise empty highway. Jen had stomped on the brakes, knocking Pal and April back in their seats. The boxes of mementos and odd-and-ends and this-and-that avalanched into the way-back. April was momentarily choked by her seatbelt across her throat. Jen had swung her arm out to catch Pal in her chest, she she'd done Gabe and Raffy. When it was confirmed that all was well and the van was undamaged, they'd sat in dazed silence, watching the horse, enormous, grey, white speckled, goggle-eyed, amble to the other side of the road. It gave them a stern look, as though this were a crosswalk, and harumph-ed over the guardrail and into the trees.

"That did just happen, didn't it?" April had asked.

"It certainly did." Jen inhaled, exhaled, put the van into drive.

Now Pal was behind the wheel and asking, "Is she asleep?"

April played possum, even added a twitch that could pass for involuntary. If there's anything to be said, say it now while your mother is a beautiful dreamer. She listened.

Pal told Jen that she'd been having some, what she called, ugly thoughts. Jen's silence articulated that these ugly thoughts were nothing new. Or nothing surprising. April pictured her older daughter nodding in that therapist's way she had, that would April into a tight coil. Like Pal shaking her head and refusing to tell her mother that she hated her. Jen would nod and, arranging her face into the cool calm of a Marian apparition, utter but two words: OKAY and YES. What was April meant to do with that?

Pal, the driver, was a disembodied confessor. April cracked an eye and tried to see around the captain's chair. "You know those stories you hear about on the news?" Pal was saying. "I mean, home invasions."

"Yes."

"Like."

"You don't want to break into somebody's house, do you?"

"No."

"Okay."

"It's like a fantasy."

"Okay."

"You know *In Cold Blood*?"

Jen nodded. "Yes. You mean the book? Or the actual event?"

"Just. You know the premise. Two guys break into a farmer's house because they thought he had a safe. They blow away the whole family—then they figure out there was never any safe to begin with? They wind up going through the wife's purse and they come away with something like fifty dollars?"

"Okay."

"Well. Here's my fantasy."

A bold choice of wording, April would have said. But she wanted to know what her younger daughter thought about, never having had the guts to ask.

"The fantasy is—" Pal slowed for a passing cop car, sped up when it was out of sight. "—it's that the same thing would happen to us. We'd be kids, still. I guess I'd be five, you'd be fifteen. And someone would come, no real reason that I can come up with. Someone would come and blast April and Daddy in the head.

But we'd be hiding in the dark somewhere. We'd knock him out somehow. Like, we'd truss him up in a chair, duct tape all over. We'd close the blinds."

"Okay."

"And we'd get that big knife. You remember that, whatever it was, that fancy, samurai style chef's knife that Dad had?"

"And never let anyone touch? Yes." Jen laughed. Her parents were theoretically blown away, and she laughed. I'm glad you find my demise funny. Jen scrunched up her face and mimicked Juan's voice. She knew to keep just a hint of an accent. "Don't touch it. Don't look at it. Don't even think about it, or I'mma cut you up. It was five thousand dollars."

It was five hundred dollars, actually. God knew what possessed him to buy it, they had knives aplenty. Juan had a surgeon's eye and would slice bell peppers in uniform strips. Tomatoes in wafer thin sheets, peaches and apples and onions in perfect half-moons. Before he offed himself, he'd cut his thumb getting together the makings of a chili. He insisted finishing the prep work before passing out. April had had to throw away cups and cups of bloodied poblanos, much more than the recipe called for.

Pal went on. "The fantasy is, we'd use that knife and start slicing him up. The point is, the guy would have to have done something to deserve it. Maybe there was a Nazi flag in his car, too, something like that."

April closed her eyes again because Jenny was shifting to look into the back. She heard Jenny ask, "How bad does this guy have to be to warrant being cut up?"

"I think we can agree that trespassing on someone's property and blasting people to Jesus makes for a pretty bad character."

"Yes."

An interval, studied quiet. Since the girls assumed their mother was asleep and could not hear, they resumed *Ten Summoner's Tales* and hummed along to "If I Ever Lose My Faith in You".

Then, because comic timing was a virtue, Jenny asked, "Mars would live, too, wouldn't he?"

Pal snorted. "How else do you think we're getting rid of the body?"

Jenny choked on her Diet Coke, because if that animal could eat a sock (one of Juan's dress socks, no less), she could only imagine that putting away an intruder's flesh would be a real treat.

It's a dark day, April thought, when you find yourself jealous of the family dog.

More than that.

To find herself ranked lower than the family dog was superficial. Here was the real concern: The arm's-length approach, the touch-me-not slapping away of embraces, all those times she told her girls to stay out of her bedroom when they were small—despite all that, had her foulness permeated the air of the Nimitz house? Had it managed to rub off anyway?

A jolt, a contracting of her stomach. Suppose they had crept into hers and Juan's bedroom? Suppose one or both of them had gone into hers and Juan's shared walk-in closet? Shoeboxes abounded, only one of them filled with something other than shoes. These were mementos that did not deserve remembrance, photos of things that she had wanted to forget, and now that the incidents themselves had evaporated, the images were as sharp as the day they were taken, decades before. You did not have to guess at what was happening in them. They were of April. The others she and Juan burned once they left the Farm, and she tried easing herself with the idea that its subjects (MAUSI, SPATZI, SCHNECKE, BLUMI, in Juan's precise, demonic hand on the back of each photo) had, too, been eliminated.

She could recall the pricing: A glamor shot was sixty cents. With today's inflation, that came to about seven dollars. What Juan called a tease shot, one that closed in on a single portion of the body, no face, was then seventy cents, now around eight-fifty. A full spread was one dollar, now twelve. A group portrait was three dollars, now thirty. A decade of jailtime if anyone knew Juan had them.

She could not recall who she was with in her group shots. She could not recall their names, nor, really their faces. Every so often, a fragment would surface in a stranger, a gap-toothed smile, a bulbous nose, a cauliflower ear, a poxy hand. In much the same way, a still would make itself known in her mind, a flash, not of herself. If you will, Exhibit A being Blumi's mouth, very full. Exhibit B, Mausi's hair and a stranger's hand in it.

April would have said, truthfully, that she did not know. She only procured. She introduced clients. She delivered the product. She collected what was due. Of course, she did not watch. You could say that April had been a busy girl, a shrewd business woman at seventeen. Another way to say it was that she was simply following orders.

"I didn't put a gun to your head," Juan once told her.

There was such a thing as free will.

There were shots of April's feet and mouth and bosom. There were close-ups of her fur and skin and fluid. In one of them (sudden flash, overexposed) April could recall vomiting after the click.

You might ask April why she kept these, now that Juan was gone. As for Juan, only April could ask him. She tried now, and he still didn't have an answer.

April had one: Lest she, lest they forget. Never mind that these images were stowed away in a shoebox. They were solid, Exhibits A through God knew how many. Lest they make a mutual pact of delusion that the passage of time would keep the deed in another, very remote decade. People said, "It was a long time ago." April's mother said, "No need to dwell on the past." Juan quoted Macbeth, "What's done is done."

Well, here, April wanted to tell these mouthers of pithy absolution, here's the past creeping up to bite you. She nudged Juan and pointed to their daughters.

"Have you been listening?" she asked.

Juan, silent.

She wanted to know what, in this grisly fantasy of Pal's, the girls would do if they knew that they were in no danger from an intruder, but that creatures just as deserving of live butchery slept under the same roof? April had once compared Pal to the child sociopath in *The Bad Seed*. Suppose Pal knew that the rot which had taken root in ugly thoughts was not organic, not inherited—could you say that her ugly thoughts were contracted, as in a disease, making April and Juan the infection?

No further questions.

It was a few miles and another cycle of *Ten Summoner's Tales* when Juan allowed, "Pal wouldn't do anything. Jen's the one you better watch out for. If anyone's going to blast anyone to Jesus, it's Jen." He called her Mama Bear when the boys were newborn. He told April he was tired. "No further questions."

April persisted. One more thing: Wouldn't you want to pass judgment, if you could? Even on your own parents? "On Bärbabba?"

Juan slapped her. "No one asked you about him. So, you don't talk about him. And you don't make me talk about him."

April slapped him back, and he was gone, and she opened her eyes and the van was parked at the

Number 5 pump at a Chevron station. 87 grade fuel, French fry smell from the Arby's. Jenny and Pal were scrubbing the windshield down and cackling.

She was unsure if she could keep up the illusion of chronic napping. She figured that if she went through the motions, sooner or later, she might fall asleep for real.

Maybe I'll get away with it after all.

When a cold snap set in at the Farm, and there was nothing going on, April sat on the risen platform with Juan. They watched April's father build a bonfire in the pit he and a few of the Federal High School boys put together out of concrete blocks. A few of the fellows wandered in when the whistle blew and the lunch break was called. December, unlike hot November and hotter October, was gelid, and folks bundled into big coats and mufflers. There was no snow, but there was frost. Juan chipped at the ice around the windows in the room he shared with his father.

The old man had lost his fire in a matter of weeks, and had to be helped to squat over the chamber pot kept under his bed, leaning on Juan's shoulder. His great height did not allow for much bulk, and before long, he'd gone from a Titan to a seven-foot-tall scarecrow. His appetite was not up to much; Juan maintained that it was because of the old man's weak sense of smell, it ran in the family. "I can't smell either," he insisted.

Still, it was Bärchen who assembled the meals Mrs. Hesse prepared on a tray and sat at Bärbabba's bedside, coaxing one more bite, Bärchen who changed his sheets and made his tea and took his whispered orders. He handed Bärbabba his earnings, which the old man would count three times (his small eyes, one cloudy) before he was satisfied.

Juan stuck close to home these days, and now it was April who made introductions and collected what was due.

But Christmas was in sight, and the men put on cheap faces of apple-cheeked goodwill for the benefit of their wives and kids. You'd never guess what these fellows got up to and, by accepting Jimmy Stewart as their personal savior, they thought it would stay that way. Juan predicted that business would be slow until after the new year. "It'll be like this around Easter, too," he added.

So, they sat in the unfinished Arizona room, warmed by the firepit, and talked about things that frightened them. It was a bold thing to ask, but the topic had come out of a magazine, an article titled, "Are You Afraid of Mice?" It centered on the idea of superficial fears, such as mice or the dark, and tried to extrapolate from them the *real* fear, the root. It was very Freudian. Fear of mice suggested a fear of emasculation in men, motherhood in women; fear of the dark suggested a fear of being infantilized, et cetera. Though it smacked of horse-hockey, the two of them got pencils and paper and made out lists. *Heights*, they wrote. *Needles, very deep water, fire, bees, sleepwalking, hard candy, dentures.* The article had the answers for some (very deep water equaled a fear of "personal growth"), but not all. It seemed that *dentures* and *hard candy* were a bit too specific. So, they wondered aloud what it was about these things that sent shivers down their spines. Then, with the eraser end of his pencil, Juan pointed to a line in the fourth or fifth paragraph, discussing the fear of heights. "To fear heights is to fear our impulses," the article read. "There is nothing so disquieting as the mistrust of your own mind. For when you are at the edge of a high diving board, or on the observation deck of the Empire State Building, do you feel a strange itch, very fleeting, but very insistent, suggesting the urge to jump?"

"Everything," he said. "That's it. Everything."

When April saw a bonfire, hadn't she ever wanted to jump in? When she saw a needle, didn't she once, for less than a moment, think of what would happen if she pushed it into the green prism of her eye?

She clapped her hands over her face, covering her nose, her mouth, her green eyes, chilled.

When your own hands want to wrap around your neck.

When your own feet carry you over the edge of a cliff.

When you sleep in the same skin as your enemy.

What Juan felt, so too did April.

The Arizona room had evolved by now from a mere naked platform to a caged structure, semi-detached, that you stepped onto from the galley kitchen. Since the first Sunday of Advent, April's father semaphored to his wife that he was turning over a new leaf, and busied himself with home improvement projects when he was not at his camp job working carpentry and maintenance. For a while, he did not speak to April, much less look at her. But the holiday neared and he could bring himself to show her the plans he drew up in school copybooks. The supplies he'd gotten from work migrated, piece by piece, to their proper places and fixed their positions with the help of the high school boys, from Juan, from April herself. She learned to use a level when the Arizona room was yet a skeleton, to pare chicken wire. "We'll have to stay on top of keeping the screens mended," April's father sighed. It would be enough to sleep one, maybe two, provided you lay on the floor. Small as a water closet, no room for cots. "We could bring a mattress out there," April's mother put in, and that brightened the mood even more. "We're due for a warm spell before Christmas." Juan brought up the idea of making a lounge chair for his father, "When he recovers."

Across the way, the Ogawas and the Engelses were spraying cedar branches in white paint and garnishing them with red velvet bows pulled from Rossi's Sunday dress.

The girls were good at keeping their other lives quiet. Their parents were the kind of folk who blotted out the bad with a long succession of parties: bridge parties, boo-ray parties, mahjong parties, dominoes parties, dinner parties, supper parties, costume parties, all of which amounted to a single, drawn-out cocktail party. You could smell the hooch from here. Former Junior League ladies could be seen vomiting into flower pots. They were not above buying from Juan. Mrs. Ogawa dropped by, ostensibly for a chat, and she would sit tapping her fingers next to the cup of tea April's mother made for her until Juan came in, smelling of pickled fruit, and she brightened right up.

Where were all the grown-ups, you might ask.

Mrs. Engels stole the altar wine from the chapel when the moxie ran out.

Were it not for her close proximity to the Ogawa-Engels house—one step and you were in their yard—April could say she did not know them, and they did not know her. She could go about the day, peeling potatoes, hammering and prying, washing and ironing.

Some days, the burden lifted and her memory was a blessed fog (enough moxie could do that) and she forgot her own name. Until a man crept up. Or a girl would stare. A recognition fixed. Yes, that was her, that girl, that April. That Hussy, better known as Hasi. At which point, the freight of her sins ran her flat, chugging and whooshing, and it did no good to pretend that it barreled her down of its own accord.

She pulled hair, she knew that. She threatened to put out someone's eye. It was Milly's ear into which she'd snuffed a cigarette, Emmi's finger she'd broken.

When had it ever really been about money?

Why could she never remember the things she did when she did them?

What a relief it would be to step aside, renounce her name and place the blame on this other, this wretched succubus, also called April. A fiery court. A jury of imps. The succubus, bat wings bound, defanged, in the stand. April herself played ha-Satan, the accuser: For how long did the succubus think she was going to keep this up? Did she want to be caught? Was she pleased, degrading another girl, excited to watch her become further degraded?

The succubus answered, dull: Until they let us out. Yes, yes, and yes.

Sores abounded. Going number one burned. Going number two bled. It hurt to walk. Forget extra cocoa rations. I can't fall from grace all alone.

Until they let us out. Yes, yes, and yes.

And she would see the wadded bills and scrip in her vanity case, under her sanitary pads, and under the cash the rubbers that Juan got for her, somehow, somewhere.

And, of course, she saw Emmi, Rossi, Milly, and Flossy every day, in class and walking home. By now, everyone knew; these were the girls you talked about, not with. In their humiliation, they'd grown quite chummy, often seen sharing lunch at the camp dining hall, studying (a pointless endeavor, April thought), whispering, comforting, embracing in the privacy of the girls' washroom. There was none of the underhandedness that might have happened, had they been in a regular public school. No cattiness here. Their new rebellion evolved into a sisterhood.

You caught bits in passing, of their likes and dislikes, favorites, longings, crushes. They adored Jimmy Stewart. Flossy had a record player and they jitterbugged in the bedroom the four girls shared. April could see them across the way, a warm window, Benny Goodman's "Down South Camp Meetin'".

April did not want to listen, but she did. In the dining hall, she sat in her own stink, bodily fluid and penicillin, picked at the camp fare. Her ear felt like a big shell.

Flossy wanted to go to Australia after the war, maybe India, to be a social worker, maybe a doctor. Milly was taking a correspondence course in French and rumor had it that she was filling out applications to the big eastern women's colleges, maybe she would get a job at the embassy in Paris. Emmi and Rossi, who were daily communicants, talked about going to Palestine; Emmi considered taking the vows, Rossi wanted to become a curator or a historian or an archeologist on biblical digs. They dreamed, now that they were left alone, now that the end was near. White flags and peace treaties. A breath of fresh air, a sobering up. They sang that song, *"Hitler has only got one ball/ Goebbels has two, but very small"*. Plans changed, ambitions shifted, the end goal a fixed point: Their futures, all varied, all bright, involved exodus from the Land of the Free, as soon as possible.

April, on the other hand, lived day to day.

They were a quartet and April had Juan, whose prowess she was beginning to doubt. For the four of them to jump her would be easy. And who would care? She told this to Juan, one day when they were stapling chicken wire to the beams. She wouldn't have said anything at all, but she caught Emmi and Flossy, Milly and Rossi, then the four of them together eyeing her, quiet when she came into a room. Emmi held her gaze a bit longer than the rest—had her lips curved into what was not quite a smile? A grimace, a baring of teeth, like a dog? Could a smile be poisonous? This from Emmi, rumored to take the vows.

They were plotting, April declared.

Juan sighed. He had other girls, he said, new ones who were ready and willing and, in two or three cases, came with some experience. Mausi and Spatzi and Schnecke and Blumi had done enough and earned enough. Mausi and Spatzi and Schnecke and Blumi were names that could be reapplied to any face, at any time.

It would be another twenty years before Iceberg Slim released his book *Pimp.* April got ahold of a copy and she and Juan leafed through it. ("*Are* You Afraid of Mice?") At the front of the book was a glossary. Well, well. There was a language for what she'd been and what she'd done. Should she take notes? She, for example, was Juan's Bottom Bitch. Juan, had he been more Americanized, might have been called Daddy until Juan reminded her of Bärbabba's standing, ill though he was. A date was the meeting of a girl and a man in the chapel. The group of them, Hasi, Mausi, Spatzi, Schnecke, and Blumi, made a stable. What a girl did with a man in the chapel was a trick. Altogether, this bizarre business was called the Game.

Juan liked that, the Game. And once the business folded, it was no big deal. It was Game Over. No strings, no tracks, no consequence.

It was Jenny's copy, not the type of thing she usually read. April put it back where she found it, wedged in her bookcase, still packed with childhood favorites, *Betsy's Wedding* and the C.S. Lewis books. When April looked again, it would be gone.

Juan knew not to push his mileage on a girl, that is, to know her limit before she lost her mind. He did not believe in it, he said, as though this put him a cut above the rest. He knew, also, the importance of the exit fee, or, the amount a girl was obliged to pay for her release. Note, obliged.

April nodded.

"You're the mean one," Juan said, cupping her face under her chin. He meant it affectionately.

She had no questions, only when she ought to collect and how much she should expect.

Juan told her the amount, adding, "The sooner the better."

"Should I go right now?"

"Wait til after the hullaballoo," he advised.

Really, she did have one question: Was there another Hasi lined up, too? The idea pained her, and she locked herself in the water closet to grit her teeth and weep with jealousy over a girl who was, as yet, a phantom. She drove her brain to the boiling point with the energy it took to consider every face of every girl. Was it her? Or her? Ha-Satan told April the succubus that she was a fool. Ha-Satan suggested she keep her wrath for the man who ran the stable. But Juan eluded her, which made him irresistible. And it was easier to hate a girl like her.

To her knowledge, Juan had only ever been with April. To her knowledge, Juan had never been with the other girls, or any other girls at Peralta Farm. To April, this meant that Juan belonged to her.

For a week, she trained her eye on a pretty redhead who worked in the dining hall. One lunch hour, when the pretty redhead turned away from mixing a ham salad for sandwiches, April seasoned it with rabbit turds, dried and shredded, and a hint of fur for good measure. She laughed when the redhead fell ill. Never mind the handful of others who chose ham salad that day.

By now, it was the third Sunday of Advent, and the Federal Schools had let out until January. A breeze from the south erased all hints of the previous frost and it was warm again, almost hot. Mr. Ogawa and Mr. Engels prophesied a heat wave that would last after Christmas. The change of weather put everyone, inmates and guards alike, in an even jollier frame of mind. The congregations, Catholic, Methodist, Baptist, Adventist, Witness, even the queer, cloistered Russellites from whom the Witnesses had sprung and who did not worship in the chapel, pooled together after sampling hymns of shifting tones, "Adeste Fidelis" followed by the old favorite, "A Mighty Fortress is Our God", followed by "Love Divine, All Loves Excelling". They saw a commonality. What they all needed, they decided, were carols and tinsel and kinship. There would be candles. There would be children haloed and winged in gold. There would be cider and doughnuts and tamales and potato soup and cornbread.

Mothers made wings for their children out of plywood and glue and turkey plumage. For haloes, they wound spare copper wiring around their heads; April said, "Here's hoping there won't be a lightning storm." Grouped together, the kids had the look of a mission from outer space.

The Ogawa-Engels opened their home for these costuming sessions, put on Tchaikovsky, and made hot milk with cocoa rations for the children. (The adults had a vat of mulled altar wine going. Juan played Santa Claus. He'd worked out a deal: In exchange for a go at April, the priest and the pastors blamed high school hoodlums.) Mrs. Ogawa, swaying slightly, told them the story of Kaguya-hime, a princess from the moon who was found in a bamboo stump by an old woodcutter and his wife. She threw in a bit of scripture, adding, "*Forget not to show love unto strangers: for thereby some have entertained angels unawares.* So, remember that when someone asks you the time of day."

Peter Engels spoke up, "I thought she was a Martian."

Nikki Engels put in, "A moon Martian."

As soon as the young ones finished their costumes, they, all but Hasi, Mausi, Spatzi, Schnecke, and Blumi, were going to the dining hall. The children were going to give a chorale and the more confident musicians would play carols in the chamber music style. There had been talk of doing a nativity play, but the idea was scrapped when the Catholics wanted to put a crown on Mary at the Annunciation, and it turned into a debate with the Russellites about graven imagery. No one booed the idea of a jolly Saint Nick, and April's father gladly took up the role, and let his beard grow out until he looked like a Persian cat. April's mother fashioned a cap from her red Chinese bathrobe and a clean white terrycloth. He'd gone to the dining hall early to set up Santa's workshop.

Juan had to stay with Bärbabba.

April's mother told her only daughter, "If you're not going, you can help the What's-their-names, those girls."

Not above knocking back moxie, too good to admit that her daughter was a Madam, those girls her stable. Surely, she knew of her husband's penchant for "those Jap girls", as he called them. April wanted to tell her mother that she had it rough, too, that of all things, her father turned out to be one of those guys who fancied girls from across the Pacific to be natural comfort women.

So, April slumped into an overstuffed armchair in the Ogawa-Engels living room, which doubled as a bedroom for Mr. and Mrs. Ogawa. Their camp cots were folded and crammed behind the sofa.

Milly Ogawa glided through, offering to top up their mugs of cocoa, while Flossy worked in the kitchen. She leapt from stove to counter, stirring the pot of mulled wine with one arm, crushing crackers for mock apple pie with the other. There was a bowl of mock whipped cream ready, made from margarine, corn flour, powdered milk and water. The Engels girls chopped walnuts and warmed applesauce. They were prepping for Christmas dinner the next day.

The grown-ups chased their goblets with tumblers of moxie, another gift from Juan-as-Saint Nick. They did not know its withdrawals as the girls did; not a day lapsed, it seemed, wherein a tumbler of moxie was not tossed back.

Years later, out of the blue, April asked Juan if he ever missed the taste. He told her he might die if he ever so much as smelled it again. "I get nightmares about that stuff," he said. "Of all things. I dream I'm at a convent or a monastery, somewhere holy. And instead of altar wine, they're passing out moxie. And the Mass turns into a party, big and raucous. You'd think something like that would be funny, but it never is. It's horrible; there's too much light, too many colors. There's party lights, but they're tacky, and they're wrapped around everywhere, the Virgin, the grape arbor. People are passing out in the grotto, altar boys are rolling up to see a nun striptease. God, the taste. And then, split second, there's this silence. The light changes, it's morning and it's grey. Everyone looks at each other, gathers themselves together. I'm usually missing something of mine, like my pants or my shoes. And they all start talking about getting everything picked up before Mom gets home. Always Mom." He went quiet. Then he said, "There's one for the Freudians."

Behind their goodwill toward men, Milly belched, Flossy moaned, Emmi sweated and held Rossi's head over a mixing bowl. Rossi realized a minute too late that the mixing bowl was actually a colander. She sobbed when it oozed vomit onto the floor.

They could not work if they did not drink, and reefers, the preferred agent, were hard to come by. Now, due for release, they'd gone the temperance route.

No pink elephants, but the DTs ran like a shock treatment through one ear and out the other. April knew. Food was as feces, or else full of maggots. That was the worst of all, for a loss of appetite did not equate an absence of hunger, nor its pangs, nor its subsequent exhaustion. What you kept down you passed. What you passed was murky, pure liquid, with an acidic element that irritated any fissures. Juan compared it to having your anus blowtorched. Sometimes there were hemorrhoids, and when you wiped the paper was spotted. She suspected there was more to moxie than just fruit and fermentation; she'd heard stories of people drinking engine coolant.

What else could you do?

To April, it was wiser to keep the stupor going. To April, the world around them blurred and, when it regained its edges, acquired an iridescent halo that connected all things, wall to standing lamp, lamp to Nikki Engels' rabbit slipper, slipper to Mrs. Ogawa's plump hand, to the spark in the diamond of her wedding ring. Mrs. Ogawa herself misjudged the placement of the sofa and took a thudding seat on the rug with the kids. Nikki and Peter, crowned in copper wire and not knowing what else to do, howled and clapped. When Mrs. Ogawa began to snore, they poked feathers in her hair.

"Turkey turkey turkey from the moon—" Nikki sang.

Peter joined her, "Turkey turkey turkey lady from the moon—"

Their mother, meanwhile, made it to the sofa, pressed a hand to her eyes. In repose, she snapped for quiet and was out a minute later. Nikki wet the last of the feathers with leftover cocoa and Peter stuck them to Mrs. Engels' face to make a beard. Pausing, thinking, they found two very tufty plumes, and fixed them in a moustache to her upper lip. They stood back, pleased. When they were sure their mother was in no danger of waking, Nikki leaned into her ear, and she whispered with more vinegar than April had ever heard such a small girl, "That'll teach you. Old turkey bitch."

April would say, "There's nothing creepier than a kid that knows how to curse."

Juan would ask, "What about a kid that smokes?"

April would tell him, "Still creepier."

Finally, Mrs. Ogawa snorted, stirred. She blinked. The children froze. They'd gussied themselves up in their wings and haloes, and for a moment she let herself be dazzled. The copper and the gold foil caught the light and cast it about the room in splinters. It was a spectacular effect of itself. To the drunken eye, it must have suggested the presence of the Holy Ghost. It made Mrs. Ogawa weep, and when Mrs. Engels jerked awake, she wept, too.

"These babies," Mrs. Ogawa wailed. "So beautiful."

"And so BIG—" Mrs. Engels was beside herself, perhaps at having remembered that these were her youngest children. She put her hand to her cheek, drew back sticky fingers and sour-smelling down. "What in the hell. What the hell is this?" She peeled layers of feathers from her face while her big, beautiful babies cackled. To April, they'd become two hens from Hades.

Something struck, jigging memory, releasing whatever chemical reserves the brain had to sober up two tipsy housewives, and it inspired them both to look at the clock on the kitchen wall. They sprung to action. They were in danger of missing the chorale, which had already begun, as Mrs. Engels had fretted when she went to the window.

Outside, the children, save for Peter and Nikki, had assembled and were winding up the avenue toward the dining hall, all gilded, all haloed, gripping real candles with real flames and trembling. They sang, not well, but they sang. *Still, still, still, weil's Kindlein schlafen will.* They stumbled through the German as best they could.

April, who had been sipping from the mulled wine, then the punchbowl of moxie, lit a cigarette and asked why the kids weren't singing in English. "It's all scheisse to them," she put in, one of maybe forty words in her German vocabulary. No one appreciated her joke or, more likely, no one noticed. She laughed anyway. She wished Juan was here; he had even less reverence for the whole tinseled farce than she. He'd say something sharp to her about the housewives, their last-minute trial of having to pull feathers from their hair and chins. Mrs. Ogawa scribbled over her lips in red, Mrs. Engels pushed past the girls in the kitchen to douse herself with water from the sink, and for a towel, she snatched the hem of Rossi's apron and ground it across her face.

"The hell were you doing when you were supposed to be looking after them?" Mrs. Engels flapped one hand at her two youngest, and used the other to powder her very pink nose. She thrust the Pond's case at Emmi. There was time yet, in between getting her coat and changing her shoes, to dispense thumps unto Peter and Nikki, blunt on the back of each head, careful of their haloes.

Mrs. Ogawa was already outside. She shouted, loud enough for April to see the words in big blocks, "LET'S. GO." April heard her sigh, mutter oaths of damnation and other terms of impatience, when Mrs. Engels stepped onto the porch with Peter and Nikki. A small transformation had taken place, Mrs. Engels made up and respectable in her marmot box coat, the children exorcized of all demons and beaming. They staggered up the path in time for Peter and Nikki to bring up the rear.

Wir, wir, wir tun rufen all zu Dir:
Tu uns des Himmels Reich aufzuschließen
wenn wir einmal sterben müssen

April knew a rough translation: We call Thee to open the heavens to us when we die. She smirked. It was a far cry from "Santa Claus is Comin' to Town".

Suddenly, everything got very quiet. The singing had progressed into the dining hall and was now there contained, yes. The children were gone, yes. And their mothers were gone, yes. Someone had turned off the record player, and now Tchaikovsky was gone.

This meant that April was alone with her stable. Individually, Mausi, Spatzi, Schnecke, and Blumi were as their endearments suggested. They, on their own, were small. April did not fear a mouse, a sparrow, a snail, or a flower. April, the rabbit, could overpower them easily. She carried fire in her like a coiled spring. She was small, too, but quicker. And because no one expected a girl so small to have such a strong backhand, it rocked them back on their toes, too stunned to fight back when she reared up to hit them again, and again, and again.

But what if you had a quartet?

Milly, Flossy, Emmi, and Rossi scowled at her from over the kitchen counter. April heard them drawn breath, in and out, in and out, evening out, sizing her up. And it seemed that now for the first time, they could take her measure and know for sure that April Hussy was not much to contend with. She was five foot three. Milly and Flossy were five-six and strong from farm work. Emmi and Rossi, embarrassed by their giantesses' height of five-eleven and were always slouching to hide it, now stood erect, shoulders back. They could wipe the floor with her if they wanted to.

The strange thing was that they didn't. They did not move from the kitchen. They did not take their eyes from her, and went on working, crushing crackers and chopping walnuts, a mechanical assembly line. April waited until Milly rinsed the knife and put it back in the butcher block to light another cigarette. She waited until Rossi put the mock apple pie in the oven and started on the dishes that she got up her nerve and strolled across the room.

"This is the first time, I think, we've all had a chance to socialize—" April tried to keep her voice breezy. She chuckled and added, "Extracurricularly."

Milly and Flossy joined Rossi at the sink. Rossi rinsed, Flossy scrubbed, and Milly dried. Emmi stacked bowls and pans by the stove and stowed glasses and mugs in the cupboards. One of them made a grunt to show they'd heard April; she wasn't sure who it was.

"Juan says you all are fixing to retire," she went on. She observed her ways as though she had stepped outside herself and taken a seat at the table, her own audience. She made a poor impression of the cool customer. She was too stiff, too light, too bright, too drunk, too shaky on her feet. She tripped over the other rabbit slipper, trying to lean against the counter. In doing that, the ash from her cigarette, grown quite long, flaked onto her arm and burned her there. Too surprised to ignore it, April yelped and jumped and bent to blow on the spot.

None of them laughed. Thank God for that. But perhaps this was worse, to have them all peer down at her from their comparably great height, at this pint-sized bitch, playing at adulthood as would a little girl who gets out her mother's high heels and clops around, insisting she is grown up. They were not amused. Flossy ran a cloth under the faucet and handed it to her. The rest of them released a collective sigh, and April thought she saw Milly shaking her head. This, April knew, was pity.

Then Milly spoke. "We quit, more like."

April tossed the cloth over the counter, hard enough to make it snap. It struck Flossy in the chest, a small victory. "Did anybody talk to Juan about this? You don't think you owed him that?"

For his sake, this imaginary Juan, who had a volcanic temper and a keen sense of what was his, she was outraged, and this gave her some backbone, enough to come around the counter and into the kitchen. The girls backed away, afraid, but not as April felt they should be. This was what you did when you found yourself cornered by a rabid dog. It was frightening, to be sure, and you knew you had to watch your step so as not to get bitten. Prevailing, however, was the feeling of how pathetic this poor creature was, how beyond hope.

There was only one way to take care of a rabid dog.

Four of them and one of me.

April remembered and stood down.

Quietly, sadly, as if trying to make April herself understand, Rossi told her that they did not owe Juan a goddamned thing. She said the word We as if to include all of them, mouse, sparrow, snail, bloom, and rabbit. "We don't owe him a goddamned thing."

Of course, Juan would not seek retribution if they did not pay up. April doubted that he would try to collect from them himself. He would move on, simply fix new names to new faces. They were expendable, and so was April. That was the truth of it. April, who was loved as the mean one. April, who hadn't a leg to stand on and who had nothing to return to, save for Mr. and Mrs. Hussy, having revealed themselves to be made of what amounted to shamefaced marshmallow. The idea of her replaceability, now that she'd narrowed it all down to Juan Nimitz, weak as he was in his own way, could not, would not stand. Without Juan, she really would be alone, wouldn't she?

Think on your feet. Look them in the eye. Don't let them think they've got you.

April set her jaw, breathed. She explained the required exit fee, the amount. Thinking on her feet, looking them in the eye, running them down and then getting them, she prided herself for remembering the photographs. There were snapshots of the girls with or without clothes, with or without a man, exposing or concealing, bound or unbound. They knew Juan had sold some, only to customers who paid extra for them. And they knew he had copies. April repeated the amount, adding that if Juan got it by midnight, he and April would be obliged to destroy every last shot. "Poof," she uttered, flicking her fingers like a magician.

Milly and Flossy, Emmi and Rossi nodded, mulling. They traded glances, again nodding, again mulling. It had gone over so easily that April worked to detect a hint, a signal that the four of them were telegraphing something ugly amongst themselves. Perhaps they meant to keep her here. They might break her and snuff cigarettes into her flesh. If it came to that, April wouldn't blame them for it. A portion of her mind champed at the bit, for that certain elation was at hand, that which excites the condemned before the punishment, that which she knows she's had coming to her, is handed down. Everyone knew that from a reckoning, especially one that was sure to be painful, you came out the other end, having paid your due. You'd endured, it was over, and you were saved.

It was Milly who said, "All right."

The elation dampened. Redemption was denied. April shook her head. Had she really wanted them to give her the thumbscrews? She swallowed. She lit another cigarette, the last in her pocket. "All right?" she asked, grasping for her previous tone of the cool customer. "All that by midnight tonight? You can get your hands on that kind of dough?" She didn't know why she chose midnight tonight, probably something she'd heard in a gangster movie. She noticed her mouth twitch and shift and, stepping out of herself again and observing from her seat at the table, she wanted to laugh aloud. Did she think she could scare them by talking like a gangster, too? Working her mouth to the side, channeling Humphrey Bogart. April Elizabeth Hesse, who came from a pretty little town in the Hill Country.

"We had some extra," Milly went on, "We'd been stashing it. You hadn't noticed so far, so we thought —" She let her head droop, knocked the toe of her shoe against the floor.

Looking back ten, twenty, fifty years later, persistent unto her deathbed, this would be the thing that kept April awake at night for the embarrassment of it, the consummate stupidity. She should have known. Fifty years later, April would play through this exchange, pause it, and catch this or that detail, a look that was too humble, a gesture that was too on the nose—Milly's toe scraping, for one, she might as well have said, "Aw, shucks." She would tell Juan, "I told you they were plotting something. I told you."

Emmi added, "What we have, though, it's not enough. Mama keeps cash in this lockbox."

"She has the key," Rossi put in.

Flossy said, "We'll have the money for you."

"Once Mama gets back," Emmi finished. "After she's asleep. She won't miss it, she never counts it."

April could have demanded they break the lock now. They had plenty of kitchen tools that would do the trick. She could have, really should have, asked to see this lockbox.

The fact remains, she did not.

Juan, sallow faced and purple eyed, snapped at April for the first time. "A lockbox? What on God's green earth is a lockbox?" He had Bärbabba's chamber pot in his hand. Usually, he dumped the waste in the outhouse. On this night, he cast it, the whole foul mess, into the yard. It sprayed the carrot tops and scared off the rabbits that had been chewing them in the dark.

Seeing herself, shrunken, April asked if she ought to go back. She followed Juan inside, watching from the doorway as he wrested a bar of soap into pink mush. He worked it back into some kind of shape, and this seemed to settle him. Placing it in its dish, breathing, turning to her, he told her no, "No need to go back. We'll wait up through the night, we'll wait and see. If there's a problem, I'll take care of it." He smirked. "I mean, it is Christmas."

"How's him?" April nodded at the back bedroom. From here, she could see a foot dangling over the brass bedstead. She wanted to tell Juan that he ought to cut his father's nails. The ones on the toes especially looked like horn and were beginning to curve under.

Juan tried terseness. "He'll live." His face crumbled, gathered to the tip of his nose. Then he swallowed and was all right again. He ducked behind the curtain that closed the washroom off from the rest of the cottage and came out with a fresh batch of moxie. It sloshed in an old Pepsi-Cola bottle. Juan had added canned rhubarb pie filling to this brew, tinging it pink, and a scummy foam piled on top like cotton candy. April found mugs, Juan topped them off. It overflowed and sparked and hit April's self-inflicted cigarette wound.

Juan asked what had happened there. His thumb scraped over it, rubbing in the pink.

April mashed her lips together. She said something along the lines of "Nothing I couldn't handle", something to imply that she was made of nails and steel, that it was someone else's unsteady hand and their cigarette. Juan would laugh and call her cute when she told him how she'd actually gotten it, years and years later. "You're a real little psychopath," he'd say, "you really are." To think, after everything, she would be ashamed to tell him of how she'd slopped her own cigarette.

The porch was looking like what it ought to be now, less like a lean-to and more like a birdcage. It was a fair night, there was a star in the east. From the dining hall, a lull had settled in between chorale hymns and in its place came the chamber music, two guitars and two flutes, one violin, one cello. This carol escaped April, on the first few notes. It was perky, vaguely pagan, and conjured holly and ivy as heralds for the solstice, rather than any messiah. She gulped moxie and it was a thousand years ago in the crystalline age of lords in the manor and mummers in the village. She had a goblet of cider, turned fiery in its aging, and wore a pair of poulaines, red velvet, with the toes so long they turned up in a curl. In the previous millennium, it was the custom to don masks and cloaks and dance wildly around a bonfire, for the air had changed and the cold set in and the moon was so bright as to suggest a veritable crack in the sky. Like All Hallows' Eve, this was a time in which the partition between this world and the other was at its thinnest. There were ghosts on Christmas, too.

It brewed in her gut, not an urge to dance. Her fingers twitched and she recalled having practiced this song when she was a young squeezebox student. She whipped around the porch and went indoors and emerged with the accordion tight to her chest. She took her usual position. Once she began, she was surprised at how much of this song she remembered, better played, now that she knew what to do with the instrument, how to cradle it. On her stool, she rocked, one heel and one toe touching the planks beneath her. It really was like manipulating an organ, external, namely with her fingers, in addition to her whole body. The vibrations possessed her, in one long thrum to her groin. She did not care how poorly she sounded, or if Juan was watching. No, strike that last. Her hands fluttered over the buttons, the right creeping to the lower notes as to suggest her fingers grappling for herself, down there.

"Gagliarda", this one was called. From the sixteenth century dance, the galliard.

Juan got up and she kept playing. The romantic in her thought he'd gone to get his guitar; perhaps they would perform a duet. She lost herself in the vibrations and pressed against her instrument, her organ, and had not heard Juan's footsteps returning. She knew he was there when he slipped one finger, then two, inside her. She'd not worn underwear on this day either. He was behind her, a bit farther this time so as to accommodate his hands, which were busier now. He worked both holes, front and back, as she worked the buttons, the bellows.

She did not whimper this time.

And neither did he, when she'd finished and it was his turn to play her.

A fair night, the howling of wild animals. Could it be a bear mauling a rabbit? They did not worry about anyone seeing because everyone was at the chorale. And anyway, they had the dark on their side for a curtain over the naked chicken wire.

April fell back, laughed. She heard an echo of years passed, her father's scolding: *That's no way to treat a musical instrument, young miss.* He would know. She grabbed the Pepsi-Cola bottle and saw the shimmer around the edges of things. The rhubarb made her saliva stringy. Her mouth and its sores burned, and other Christmases showed themselves to her, no lighter, but it invoked familiar colors, midnight Mass at Osanna of Mantua, a carol's name that she could not remember but knew the part of it that went, *Turelurelu, patapatapan.* Had she been wearing wings, a halo of gold?

Juan patted her thigh and pulled her to her feet. They peeled April's mattress from her bed and dragged it outside before they were too groggy to do anything else. Agreed, it was too hot this fair night to sleep indoors.

An hour, many, but no one had come home yet. The air held faint notes of the children's choir, the last verse of "Kling, Glöckchen". The bit that went *klinge-linge-ling* was punctuated by a tinny jumble of the youngest, the toddlers, ringing bells borrowed from the school and the chapel.

April woke on the mattress in the Arizona room, damp. She wore her undershirt, her dress balled under her head. Her legs were sticky. She disengaged from Juan, who slept with his lips parted. His lashes were long and she kissed his closed eyes, his parted lips, and went into the cottage. All was cool, now that the house was empty. The little French press that her mother kept by the stove held a cup's worth of coffee. In the mug it looked thin and fecal, but it made April's eyes open all the way and she delighted walking through the cottage's two rooms half-naked.

She swallowed the dregs and was still fuzzy yet when she heard music, not from anywhere outside. It brought her to the edge and woke her up completely when she understood this music, a guitar, to be coming from the second room. Peering through the kitchen window, seeing Juan where she left him, sticky like her and snoring to beat the band, she moved to the farthest corner, by the water closet, where she knew she could get a full view into the space that Papa Bear shared with Little Bear. She could see him, but he, Bärbabba, could not see her.

And it was him, risen, thanks to some reserves that got him to the edge of his bed. Under the guard tower lights, Bärbabba was a shape. Seated as he was, hunched over the guitar, he approached the instrument with halting ferocity, finding notes and losing them, growling, hissing when his beard caught in the strings. She did not know she was naked until he'd stopped playing. She did not know if he knew that she was there when he set the guitar across his lap and, with hands like great paws, began to take it apart, the wood splintering, creaking in weak protest, starting from the sound hole and ending only when Bärbabba had the three steel strings in his fist. The nylon ones curled from the carcass, snapped, stupid little twigs that made no noise as Bärbabba stepped on them. He, having taken nourishment this last month in the meekest bites, was like a winter tree made mobile, all angles and snapping branches, an energy in him working from a place of wicked enchantment. In shadow, he was bigger than April remembered him to be, and the nails on his fingers and toes curled like horrible winklepickers. It made her think, too, of Frankenstein's monster, who was made to live beyond the span of its parts.

God forbid, she prayed, I grow so old and broken that I waste my rallying moments tearing apart a guitar. *That's no way to treat a musical instrument.* God forbid I live to see the tantrum stage of my senectitude.

It made her laugh—well, it was not exactly a laugh. It was a noise, involuntary, that bubbled in her throat and would hurt like hell if she did not let it out. She had to make light of it somehow. She had to make light of it or she would die there on the spot. Spontaneous combustion, a lightning strike. How it happened didn't matter. She understood now, this was why people laughed at funerals.

Crunching underfoot, wood and strings. Bärbabba's gait was off to a slow start, but again, he summoned his reserves, and April had an idea of what he must have been like in his prime. Two strides and he could cross a room. His closeness did not make his features and clearer, and so April could not have said what his eyes were like, what his mouth was doing. Was he smiling? Would he rape her? He was already looming over her, craning his head. He had claws and a beard that was like fur and he smelled of disease, sour and sweet that combined to make April gag.

She held her breath.

Here was April, having come to this very moment with such force that she felt nothing so strongly as the urge to scream. She was indeed a little rabbit. She was meek, as in a dream in which she tried to talk but it all came out as lisps and squeaks. She would be powerless to stop him if he decided to pick her up by the hair, wrap his claws around her throat. If that was what he wanted. And here was that elation, that prisoner's excitement at knowing that the blade will fall, the trapdoor will open, the switch will flip and she in the chair will cook. April readied herself.

But Bärbabba did not move. He inched closer, yes he did, enough to put a hand against the counter, leaning into it as though in exhaustion. And wasn't everyone here exhausted? Wasn't everyone here disheartened? What made Bärbabba any different?

For all his height, he seemed unable to do a thing to fight it. And it brought the revulsion back in a different way and April forward, tiny steps, up to his nose, to get a good look at him, this dumb, weakened creature, good for no one, parasitic, not a man at all, but a beast that followed and came and did whatever it was told and then stewed, happily, in its own waste. He was not human, not a bear, less than. There were people like this, April knew, people who enjoyed misery. It relieved April, enough to make her smile, and she did, looking at him as though he were in the Arizona room, built as it was like a big cage, and she were outside.

And then he did something. It was so quick that April could utter only a noise like a lisp or a squeak. Bärbabba's hand was sure and quick. He cut his throat with the same deliberation he gave to playing a song. One of the strings was a steel one, borrowed and fixed to his own guitar when the old one had broken, too warped to be tuned anymore. It had given his music a chilly edge. And now he had drawn it across, emptying himself in a terrible spray from which April had been shielded by her arms, fast to cover her face. She was clean, save for a thin line that shot through and landed on her upper lip. She licked it absently, the taste of meat.

When he was on the ground and did not move, April stepped over him. As though this were a normal day and as though she were soaked in something equally sticky, equally smelly, but ordinary, moxie for example, she bent over the sink and scrubbed her arms. When she smelled of pink soap, she went back to the Arizona room.

She saw the red bow and sprayed white cedar branches first and did not connect it to anything until she remembered that this pile of junk, under its festoonery, had not been here when she went to sleep and had not been there when she woke. Two strides and she knelt. The odor made her clap her hands to her nose. She covered her eyes, peeking through her fingers when she knew she had to. It was her accordion, the bellows gutted and the mother of pearl buttons smashed as if by a hammer. Inside the bellows, where the tear was widest, she saw the soft tips of long, long ears poking out. Stuffed with rabbits, it was—No, rabbit pelts, those that the guards sold and reserved for any inmate taxidermists. Mr. Ogawa had taken up the hobby and brought home a bunch. He had rabbits in repose, rabbits erect with one ear cocked, rabbits in loaf position. These were the ones he had not used, and, as April read on the note attached: "Here's to a bright and musical future. You and Little Bear are a match made in hell. God have mercy on your souls. Merry Christmas and fuck the both of you. We quit. Love from—" And there was no signature, but little doodles under the sign-off of a mouse, a sparrow, a snail, and a flower.

She lay beside Juan, who had not stirred, and slept.

"You're a vampire," Juan told her.

"I'm a what?"

"You're a bloodsucker."

Jenny was in her room and they heard Pal padding across upstairs. Then, Jenny was an apple in April's belly, and Juan was shrieking in her face.

Juan, who became a good boy upon release, who talked his way into the state university, who went to confession because he didn't like the idea of analysis, and who became a credit manager for Wells Fargo and eventually one of the top dogs at the Andermatt branch. Juan, who was not and never had been called Hans, and whose missing fingerprints were the result of an accident, a fire, he was trapped, had to bang on hot metal to get himself out.

Juan, who had the nerve to call April a vampire.

April, who had begged her mother to let Juan live with them once he graduated. April, who let him collapse into her when he woke and found Bärbabba, stiff, purpled, on the floor, the kitchen a bright chaos. April, who put her lips to his neck where she'd bitten him, and told him she loved him. And whether he was too distraught or whether he really meant it, he told her he loved her, too. April, who took him home with her at the end of the war because he had no one else.

Juan put his hand through the dining room wall. April patched it the next day. You could see the indent in the years following, even after they'd repainted the room primrose yellow in the late eighties. "You could've just let me die, too," he howled. He was withdrawing and he'd entered the inferno. He'd calm down, eventually, after enough water and carrots and daily Masses.

"Well, I didn't," April said.

I guess that's my punishment.

She woke one time at another drive-through break, this time at a McDonald's. Jenny ordered coffee and chicken nuggets for them all to share. April played possum and the girls let her. It was decades and minutes in between eavesdropping, and she was confused at how Pal could move so seamlessly from talking about dissecting a home intruder to talking about the Spice Girls, making Jenny laugh.

"There's Junkie Spice and Crusty Spice and Ganja Spice and Gnarly Spice and Bleach Spice and Spacy Spice and Pumpkin Spice—"

"Aren't there only four Spice Girls?" Jenny was asking. "That's like ten."

Never mind the intruder who'd shot and killed their parents.

I'm glad you all can just move on.

Napping, a blank state of being that is the closest you get to the experience of a sensory deprivation tank. You can't see or hear or speak. Nor are you really asleep. You can swim to the surface when you want. Or you have the choice of turning inward, where you gather flashes of images, not quite dreaming, though what you come up against are, for an instant, fully formed. You might as well have gone to another place. It's usually a fragment of an old nightmare, being chased and your inability to run, trying to shout and having it come out muffled, knowing that something is creeping up right behind you and you don't know what it is. The anticipation. The split second before you run off a cliff, get caught by the monster. And then I woke up.

April had the image of herself in her bedroom. Very clear, it was. She had the peacock tail wallpaper, jade green and gold; she had the little porcelain animals she collected from boxes of English tea lined up on the windowsill, an eagle, two elephants, a herd of sheep, an owl; their oak hutch with her perfumes and his shaving stuff; even the odor of the bathroom, the apple-cinnamon Fabreeze spray, which had never entered her dream life before.

She was in bed, Juan next to her. She had woken first.

She came to and the girls were listening to the messages Juan had left. They must have stopped again for Jenny or Pal to dig the box of answering machine tapes out of the trunk.

"Tag, you're it."

"Tag, you're it."

"*Dónde éstas?* One of you goons forgot to put gas in my car and now I'm stranded in the middle of nowhere—Well, by nowhere, I mean the Walgreens. Come on out before the sun goes down."

"It's about five o'clock on a Tuesday."

"It's two-O-two on a Friday."

"Did he just call April in the middle of the day?" Pal asked. "Like, it's two-O-two, time to harass my wife."

"It's O-nine-hundred hours on a Monday. Supplies are low. Morale remains high."

"Tag, you're it."

"Tag, you're it."

"Tag, you're it."

"Phone tag," Jenny tittered.

"Are these all just for April?" Pal asked, "Aside from the one where he's at Walgreens." She paused. "That was on me."

That message was from five years ago or more. Pal was home from school (undergrad or med school?) and running around, errands, visits, lots of aimless driving. Juan watched the sun go down in the Walgreens parking lot, leaning against the car and drinking a Dr. Pepper. April was so taken by the picture he made, she brought him straight home and fell on top of him.

"You creature," Juan said.

April started. "Who? Me or Pal?"

"You."

She dreamed the same half-dream as before, the one where she woke in their bedroom. Everything was as it had been the first time. Juan was still beside her. It must have been early morning because she could hear the school bus whining to a stop down the street, the gasping of the doors, kids' chatter ("—cuz there was this lady who did eat that part and she died—"), the grunt as the bus moved on.

Pal would be robbed of her fantasy.

Who would she cut up, if her parents were dead in their home, but there was no intruder?

April came back and Jenny and Pal were talking, appropriately, about death. Specifically, they were talking about the concept of an afterlife.

Pal, the atheist, believed that matter was finite. She had seen it for herself on the body farm. Human decomposition went as follows, in four stages: Self-digestion, bloat, active decay, skeletonization. Self-digestion occurred within twenty-four hours, wherein the tissue had turned necrotic and begun the process of consuming its own cells, starting with the organs. Bloat, during which gases expanded and dribbled fluid from the nose and mouth, set in by day three or four. Active decay cemented in the observer's mind the point of no return, the body's revelation of what it had always been: meat, now rotting. Hair and nails did not continue to grow, despite the old wives' tale. The skin would recede, giving the impression of growth, but eventually, the hair and nails would fall out. Bugs feasted, buzzards pecked. When the meat melted, the scavengers would leave, having picked the bones clean.

Jenny, a Jew, held to their parents' idea of what heaven would be. April perked up at this; it was one of hers and Juan's better inventions. Heaven, according to April and Juan Nimitz, was much more crowded than folks let on. In fact, Hades was the empty place, made for people who were really and truly past hope. Jenny combined this notion with the Maimonidean belief that the really and truly wicked were so consumed by the shame of a squandered life that they simply burned themselves out from humiliation. C.S. Lewis had said the same thing, that hell was not meant for people, only waste. Heaven, meanwhile, was perfectly intact in Jenny's mind. In heaven, you had the best of everything. It was not in the sense of Everything that included a mansion in the sky or streets paves with gold. Jenny's heaven had a lake and thick, breathing forests. In heaven, you could talk to animals, the way humans did in the time of the Garden of Eden. In heaven, you never went hungry. In heaven, berries never went out of season, though you did not need to eat.

Pal liked the beach and asked if heaven could have a beach instead. She was twenty-six years old and four years old, in this Astro and on April's lap. Would there still be music? Would there still be language? It was logical to presume that humans would not need to speak if they did not need to eat.

Jenny repeated Juan, word for word, "If you want it there, it'll be there." She clarified, "The key phrase is that we will no longer need to do this or this or that. But if we want to—"

"—if we want to," Pal finished, "—we can still do this or this. Got it. I'd definitely still want that blue raspberry thing they used to have at the general store —"

"They still have that—"

"Yeah, but they changed the recipe. It's really syrupy now."

"You'd want blue raspberry frosty from the general store?"

"Yup."

"Would you still want the general store to be there?"

"Of course."

"Would you still pay for it in change scrounged from under the car seats and stuff?"

"It's part of the experience."

Jenny snorted. "You won't need money, you know."

Pal said, "I know that, but what I want is the experience."

April remembered when they changed the blue raspberry frosty recipe. It was the day the owner was arrested for child molestation. It was a stepson. There was Robitussin. He'd duct taped a bag over the boy's head and took pictures. The boy had been telling people for ages, but it was all so—well, so out there as to suggest having been lifted from a nightmare.

April asked whatever happened to the stepson.

"Went to live with his grandmother," Juan said. "In Virginia, I think."

"What about his mother?"

"She died. Don't you remember?"

"No."

"You don't remember? It was a big thing. She was parked in front of the doughnut place on the main street. And she'd had a lapse of memory and forgot which was the gas and which was the brake. And she plowed right through. She landed in the creek behind the store."

"How do you know she forgot? How do you know she didn't do it on purpose?"

"Because Simon Fielding told me she'd just got done talking with her divorce lawyer, and then she had an appointment to talk with him at the bank that very day."

"What about?"

Juan shrugged. "How would I know?"

There had been something of a problem in Himmel Creek with cars driving through buildings, April recalled. This was one of them. The girls recapped them all; they laughed, in the way that you do when you just can't believe it. The second was an old man who'd put his car into drive rather than reverse at the chicken place. The third was a high school girl full of boxed wine who burst through the garage door of the neighbor's house, thinking she'd made it home. The fourth was a college boy who, unable to handle his girlfriend dumping him, barreled into the gardening outfit at which she'd worked; he meant only to run over the topiary animals out front, he'd said.

The second, third, and fourth occasions had the element of cautionary tales at play. After enough time had passed, they could even be funny, the poor old man, the dumb drunk girl, the idiot boyfriend. They, the poor old man, the dumb drunk girl, the idiot boyfriend, had acted irresponsibly. They had stepped back, last minute, from doom. The poor old man got his keys taken away. The dumb drunk girl had to pay for the neighbor's garage door. The idiot boyfriend got arrested and, because money talked, took mandatory anger management classes in lieu of jail time.

On only the first occasion had anyone died.

Would Pal still want a blue raspberry frosty after she knew all that? Would the owner of the general store be in heaven to make her one? Or would there be someone else behind the counter? Did that make it the same experience?

More to the point, would Pal believe it if April told her why the blue raspberry frosty had changed and why the general store's management had changed, too?

Point blank: Would Pal and Jenny believe it if April told them—well, told them everything? Right here, at seventy-five miles an hour, with farm-dung smell and trees outside and a disembodied voice inside, saying, "It's twelve-eighteen on Wednesday. Tag, you're it"? The camp, the chapel, the men who peeled off their disguised wholesomeness and did what they wanted with girls who were not yet out of high school. The accordion, the guitar. How Papa Bear departed this earth. And how none of it might have happened if Juan had just left their mother alone.

There were people who believed that the Holocaust never happened.

There were people who knew that the camps in America happened. They told you that they were not for forced labor or extermination. They told you that, yes, it was hard, but many things in life were hard. It was a long time ago. They told you to make do, to pull yourself up by the bootstraps. These were the devotees of the Protestant Work Ethic. These were usually, of all those interned in the second world war, the Germans. They told you to make it so that the problems of this world did not apply to you.

By contrast, the Japanese banded together. They wrote letters. They demanded apologies. They fought back. They talked about food shortages, rubella, fleas, lice, the cottages that housed two, four, sometimes five families in three rooms. By the sixties, people were tired of keeping their heads down. Times changed. Maybe it was the war or the bomb. Maybe people saw the Protestant Work Ethic for the crock it really was. Of course, the public was shocked. Of course, we could not allow this kind of atrocity to happen on American soil.

Yet again, time passed. People heard enough about suffering. It bummed people out to hear about atrocity on American soil. It might not be the Protestant Work Ethic at hand, but the sentiment remained the same: Just move on, it was a long time ago. We built the memorials. What more do you want?

Mrs. Glau showed April her mother-in-law's deed, granting, selling, and conveying the ownership of the first Mrs. Glau, then four years old, from an Irish called McCuistion to a plantation man called Hatfield. Her reason for keeping it: "Because it happened." The second Mrs. Glau had a grandmother from the same plantation, as it happened, having been granted, sold, and conveyed from a merchant in Louisiana. The second Mrs. Glau did not have powder her face and hands and fix her hair as her mother-in-law had, though she was told never to mention that her grandmother was, during the state's twenty-year engagement of this type of commerce, a slave.

Had there been any fear that Mrs. Glau, the younger, would not be believed if she said anything?

Had there been any fear that Mrs. Glau, the elder, would be punished if she said anything?

Juan's voice, not on the tape deck, but in her ear: "Don't compare yourself. You'll make me sick." He wasn't wrong. To connect her place in American history to those who had survived far, far worse laughable.

April and Juan did not have to write letters or demand apologies. They were able to go right back to where they'd started.

In Juan's case, really, he had the opportunity that many sought and few achieved, which was full-fledged, whirlwind metamorphosis. He could move from small-time procurer to a Wells Fargo banker, by virtue of speaking nicely, of having good teeth. He had an MBA. He had an accent, but in time that was gone. He spoke four languages, once a point of suspicion, now useful, even exotic. He was a good boy.

April held up her end of the bargain and bore his children, looked after her mother after Daddy passed away from (according to the story) a heart attack. She took a typing course, then another course on the Dewey decimal system. She worked at the library when Jenny was old enough to be on her own. She worked at the Andermatt County courthouse when Pal was old enough to be foisted onto Jenny. She gardened. She gave dinner parties. She mixed cocktails and made Caesar dressing from scratch. People talked about her chiles rellenos, her primavera, her pesto, her sangria with pureed raspberries. She wore sterling silver and simple gold jewelry and did not fuss too much with her hair. She swam forty lengths at the racquet club pool four times a week. She did aerobics. She had a quick wit. She was good fun.

I once roped a bunch of underaged girls into selling their pussies.

Imagine saying that to the folks at the racquet club. They'd laugh, in the way you do when you just can't believe it.

They'd laugh because there were too many questions, April figured. It would be exhausting to ask every single one of them. Leave that to an investigative journalist, who will have all the answers in plain language.

April asked Juan now, "Why do you want me to die with you?" Not even the most astute reporter could wrest this one from him. April could.

Juan told her, "You're as bad off as me."

They'd been unhappy. Not with each other, it seemed. The melancholia came from outside, it seemed. It was persistent, of insatiable appetite. It did not sniff around them and worm its way in, as it had done before. This time it was different. It fell from out of a clear, blue sky. And as a result, a clear, blue sky had become unbearable to either of them, a mockery of the first thing that put human life into motion. It was too bright, too blank, too placid, too static, too still. How could everything keep going at the same pace when, in one fell swoop, Juan and April Nimitz were falling apart? They were sixty-something one day, seventeen and twenty-four the next.

April started throwing up anything she ate.

Juan could not touch any food.

Her teeth turned yellow. He lost weight that he did not need to lose.

The demon in him and the demon in her asked each of them, "You were never bothered about all those things before. Why now?"

Why now? Was exposure imminent? Was lockup? Had they spent their freedom so preciously that damaged reputations or jail would be considered unthinkable to them? As it happened, no, no, and no.

Chewing it over, they decided that it might be a relief just to tell somebody. A fair trial, a fair punishment. No entitlement, no self-righteous fight to clear their names. No more condemnation heaped onto them than need be. No disbelief. Would it really be so far-fetched to learn that perfectly nice people could do terrible things?

"I think that's it," April said finally. "No one would believe it."

Juan said, "No condemnation, no absolution." He sounded like he was quoting something. He said again, "I can't do it by myself."

Imagine: Telling someone your laundry list of sins. You could pick anybody you wanted to tell, the police or a perfect stranger. You lay everything out. You give them the who, the when, the where, the how. The police might tell you that there is a statute of limitations. A perfect stranger might tell you to sit quietly while they called an ambulance. A priest might tell you to say an Our Father and fuck off. A friend might laugh.

Fifty years was well beyond the statute of limitations. By the time a clear, blue sky looked to you like a mockery, the burden of fifty years had grown too heavy. You couldn't do one more day of schlepping it. You hadn't the energy. You hadn't the mendacity. You could not say that it was a long time ago because here it was, galloping in with the same vigor it had decades past.

And then you had a reprieve. It really was a long time ago, you got to thinking. You could barely remember faces, let alone names. What was the point? It was a bummer, dwelling on it like this. You got away with it. You felt confident, that is to say, arrogant. That was one of Jen's words, actually, as in, "The level of arrogance is appalling". You wondered at how people could be so stupid.

And then it would repeat from the start.

"I can't do it by myself" was as good a reason as any.

A soul in hell only burned from humiliation. Was humiliation the worst thing? No, no, of course it wasn't. April could have made a list of all the fire-and-brimstone believers she knew who would tell you that they'd take public shaming over the thumbscrews, the rack, the red-hot pokers any day of eternity. But in this Dantean drama, hell was at full capacity, shrieks up and down its grim corridors, the moaning condemned, the yelping laughter from imps and devils. You were in pain, but you weren't alone. That was the thing about humility: You're always made to feel as though you're the only one who has ever done this or said that. Backs turn. Folks step away, firstly, so that you cannot touch them, secondly, to observe the burning of you and the smoking out. You were not a person.

"Just give me time," April said.

Juan nodded. He knew as well as she that, while ordinary things like a sunny day could become unbearable, and while they felt unfit to live among ordinary people, the pleasures of life on earth were so plentiful, so simple, so breathtakingly lovely that they succumbed to it when they could and basked. They did not want to be anywhere else, just yet.

She made a list of things she would take with her, if heaven let her in: Raspberry sangrias, chiles rellenos, peanut butter sandwiches on toasted ten grain bread, a lake or a beach, dogs, cats, parrots, horses, summer and fall, a linen dress, some nice shoes.

When she next woke, it was when the Astro had eased off the highway and onto a winding road. She cracked an eye and caught sight of green. She lifted her nose and breathed piney woods, beyond that something elusive, meaning movement, meaning water.

She yawned, her jaw snapping. "Are we still in Kentucky?"

"Kentucky was a while ago." Pal was driving.

April righted herself and found a pair of sunglasses digging into her hip under her. They were

the Jackie O kind, with big frames and smoked amber
lenses. They could go with a herald print scarf around
your head. They were classy, not snazzy. That was
April's phrase, and she was glad her girls had stuck to
it, to dress classy, not snazzy, in sterling silver and
simple gold. She wondered if they belonged to Jenny
or Pal. Never mind. She put them on, they were hers
now.

She asked, "Are we still in Tennessee?"

"We're near a lake." Jenny was smelling the air.

This by way of an answer.

April lifted the sunglasses and took a good look
out the window, hunting for clues. She had a
panorama of trees, a nice mix of pine and oak and
maple. It was warm, not muggy, not dry. There was a
cool gust that came through the woods, bringing
movement, bringing water. She sat still a minute
before craning her head and found that the road on
which they were driving was unpaved, packed dirt
and sand and pine needles.

She figured that, since the girls weren't inclined
to tell her anything, she could put these bits together
for herself. What state had trees and lakes and
unpaved roads? Many states, she reasoned, had trees
and lakes and unpaved roads. Let's try again. What
state was green and woodsy and this cool in
summertime? That seemed to narrow it down. She
had been to Lake George and the Finger Lakes in New
York. She had driven past Lake Champlain in Vermont
with Juan, on their way to Montreal.

They had stopped at Cedar Lake in Connecticut. It was Juan's last trip up there before Jenny and Mo and the boys went to England. It was just after Christmas, they were visiting for New Year's. They often went during the winter months, when snow was supposed to lay like icing across yards and fields and ponds. But, as luck would have it, it seemed that April and Juan would bring the sun with them from Texas and by the time they arrived in New England, much of the snow was scraped away and what remained clung like scum to the curbs, grimed by car exhaust. It hadn't impressed April, who was beginning to think that snow could be found only in the movies. She nearly lost hope, stepping from the plane in Hartford, groggy and sour, when she suddenly woke with delight. That December, the expected warm front had given way to a light snowfall, then a proper blizzard, and the airport runway was covered in the first half-inch. "It was all supposed to blow out to sea," Jenny had said. They drove through winding highway and iced trees, from Hartford down into Chester, where they spent the night in a little motel by the lake. They put on Mannheim Steamroller. They ordered pizza, real brick oven style pizza, from a place run by fifth generation Italians, too stubborn to close on account of the snow. The boys, Gabe five and Raffy four, were too wound up to sleep. When the storm passed, they all crossed the road, wading through drifts up to their shins, to look at the moon from the beach at Camp Hazen. It wasn't until they were standing in middle of the lake, frozen six inches thick, when they realized how far they were from land. It was what April imagined being an alien must feel like, in the best sense.

Juan had called the pizza crusts bones. "Y'all are leaving the bones," he said when the boys laid their uneaten crusts aside. April had heard the boys call pizza crust bones when they ordered Dominos after Juan's funeral. Since they did not remember Opa, it was unlikely that they remembered it was Opa who called pizza crust bones. She was glad that stuck with them.

Wait.

What did any of that have to do with coolness in summertime? It had had the same feel of summer, that was true, wherein she'd felt that she had stepped outside the normal order of things and behind a curtain, and was exposed to an enchantment that was otherwise hidden, though just as real.

Jenny had been there, and Juan had been there.

Where was Pal on that trip?

Had she refused to come? April had a foggy notion that it was because she was not speaking to Pal or Pal was not speaking to her. They were not speaking on that trip, that much was clear. For what reason were they not speaking? Another notion, less foggy, wormed in. It was something to do with Jenny, Jenny having orchestrated it, Jenny having read something somewhere about going No Contact and telling them (telling April) that it was, for now, for the best. It had been Jenny who had lifted the decree of No Contact, without any formal announcement. Pal had simply shown up at the next gathering, a barbecue holiday, a lesser holiday, Memorial Day or Labor Day, a garden party at April and Juan's. She had simply come around the corner into the backyard. As if nothing had happened. All was well.

April had appreciated it then.

It made her sour now, and she did not want to be sour. Suddenly, there had never been anything more desperately that she did not want. It struck her, the way it had when she'd opened her eyes and found herself in her bedroom in Himmel Creek, Juan beside her.

Then it passed.

Better to just move on. Better to leave it in the past, along with this namby-pamby nonsense of having to come to a round table discussion about every little thing. Pal was talking to her now and Jenny was talking to her now. And Juan would move on, too, into the ether.

She decided that this foray into these woods, on this road, at this hour, some kind of redemption could be made. She did not know where they were and Jenny and Pal did not want to tell her. And April decided not to press it. It peeled back the curtain. It made it—not an adventure. That wasn't right. There did not appear to be any danger involved here, as adventures are wont to have. This was a reprieve. What ill could befall anyone in a place so lush and green, a place of enchantment?

April put her feet up as best she could. Her breast did not hurt. She bet that her clothes, when she unpacked them, would be clean. She bet that if she were to call Beverly Across-the-way, all would be forgiven. No, all would be well.

Juan hummed, "All shall be well, and all shall be well, and all manner of thing shall be well."

April asked, "Is that from Psalms or Proverbs?"

Juan shrugged. "I just thought it sounded nice."

April concurred that it did sound nice, wherever it was from. She sighed. "Get a load of these trees," she said.

"I see them."

"We never had anything like this back home."

"No, we didn't."

"Are you going to enjoy this? Or are you just going to mope?"

"I'm not moping."

"You're being a real bummer, that's for sure."

Juan smirked. "Listen to you, with your hip lingo."

April sniffed. "There is no other fitting word. The fact is, you're being a real bummer."

"Fine. I'll take it. I'm a bummer. You're a bitch. And I love you."

"I love you, too. You can die in a fire."

"Okay."

"I'm going to have a good time."

Juan applauded. "I hope you do. I really do."

"I will."

"Mothers, lock up your sons."

April pushed the sunglasses over her eyes, resolute. "You better watch out."

When she next opened her eyes, it was to a gentle slap-slap-slap, far away, of kayak paddles and sanguine limbs treading water. It reminded her of camp, summer camp in the late thirties and early forties. One year, just before the war, she went to camp in Wisconsin. Her parents stayed at a lodge on Lake Michigan, and she would wave to them from her canoe. Up at dawn to say the Pledge of Allegiance, badminton and tennis, hot dogs and hamburgers, a jamboree in the dining hall with the boys' division where they danced to Benny Goodman's "Down South Camp Meetin'".

It had been Camp Carl Schurz when she went. You would never know it had been Camp Hindenburg the year before.

Camp Carl Schurz no longer existed. And there was no trace of Camp Hindenburg.

It was a long time ago.

At any rate, it was not Wisconsin. Wisconsin, to April's knowledge, did not have such heavenly, heavenly hydrangeas, dreamy blue and cream colored. It did not have advertisements for real maple syrup and lobster rolls and places you could get real brick oven style pizza. You could go further south and gamble at one of the casinos run by the Mashantuckets or the Pequots or the Mohegans. You could drive to Katharine Hepburn's house and spy on her during one of her legendary Long Island Sound swims. Or you could go north and play golf in Farmington.

"I guess we're in the Nutmeg State," she said to Juan.

When she opened her eyes, it was to Jenny and Pal extending their hands to her. "Mom," they mewed, "Mom, wake up."

April did not protest at the endearment this time. This was not the place. She stirred and stepped out of the Astro, onto the dirt and pine needles of a parking lot. There were blue hydrangeas. There were day lilies. There was a koi pond running with enormous speckled goldfish, and a fountain with a sign that encouraged visitors to toss in a penny and MAKE A WISH. There were folks pulling in with dogs and kids, and folks lifting kayaks from the roofs of their cars, and folks with towels and coolers and water shoes. The very air was perfumed with sunblock. At the forefront of all this, there was a great house that April momentarily mistook for one of those Russian stave churches, a stave church if designed with the minimal elegance of Frank Lloyd Wright. The windows were tall and high and paneled, the roof peaked. It was unpainted, save for the green and yellow trimming, but varnished, as though the intention was to have it blend into the surrounding forest.

LAKE WARREN RESORT AND SPA, so the brochures said.

"A spa," April breathed.

"They have horse trails," Pal read.

Jenny peered over Pal's shoulder. "They have yoga in the mezzanine."

They passed the brochure to April, who gushed, "Manicures, pedicures, AND massage therapy. God, I could go for that."

"I've never had a massage," Pal said longingly.

"Their specialty is the vanilla bean mousse with raspberry compote." Jenny looked at her mother. "Probably not as good as yours, but I think I could force it down."

"Ooh-la-la," said April.

"Ooh-la-la," echoed Pal. "That's for me."

They, with their duffels and suitcases, marched across the pine needles, stopping at the fountain to make three wishes, stopping once again at the pond to admire the speckled koi, and into a lobby that smelled of wine and wood and, thanks to the high, tall windows, was full of light. It was rustic, yet modern, with work by local painters displayed. April went around with the girls to examine them. April liked Steve Cryan's watercolor tugboats, while Jenny preferred Yves Parent's panoramic views of the Connecticut shoreline. Pal took an interest in the glass display case exhibiting a Mohegan-Pequot translation of the Bible, a joint gift from the two tribes, according to the plaque. All the while, they were serenaded by hidden speakers tucked far into the rafters, emitting soothing music like wafts of perfume, New Age music,

Andreas Vollenweider's harp, Peter Maunu's guitar and synths.

If you were here, would you be home now? Well, taking a hiatus, anyway.

April looked over one shoulder, then the other, noting that her bags were missing. She'd been about to call out when she spotted Jenny and Pal at reception. Pal was sifting through credit cards, Jenny was spelling her married name for the little lady behind the desk. "My husband's Israeli," she was explaining to the little lady.

"Oh, wow," the little lady was saying. "So, is that where you're living now? I'd love to go one of these days."

Jenny had been to Tel-Aviv and Jerusalem and Jaffa, where Mo had family, and added that he'd grown up in France. She'd been to Arles and Saint-Tropez and Grasse, where Mo also had family.

"Now, I've been there," the little lady said of Grasse. "The place where they have all the perfumeries? My late husband and I had our honeymoon there. Did you get a chance to take a tour of the perfumeries?"

Pal put in that she and Jenny both had. "I had my own scent made there," she told the little lady, and bent to paw through her knapsack. April squinted at the vial between Pal's fingers, round and a quarter full of a liquid the color of Chardonnay. It had a stopper shaped like a fleur-de-lis. "Jasmine, basil, and mandarin." She held it out for the little lady to smell.

April came upon them, making all three jump. "Since when do you wear perfume?" More to the point, when did you go to France? She twitched her nose. "Was that what that was? Stinking out the car?" She pushed past both girls to thump her own handbag on the desk. "Put your money away. I got this."

She waited. She waited because if this were any other place, at any other time, she could expect a fight. She steeled herself. She knew that it was an odd thing to create an argument over who was going to pay, in the format of "Let me do it", "No, let me". What no one else seemed to get, save for her and Jenny and Pal, was that following an insult with a treat negated everything. You assessed the situation, which you had instigated, and you made it better. You held it, through memory or through souvenirs, by a long ribbon over their heads when they had the nerve to take you to task. Think of everything I've done for you, college, summer camp, horseback riding, that damn dog, this trip.

But this time, there was none of that.

Jenny and Pal, trading glances, that sneaky calm. April never trusted it.

She repeated herself, "I got this", prying apart her billfold, fingering her cash, her Visa, her MasterCard, her AmEx. Without looking, she picked one and slid it across the desk to the little lady, at whom she had also not looked.

The little lady peered through April at the girls. Peered through as though April Nimitz were made of gossamer, and the fact of her transparence caused her teeth to gnash behind her prune-y, puckery lips. Had the little lady heard her at all?

It was Pal who said that it was fine. "She's got this."

The little lady nodded at Pal, nodded at Jen, took April's card.

She, the little lady, had spotted hands and skin like paper. Now April could stand back and take this time to study her. It was something she'd come to enjoy doing, after a long gap between the years in which she silently critiqued and the years in which she did not. She'd forgotten how delectable it could be to put, say, her skin against that of another, to compare smoothness or freckles or moles or whatever it was, and report to herself a victory. She had aged nicely, you hadn't. Take this little lady here. Her hands, as aforesaid, were too spotty, her skin too thin, too pasty. Her eyelashes were all but gone. Her teeth were too yellow. There was a whisker under her chin, a puffiness about her knuckles. Her hair was nice, April gave her that, prettily bobbed and let to turn silver. Her back was humped. She sounded like a grandmother. Her clothes were trim and professional, as befitting a manager. That was what her tag read.

That was what her tag read. MANAGER, and above that in larger letters, MILLY.

Milly.

Milly, who lifted her head from her work to ask all three Nimitz women if, by any chance, they came from Texas. "I'm from there, myself." But she looked at April.

Pal asked, "Is the accent that strong?"

Milly conceded that there was a little twang unique to that part of the world. "My sister and I came up here, oh, I think forty years ago." She gestured with her thumb over her shoulder, toward a door marked EMPLOYEES ONLY. "She's my co-captain, as a matter of fact. She does the numbers, I do the marketing, reservations, all that excitement. With a full staff, of course. We bought this place when it was —"

Her tag read MILLY O. WATRUS. Married women camouflaged with their husband's name. She was at that age when identity blurs, due to the depletion of hormones. Her skin had lost its elasticity, its pigmentation, resulting in general ambiguity, a figure without race or beauty or ugliness or gender. At a certain point, people become goblins. These was something that April had put a bastion against, for all it exhausted her, and there were days in which she dropped the act of eternal youth and accepted her metamorphosis, even enjoyed it because no one remembered little old ladies.

Surely, Milly Ogawa did not remember April Hesse.

It was a long time ago.

"It's been ages since I've heard anybody say Y'all," Milly was saying. "People up here look at you like you're some kind of bumpkin if you try it on them."

It was one of those things where there is no doubt. You just know.

The trick was to pretend not to.

April's credit cards had her name stamped into the bottom lefthand corner of each one. April H. Nimitz. April H. Nimitz. April H. Nimitz. Milly Ogawa would not have any reason to make the connection unless she, at some point before she migrated north, came across a little article in a little newspaper from Himmel Creek, Texas announcing the marriage of Juan Nimitz to his bride.

April Elizabeth Hesse, as she was then known, dropped the sunglasses over her eyes when another grandmother's voice drifted across the desk. She did not look. She did not look when the other grandmother's voice beckoned her closer, to look at this, get permission to do that, there was a problem with her card. Through fogged amber, April could distinguish a snappy Dutch crop, also silver, akin to Judi Dench. This individual introduced herself as Flora, not Flossy, not Blumi. Her surname was Radanovich. Her ring had an empress cut diamond. She wore bifocals and Dr. Scholl's sandals with a low wedge. She was more upright than her sister, but no longer the prettier one. The years had made fraternal twins identical.

They tried the Visa. They tried the MasterCard. They tried the AmEx. All failed. They were not expired. There had never been an overdraft on them. April had always paid their bills. She explained this to, what she took to be, her audience, perhaps her jury, which included a woman with two bull terriers, two servers in bowties and black vests negotiating a case of Perrier, and two dripping guys just in from hot yoga in the mezzanine. Her appeal rerouted to them when the ladies at the desk shrugged. As if any of them could sway the temperament of a bad credit card.

No one seemed too concerned.

For April, it left a weight in her stomach. Then it went in the other direction, leaping in a panic. It buoyed like this for a good ten minutes, or however long it took for the co-captains of this vessel to swipe each card, switching them up and trying them again in different sequences.

Is anyone looking at me? Does anyone hear me?

Might the complete dismissal of her person be a worse fate than humiliation?

Does anyone know I'm here?

Jenny and Pal and Milly and Flora were talking again, about the paintings and their prices, and April remembered a terrible B-movie she had seen once at a drive-in. In it, a woman fell in and out of existence, one minute discussing the fit of a dress with a salesgirl in a department store, the next completely ignored when she tried to speak first to the salesgirl, then another customer, then a man in the street. It was the first clue to the audience that she was really dead the whole time. It was the most terrifying part of the film, April thought, indeed scarier than any of the ghosts and ghouls in it.

"Hey." Jenny with a room key. "We're all set."

April took it. "Did any of them finally work?"

"No, mine did."

April went tight. "I said I'd pay for it."

"Well, what's done is done. They already swiped it and everything."

Jenny turned and Pal turned and they shared a secret smile. They threaded through plants and kids and William Morris reclining chairs and Queen Anne tables spread over top with issues of *Newsweek* and *The New Yorker* and *Bon Appetit* to an elevator that yawned to admit them.

Peter Maunu gave way to Sade, underwater tones invoking mermaids. It worked like a shot of something good and, combined with the general exhaustion from the trip, it settled into April's shoulders, her back and her legs. She sunk into a corner of the elevator, her mouth a perfect O, issuing breath as she would smoke.

Wouldn't they look more afraid than that, if they knew who they were talking to? Not everyone's memory is sharp as a tack.

The elevator doors stuck once before inching closed. They were of a curious, pleated design that revealed on the lobby side a delicate tableau of a scene from the myth of Princess Tamatori, stealing tide jewels from the sea gods, so the plaque read. April watched the illustration unfurl from the passenger's side, and it looked much the same to her, from the same tale, at least, if a different sequence, the waves as blue scrolls, the tentacles emerging and glinting with mother of pearl. The three of them stood in foot-tapping silence until the doors crept closer together, but did not quite close.

"Jeez," Pal moaned.

"I hope that's not an omen of things to come," April said.

"Should we just take the stairs?"

Jenny was about to nudge the elevator open when, with a jolting, mechanical wheeze, they strained and snapped shut, like the bellows of a squeezebox. Now that they were in ascension, they had the full view of the second tableau. There were waves, and there were tentacles, and there was a maiden, the same scene, but quite different. Jenny's eyes widened. Pal grinned.

"Wow," she said.

"How did they get away with putting up something like that?" Jenny mused.

"Yikes," Pal said.

And April, poor April, who might have gotten a kick out of the octopus that snared Princess Tamatori with its eight legs keeping her in place and the jewels out of her reach as its mouth feasted on her cunt, did not join in the critique. Her eye was trained on the place where the doors met, where, just before they sealed, she got a full view of the reception desk and the little ladies behind it. They behind the desk could not have been looking at anyone else in the elevator but her.

"Wow," Pal repeated.

Jenny laughed. "I guess they're hoping nobody will look too close at it."

"Probably because it's art," Pal said. "If it's art, it's classy, not trashy."

Is anybody there?

Does anybody care?

The hotel portion of the resort was smaller than it looked, with fifty standard issue guest rooms, two bridal suites, and one so-called deluxe suite that was reserved for visiting celebrities, usually actors working on location. There was a rumor circulating that Meryl Streep was the current occupant.

The standard issue rooms did not have numbers. Instead, they had names, one for each of the United States of America. There did not appear to be an order, April noted, with regards to region or admittance to the union. The Nebraska Room was next to the Hawaii Room, which was next to the Pennsylvania Room, and so on, the doors marked with a bronze plaque (New Englanders did seem to love their plaques) and beneath that a bronze pineapple for a doorknocker. (New Englanders had a thing for pineapples, too.) The Emergency signs were so discreet and delicately mounted that they did not engender alarm, more a polite suggestion of where you might like to go, should the End of Days come midway through your vacation. It was a place that still provided for smokers, and April counted the rooms that were labeled for them. Non-Smoking still outnumbered Smoking, to reduce the need for emergency exits, she guessed.

Her suitcase was on wheels, with a handle that you pulled out from the top and used to drag the luggage behind you. It was heralded as the convenient choice, which had been the seductive factor when she bought it, and at present she found herself nursing the heel that had knocked into or got caught in the mechanism that made the suitcase so handy in the first place. She would sooner have hobbled along like a hunchback with a duffel on her shoulder, as Pal and Jenny were doing. Of course, they had only packed for the weeks (how many?) they were in Himmel Creek and for however long they were on the road. April had her entire wardrobe here, and everything else she owned in the van.

Jenny and Pal had the Florida Room. It was across the hall from where April would stay, in the Arizona Room.

There was no doubt.

But still. Still, she wanted to nurse that kernel of off-chance (should she call it denial?) that it was just that, an off-chance. There were only fifty standard issue rooms, after all. It was the peak season, close to Memorial Day or Labor Day, whichever holiday it was before the kids went back to school. Even Meryl

Streep was here. They were probably lucky to have gotten rooms here at all.

But still. Still, why did Milly and Flora put her in the Arizona Room, specifically? They could have put her in the Florida Room and the girls in the Arizona Room, or put her in the Minnesota Room or the Alaska Room or the Guam Room, if there was one.

She was afraid to open the door. It was prudent, she felt, to wait for the girls to unlock the Florida Room first. It would be a test, of her courage and against booby-traps. There was a sigh of air conditioning, a breath of good, citrusy soap. She followed Jenny and Pal in, took stock of the two queen sized beds, the nubby paisley carpet that matched the coverlets, the television mounted above the rattan dresser, the mini bar, the little bathroom stocked with littler shampoo bottles and conditioner and toothpaste. The walls were papered in monstera leaves. There were prints above each bed, one of van Gogh's bedroom in Arles, the other of Gaugin's topless Tahitian ladies.

Pal sprawled on the bed under the topless ladies (classy, not trashy) and turned on the TV. Jenny knelt to root through the mini bar. It looked like a lot of liquor and a handful of dainty snacks of the cheese-and-crackers fare. Jenny found a bag of dried apricots and went to work on it.

Despite all evidence, I refuse to believe that I have not gotten away with it.

April went to the bathroom and could not find an excuse to be in there. Her heel hurt like damnation, but the wheels of the suitcase had not cut her, and she did not need the toilet. She did not want to take a shower. She did not need to freshen up. It was to show the girls, maybe, that she did not need their immediate company. She did not want to appear clingy. She did not want them to know that an awful dread had descended and was in danger of solidifying, in an arthritic, brittle kind of way. It was imperative that she be with them.

What she really came in here for was to look for Juan.

Where are you?

I can't do this by myself.

There was no reason for him to be in here, she knew that.

She made sufficient noise, flushing the toilet, pretending to wipe and saluting wasted paper, splashing in the sink, rubbing the soap between her palms. It crossed her mind to take the little bottles of shampoo and conditioner, but she didn't. She stepped back from the mirror, brought her t-shirt over her head.

She squeaked, rabbitish.

What had she expected? A gaping wound, festering with fanged larvae? A boil? A horn? At the very least, a cut?

Certainly not this. Certainly not her own hide, thin and transparent though it was, her greenish veins, her liver spots, her breast pendulous, her nipple wide and brownish rose, not puckered. Certainly not unmarked. Certainly not without a scar. She pressed her fingers to the spot, where she sensibly thought there should be a lump where the shard and the cat claw had buried themselves. All was smooth, all was well.

You got away with it.

Didn't you?

When you expect damnation and find none, you tend to look over both shoulders, one, stealthily, and then the other. April caught herself doing this. She did not stop herself when she went to the bathtub and peered down the drain, when she went to the shower and ripped the curtain back. There was nothing but a beetle. It was her only witness, and so she brought her foot down on it, one stomp and a pleasant crunch. A quick run of the water made it disappear and she waited until it was completely down the drain before she put her shirt back on.

When she came out of the bathroom, Jenny had joined Pal on the bed and they were sharing the bag of dried apricots and vegging out. The TV played an episode of *Dr. Katz, Professional Therapist*, where all the patients were comedians. This one featured Ray Romano; it explained why the girls weren't laughing. It was a Squigglevision cartoon and the mellow, pulsing lines made April nervous. She leaned in the doorway and watched. A commercial break, Pizza Hut, Raisin Bran, Fancy Feast, *Pure Moods.* The next patient was Judy Tenuta and her accordion, and that was when April suggested they all get out and do something.

"We didn't come to a swank place like this just to sit around and look at crap." She gestured the TV set.

Obediently, Jen found the remote and turned it off. She was a mother. She understood. She didn't like the idea of her boys vegetating either. She poked Pal, who stretched and groped for her shoes.

Were it not for Jenny, it was entirely possible that Pal would not have moved an inch.

Never mind that.

April held up the brochure. "So," she said, her voice bright, "what do you want to do first?"

The first thing they did, because it looked the most picturesque, was to ride along the trails. April found herself at the end of the line, audience to whipping tails and colossal bowel movements, with Jenny and Pal three, four, five horses ahead. Their mounts were velvety black with swatches of white on their snouts, sisters from the same mare, according to their chipper guide, a gal called Megan.

There was a recent phenomenon, April found, only in the last decade or so, of girls who were enamored with horses. There had always been equestrian types, those from old money who competed in show jumping and collected ribbons, and there were ranch types who saw a horse as a living, breathing piece of machinery, no different from a tractor. This was something else. This was a crowd that was really more of a cult. To them, horses were a lifestyle choice, horses were an identity. At first, April thought they must be gay, but that wasn't it either. ("Does everything have to be gay with you?" Memory of Jenny, in reference to an argument they'd had once, about what God only knew.) Like a cult, they had their phrases and their titles and their markings. For one, they all had names like Megan or Allison or Taylor or Heather or Gwen or Leah. They were all white. They disliked gymkhanas and had never seen a tractor up close. They all stressed the importance of having a symbiosis with your horse, which made it sound less New Age-y than to simply talk about being "one with" your horse. They all wore their hair in French braids. They were all quick to point out that they were not racist. They all said things along the lines of how money didn't matter, though they had all graduated from expensive schools. They all said gosh and dang, in lieu of the F-bomb. They were all pagans or Wiccans, though they did not take the Lord's name in vain. They were all vegan. They all smoked pot, which explained their Zenlike approach to the outside world. And of this outside world, they seemed to have no knowledge. They had no knowledge of the outside world because they all fell within the age rage of fourteen to twenty years old. They all believed that you could not own a horse, but suspended this belief in riding a horse to begin with. And they all, without fail, they all smelled like peanut butter.

This last was the real sticking point for April. When you rode a horse, you ought to smell like one.

Her own was a poky old nag called June. June's rider was a fusty old bitch called April.

Jenny and Pal, if they were only a few years younger, would have fit right in. They fit in now. Their horses had edible names, Strawberry for Pal and Pavlova for Jenny. They followed Megan's lead through ferns and emerald bowers and revealed personal trivia that left April stumped.

She did not know, for instance, that Pal had broken her left forefinger when she was sixteen, having survived an accident in which the junky Pinto she'd been driving had flipped not just once, but four times, leaving her otherwise unscathed.

She did not know, for another, that Jenny, only last year, had had a reaction to Motrin, anaphylaxis, as a matter of fact, wheezing and cramping and eventually collapsing in the middle of dinner at a kebab house in London, to be revived by Adrenaline, thanks to a fast-thinking waitress who happened to be allergic to bees.

It never occurred to you to tell me how you almost died?

What did April know?

April knew that when Jenny was seven, she had spelled the word asshole as "ass-whole", in reference to circumference rather than anus. She knew this from a note that Jenny had written to her mother. *You are an ass-whole.* Spurred by what, April did not know.

She knew that when Pal was in seventh grade, she'd called in a bomb threat to the high school. Pal had watched the evacuation, roaring, from the roof of the indoor pool at the racquet club. She knew this because Pal had told her. Very casually, breezing in, settling at the kitchen table with her homework and a blue raspberry frosty, answering, when asked if she'd heard about it, "There was no bomb, it was just me." What possessed her, April did not know.

What do you mean, you don't know?

Hadn't they seen you reserve the worst of your animal temper for your mate? Hadn't they seen, on two separate occasions, your wicked metamorphoses, from woman to predator? You had never touched your own children (atavistic chemistry blocked you from that). But you had crept up on your husband. While he slept, while he was passed out. People say it's impossible for a woman to force herself on a man because she lacks the right equipment. Well, they got that wrong, didn't they? It's entirely possible, if you have the right tools, if you wait for the right time. Your own hand will suffice, though something with give would be better, a knife handle, a narrow rolling pin, a candle. The butcher, the baker, the candlestick maker were all participants, and they never said a word. Juan never said a word. He fought back. He turned you on your stomach and mashed your face into the rug until your vision blurred and you could not breathe. There was a tacit understanding that it did not count if he woke and the tables turned and he was the one taking you. He'd never say a word. No one would believe it; think of the absurdity. It was about as batty as, well, a rabbit buggering a bear. To the girls, too young, observing from the gods this drama, Jenny from the hallway, Pal from the stairs, it did not make enough sense to register. They never brought it up.

You got away with that, too.

The people separating them was a group of girls, whom April put somewhere around sixteen or seventeen, maybe eighteen. They were a portion of a larger group, she learned, here for a celebration, a graduation party or a birthday party. They were Allison, Taylor, Heather, Gwen, and Leah. Their horses were Parsley, Sage, Rosemary, Thyme, and Sesame. They were mild-mannered. They were nice. One of them, Gwen, talked about how she was trying to be a better person, and the others nodded, conceding that this, too, was their main goal in life.

April didn't buy it for a minute.

April, for all her sins, had no delusions about them. She knew that she was not a nice person. She knew that what people had really liked about her in Himmel Creek was her sangria, her pesto, her homemade salad dressing, her orchestration of a good time. And they left it at that. She knew that she was a racist, not in the overt, Klansman way, more the kind who had her notions about this group of people or that, and they stuck. Perhaps that made her more dangerous. Wasn't that what folks were always saying when the police discovered a human head in their neighbor's refrigerator? Jeffrey Dahmer had worked at a chocolate factory. He had served his country, honorably discharged. He knew he wasn't a nice person either.

Better to know what you were. Better to accept your fate.

April relaxed. June huffed and moved her bowels.

Agreed, enjoy it while it lasts.

Through ferns and emerald bowers and a sun-dappled lake.

Enjoy them while they last.

April wanted to avoid going into her own room for as long as possible. She told the girls that they should take full advantage of all the resort's amenities, and they were game.

After the horse trail, they bid farewell to the nice girls and their steeds and went for a dip in the lake. Neither Jen nor Pal had brought a swimsuit and April's was too buried to look for it, so they found a secluded spot, thick with late season blueberry bushes, and stripped to their underwear. The girls crawl-stroked farther out to tread water in their panties and sports bras. April waded up to her knees, keeping her shirt.

They warmed up in the hotel's hot tub, leaning against the jets and ordering hard lemonades. They talked about nothing of consequence, not Juan, not the end of the trip, not Jenny's house. They watched birds and people. They spotted Meryl Streep and acted casual when she asked them if they'd seen a little white bull terrier come through. They said they hadn't and shrieked when Meryl Streep left. They spotted other famous folk at the poolside, Pamela Anderson and Linda Lovelace and Julie Andrews and Tommy Chong.

"What the hell kind of movie are they making?" April asked.

"A hard-core stoner musical comedy porno," Pal guessed.

They got their nails done, got mud facials, got full-body massages. In white robes and smelling of cantaloupe and cucumber, they wandered into the lobby from the salon and perched in the Morris chairs to absorb the activity. It was both a graduation party and a birthday party, as it happened, combined to commemorate a grandmother's seventieth year and a granddaughter's departure for college the next month.

Jenny and Pal, suddenly, resolutely, chummy, sidled up to the Ogawa sisters at the desk and reported back. The grandmother had battled cancer and won. It had looked as though she would not survive the year, but things had turned around, and now she was cancer free. The granddaughter had returned from a gap year in Chile, and was due to take up her studies at Mount Holyoke.

"Everybody wants to tell you their life story these days," April scoffed.

"Well, it's a special occasion," Jenny said, perusing *Bon Appetit*.

"It's not every day you're seventy," April conceded.

"I mean, she's an old, old friend of theirs." Jenny found an article about raspberry compote and Pal read over her shoulder.

"Did they say who it was?" April picked up another issue of *Bon Appetit*, trying for blasé.

"Who?"

"The friend."

"What friend?" Pal found a feature on Julia Child and a pen and went to work drawing a curlicue moustache, a large beauty mark, a goatee on the full-spread photo. She showed Jenny, who snorted and added a septum ring to Ms. Child's nose.

At once, April felt very, very tired. She told the girls to forget about it, took the pen from Jenny and knitted Ms. Child's brows together in a series of sharp, black lines. She put in a chin hair for good measure.

The lobby surged and emptied, one minute full of arrivals, people who knew each other, embraces and declarations of how long it had been since their last encounter, bags, balloons, bouquets of day lilies, chrysanthemums, yellow roses, blue hydrangeas, the next completely still, save for the echo of voices, and in another minute, those were gone, too. April waited for the old, old friend to appear. She noted that this old, old friend was singular, it was not two old, old friends. She wondered which old, old friend it might be, if it was the old, old friend of whom she was thinking, which it might very well not be.

Would the old, old friend come in a walker? Would she have hair, or don a wig, or maybe a lovely scarf? Would she be bony? Would she be upright, with some reserves left? Would she be missing a breast or both of them? Or would they have remained, pouchy, not perky, but there? Would she have scars or would they have, by now, faded?

While we're on the subject, would anyone have gone into Beverly-across-the-way's house? Would anyone have found her? Would enough time have passed to draw anyone's curiosity? Where is Beverly? Does anyone know what happened to her? Had the inquiries begun?

Well. What happened to you?

Passive.

Then urgent.

April lifted her arms above her head, netted her fingers together. She had only meant to yawn as a pantomime, but once she'd started it became the real thing, making her jaw crack, unhinging it in the way it did when true fatigue kicked in.

"I can see your tonsils," Pal remarked.

April asked if she could get the key to the girls' room. She wanted to lie down before dinner.

"What's wrong with your room?" Jenny asked.

"All my stuff's in yours." It was the best excuse April could think of.

"No, it's not," Jen said. "Not anymore. I asked them to get a bellhop or someone to move it across the way. It should all be over in your room now."

"Did you need me out of there so fast?"

"What? No. Just one less thing, you know?"

April snapped, "What does that mean, one less thing?"

Jenny folded her legs under her and settled into the Morris chair. She appeared to have every intention of staying where she was. "Just one less thing." Nor did she see, or appear to see, the need to elaborate on that point. Just one less thing had a universal meaning of which April Nimitz would have to be contentedly ignorant about.

She took the same elevator going up. Once in, she'd forgotten that it was the one with the illustration of cunnilingus on the doors. She would have to be content with looking at it. Or, stubbornly, she would not. Instead, she admired her feet, the nails newly trimmed, the opal pedicure.

(Was the argument over something silly, as they are wont to be in engendering a blow up? *Sesame Street?* She'd made similar remarks, of this or that type of person, and felt she was being shut up when her daughters told her not to use this or that term.)

Here was something else they didn't know. Something else. That as a twenty-ninth anniversary gift (the Iron Pyrite anniversary, they called it), Juan bought April a bracelet with mother of pearl inlays. The silver in the bracelet was not really silver, but a mixed metal, steel and zinc and copper and nickel. Before long, a rash had appeared, a cluster of pinhead bumps that itched and that oozed when she scratched them. It spread all the way around her wrist and a short way down her forearm. But she refused to take it off. You see, it had been a charm—or so she thought. Good things had happened following the moment she'd fastened the clasp. Juan had gotten a raise. April had gotten the courthouse job. They'd gotten a tax break. These were fairly ordinary things, already set into motion by the ones who called them strokes of luck. April was persistent: Here was proof. She would hold up her wrist, for Juan to take in the bracelet, which he could not see for the, now scaly, now scabby, rash. Portions of it had pitted and turned black. A rush to the GP, then the emergency room confirmed that, had April left the bracelet on any longer, she would not be in the emergency room receiving antibiotics. She would be in the emergency room having her arm amputated.

You couldn't see the scar anymore. It'd been a decade since it had really been visible.

Admitted, it was not quite a near death experience. But her daughters might have had to go through life with a one-armed mother.

She was at the door of the Arizona Room when she patted her thighs and remembered that she did not have her clothes. She was wearing the spa's white robe and under that, her damp t-shirt and underwear. A passing fellow from room service had a master key. He stopped her going in.

"There's a dog missing."

April nodded. "A bull terrier? White?"

"Exactly." The fellow smiled, then, sotto voce, "I'm really supposed to keep it under my hat, but he belongs to someone pretty important who's staying—" He pointed, indicating the floor where the suites were above.

Here was an opportunity for delay. April decided to play ignorance. "Who is it? I'll guess and you nod or shake your head. Is it Nathan Hale? Is it Nathaniel Hawthorne? Emily Dickinson?"

The room service fellow inclined his head to mean No, and April read his own play at ignorance for what it was: a reaction to a joke which you found equally annoying as dumb. In spite of this, you had to laugh. You were not in a position to do otherwise.

Finally, she hit on it, also sotto voce: "Meryl Streep?"

The room service fellow negotiated his burden, a tray holding an empty plate with a gritty, green smear and one bowtie noodle. No silverware that April could see. She asked if the person from whom he'd collected the tray had eaten their meal with their hands. The fellow shrugged. He appeared to be at a distance now, and April wondered how he did that without her actually seeing him take any noticeable steps backward. She asked whose plate it was. He said we wasn't allowed to say.

This was how you wasted time. You groped until you snared someone. Maybe it would turn into a real conversation.

She whispered, "Tommy Chong?"

The room service fellow frowned. He was at the elevator door now, having gently floated there. "How'd you guess?"

"Well, you know." April preened. "Him, me, and Meryl go way back."

The elevator pinged and unfolded for him, pinged and refolded, devouring him. His last words to her: "Far out." He didn't sound impressed.

Her room was open and she stuck her spa slippers under the crack for a doorstop. She thought she might dawdle. Hadn't she the right? She turned up the hood of her robe and strolled as though the hallway were a promenade. At every door, she would pause, glean what she could about the room's occupants, what was left over on their trays, what newspapers they had requested, whether or not they had left a DO NOT DISTURB sign on the pineapple knocker. It left her with a queasy feeling, akin to loneliness, as though she was the only thing out of place. Everyone else was all set and contained, and here she was, locked out. Sometimes, she got a prize, a snatch of conversation, between two people, but usually just one, the one-half of a phone call. It sounded schizophrenic, listening to the one-half conversation by phone just as much as the two-way, with both parties there in the room. Everybody seemed to be talking about different things, though their tones indicated acknowledgment. April wondered if they were all talking in code, and that this was the way people now communicated.

Or perhaps it was just more difficult for her to keep up than it used to be.

So, this was it. This was the era of inconsequence. She could not keep up and was making the first doddering steps toward incompetency. No one would notice what she did; it was a given that what she did, in its strangeness, in its singularity, would be dismissed as a symptom of her senility. She did not know where she was. She did not know what would be expected. She might take off her robe, for instance. She might continue this stroll in nothing but her t-shirt and underwear, and then maybe just her t-shirt.

Why not?

An idea came to her. One in which she would flash each closed door, with one quick sweep of her robe. She'd already lost her t-shirt. She exposed herself to Wisconsin and New Jersey and Montana and Rhode Island. She bounced her tits at California and Maryland and Washington and Iowa. She dumped her t-shirt in front of the Texas Room and her underwear in front of the Connecticut Room. She prepared to open her robe for the Florida Room because she knew that no one was in there. She undid the belt. She gripped the lapels.

She heard, "Are they pretty? Do they party?"

She was senile, but she was spry. Ducking into the Arizona Room, bringing in such gusts that caused the door to close behind her, and wheeling around to spy through the peephole. It was another fellow, this one from housekeeping, one hand piloting a trolley of stacked towels, the other wedging a cellular phone into his ear.

Apparently, he'd not been clear enough the first time, and repeated himself getting into the elevator, overenunciating, "Are. They. Pret-tee. Do. They. Par-tee."

Juan was on the bed. Never mind the décor. Here Juan was, all along, on the bed. When she'd registered the shape of him, curled on one side (which varied, sometimes it was his left, this time it was his right), she made a quick inventory of everything around her, to see what distinguished the Arizona Room from the others.

When her parents brought it up, they made it sound very grand. It was a magazine word. You imagined a conservatory.

This Arizona Room was different. It just happened to be called that, with the Grand Canyon State firmly in mind. Everybody was trying to better themselves in that era, and thought that the first step in making that accomplishment was to better the home. When the Hesses got their house back after the war, her mother stripped it of all signs and smells of the tenants, trying for an effect of suspended animation, to restore it to what it had been before they left. A deviant precision enabled April's mother to recall and replace any item that had been thrown out in their absence, any item that had been damaged by the tenants, any item that April's mother had had to discard herself. The house had not quite returned to what it had been, was instead an eerie copy with price tags still to be found on lampshades and end tables and picture frames. It was then that her mother decided to scrap everything and start again from scratch. It was a process, her word for it. She pronounced it Pro-cess. She handpicked antiques from estate sales at haciendas, and someone misheard through the grapevine that deposed European aristocrats were living among them in this part of the state, and her accent had intrigued them, and her taste had impressed them, and she let the rumor run until she grew tired of it, and gently corrected the story at another estate sale, at another hacienda. She papered the dining room wall in a pattern of red pheasants facing each other in intermittent couples on cream. This was the wall that Juan had put his fist through, and that she, as April Nimitz would paint primrose yellow.

At some point, in between scrapping everything and papering the dining room in pheasants, April's father had died.

At the time, she did not have much to say. She had more pressing matters, so was the pro-cess. She tried now to pinpoint another, adjacent event that would corral this one and put a date on it. Her mother's scrapping everything? Her mother starting from scratch? Before her marriage? After? Did Jenny yet exist—and she defined existence loosely, to mean the period in which Jenny had been conceived up to the date of her birth. Still, nothing. She knew the facts, the how and the why of it, not the when.

She'd thought, at the time, something to the effect of that it was just as well, he didn't go with Mother's new décor. Until April and Juan were married, Juan had slept in her father's former bedroom. She would find him in the bed, the same frame but a new mattress and linens, and he would be curled on one side. On those mornings when he slept apart from her, she would hover over him to confirm his breathing. If she saw a distinct rise and fall of his shoulder, she continued downstairs to do whatever she'd needed to do then in the morning. If she did not trust her eyes, she put out a hand and let it rest somewhere on his person, usually on his back. She'd had to feel it for herself, not only the warmth of him, but the rise and fall, as well.

She had stopped doing that when she joined him in sharing a bed, and she did not do it now.

The Arizona Room had cedar furnishings and enlarged photographs of pueblo ruins at Canyon de Chelly. There were prints of Navajo people in blanketed groups, copies of copies of images captured during the Long Walk, or the American government's forced marching of the tribe from its home in Arizona to New Mexico in the mid-1860s; April didn't think the decorators knew what these pictures were, only that they were of Navajos and that the Navajo people came from Arizona. There were Ansel Adams photos and shed antlers mounted on the wall by the TV. April did not understand the placement of Valentine's cards among the other decorations until she came to the mini bar. There was yet another plaque above, giving the state's admittance to the Union, February 14th, 1912. She supposed that there were plaques giving the state's admittance to the Union in every room. The ash tray was full of those chalky Be Mine candy hearts.

Juan was in bed and the television was on, a Julia Child program, not *The French Chef.* They'd had a TV in their bedroom in Himmel Creek, a tiny one with a built in VCR. They could only watch videos by it, it was not connected to any network satellite. So, they brought in stacks of videos, mostly dollar purchases from library sales. These were usually documentaries, David Attenborough's *Life on Earth* and *The Living Planet,* a series on American poets called *Voices and Visions* from which they'd picked volumes of Sylvia Plath and Emily Dickinson and Walt Whitman. And there were cooking shows. Juan had always liked Julia Child's voice, she was the perfect antidote to insomnia, as he'd said.

If Juan knew what she and the girls did to Julia Child's picture.

Julia Child was what they put on when it looked like neither of them would be able to sleep through the night. They would choose an episode, or rather a recipe, and start the tape. Sometimes they were long ones, how to make fish and egg courses, or how to make appetizers and desserts. Juan might wake at two. April might wake at three. They might turn on the lights. They might try to read or make snacks or do a crossword. They might not do anything, too crippled by a bad dream to make the transition from waking up to getting up. In those nights, they did not feel as though they were a part of the world. That is to say, they did not feel human. That is to say, they felt that they had been removed from the natural order that came with the passage of time. This night, they believed, would not end. They believed, this night, that this was where they now lived. They did not touch each other, nor did they speak. They remained as still as they could, exhausted, also vigilant, moving a toe only when the backyard shifted back into focus. When the backyard went from grey to blue to gold and green, then they could get up. On those mornings, they smelled. They smelled because they sweated and were too afraid to open a window. And all the while, they had the blue screen of the television, if not the voice of Julia Child.

And there she was now, in the Arizona Room, showing you how to roast a leg of pork.

It was the last video they'd put in their VCR at home. Juan had laid still for an hour before telling her, "I don't think I want to be alive anymore." As though he thought he might cancel their membership to the racquet club. At the time, April had felt more or less the same, of being alive and of the racquet club. It was time, she'd thought and Juan had thought. Or, in the words of a phrase that had become private to her: I'll have gotten away with it. No discovery, no reprimand, no punishment. Her daughters did not need to know every little thing about their parents. And now they never would. April had used that phrase, the public one, in a draft of a note she'd scratched onto a very nice piece of stationery, from that Jen had given her one birthday with her name in gold and a paisley pattern in the margins. She knew that was what you did, out of courtesy. You left a note. It would be rude to leave without giving reason. But one draft became two, then five, which April then shredded and flushed. Courtesy be damned, if yours was a life made of scaffolding and no real substance. "You all just come here for the food," she would say, gayly, on nights when she played hostess. Standing on the step, in sterling silver and simple gold, citrus and pork wafting from the kitchen. "You all wouldn't have set foot in here if there wasn't my tenderloin."

She had no real friends. She frightened her children. Her husband would leave, whether she came or not, for a place beyond which time could be measured.

Could she manage it, to be left behind?

Juan's face was pink, he hissed through his nose. He would hate to be woken.

So, she lay down beside him.

And she woke in their bedroom in Himmel Creek. Juan was stiff, warmish. He snored. His lips popped with any small emissions of air. She was cold. There were blankets bunched at her feet, and a queer reserve in her breast which told her that to pull up the blankets would be an indication of having woken, whether she meant to go back to sleep or not, for it would lead to getting up, starting the day with the intention of finishing this one and beginning another.

Nothing had changed. It was still bright. The trees were still green, red roses too, as Louis Armstrong once sang. There were days in which she elated in nature's persistence, in its ability to go on doing just what it had always done, despite human interruption. On those days, she was glad enough to be a part of it. On those days, it was a manifestation of a god that did not know her and did not care. A woodpecker drummed at the clapboard. A squirrel made a nest in their chimney. When she herself became extinct, this house would succumb to flora. There would be vines going up the banister. There would be vegetation, mushrooms in the cupboards, wild grapes in the windows. The hedges would blow up like foam, the asparagus poking through the soil in fingers before going to seed, and the dill and the mint and the basil would take over the garden.

That's when the horror of it would descend. As in the logic of a dream or episodic paranoia or the feeling of something intruding upon what you thought to be your regular narrative, nothing, outwardly, had changed. You had only to wait for the horror to make its presence known. Was it around a corner? Was it in the overgrowth of herbs? It was enough to freeze you in one position in your bed, despite how cold you were, how badly you needed to go to the bathroom. At last, it had come and you prepared for it. And you waited. And you waited. You almost yearned for it. It would be correct to say that you at least wanted it to come.

Her mouth was full of sweet slime.

Another school bus, this one pulling up in front of the Nimitz house. April did not move. She listened, for there were small feet coming up the walk, a tentative hand trying the door, finding it unlocked, whispering, tiptoes, an easing of the door to make it close without much noise. She could not tell who it was, only that it was a child, no, two children, at least two. The school bus had not pulled up to this house since Pal got her license and her Pinto.

Her eyes closed, one ear buried in the pillow, the other alert, she tracked them. Their footfalls went through the dining room with the primrose yellow walls and into the kitchen. There was faint commotion, drawers yawning open, the pantry poked through, a soft munching. They must have found the tortilla chips. She didn't know what other kid foods she had. There was a mechanical gasp, the fridge wide and chilled, and another gasp, this one delighted and human, an alien babbling between the two and a crack and clank of things being removed and laid out on the counters and the table. She tried to remember what she'd put in there: a carton of raspberries, for sangrias, a carton of whipped topping, the jar of strawberry jam, the jar of peanut butter, a half-full can of Duncan Heinz cream cheese cake frosting. Chairs screeched, bowls brought down, the milk found and the cereal. She did not need to be there to know the incredible mess that would come of this. A small laugh, one of them had come upon the salsa, the root beer, the cranberry juice. Another of them dropped a fork and cursed. It was a competent expletive, too, an adult sharpness to the word "SHIT". It chilled April as it would if it had been a grown man. But that was the thing with kids; androgyny made any curse they uttered sound impossibly, eerily sweet. The younger, the creepier.

The one who cursed segued into murmured, excited talk. It had a cadence, but few words. April was inclined to believe that it was another language, the kind that kids use to communicate without arousing suspicion of any grownups, Pig Latin or Gibberish.

Pal's vision of intruders was something out of a true crime series.

What, then, was this?

It would be inappropriate to rush down in her nightdress and armed with a shotgun. It was not how you confronted two, possibly more, children who had done nothing but raid your fridge. She could come down in her nightdress; that ought to scare them off. She could demand to get their numbers and call their parents. She could, at this moment, call the police. She could do the sensible thing, put some more clothes on, go down, and gently, firmly shoo them out. They were only kids.

Why, then, would she not get out of bed?

And now she could not. Not when she heard them on the stairs, bolder now, trace discretion, heavy footfalls if only on tippy-toes. They had not yet explored the second floor and their voices dropped when they came to the top. Snorting, smirking. April did not like the sound of it, wet, not at all like children who undertake to do a naughty thing and are nervous about it, trying to laugh it off. These were children who knew what they had, and what they had was a house all to themselves.

Their speech was no clearer, despite their proximity. They were bold but vigilant, still whispering, still on guard for someone to tell them that they did not belong there. Going from room to room, Pal's old room, then Jenny's, both long since made up for guests, not rifling, more like dilly-dallying through their things, they traded judgments and laughed aloud, and put everything back where they found it. There was a muffled puck-puck of their tiny hands handling a little brass clock from a bedside table, a ceramic tissue box, the tissues themselves, which the children yanked from the box with little yips. There followed grunts and gasps as they bent to gather them up. April heard one of them say, "They'll never know."

Through all of this, Juan was very, very quiet. He'd stopped snoring and hissing. The texture of his sleep seemed to have evened out, and now it would be impossible to wake him.

"They'll never know—"

At this, April shut her eyes and slowed her breathing, trying to look asleep herself. They were in the hall. They had been outside, and now they were coming in. The television, bare static, was switched off. One hushed the other, or others. Now they were silent, perhaps out of respect. April imagined a couple of, then three diminutives, in mourner's or morgue worker's clothes, uniformly straight-backed, poised, their manners perfect. But that was all it could be to them, an observation. April heard a buzzing of lips that could not be mashed together any longer, and following that, a great big wheeze, and another. It became a chorus of raspberries. Could it be that they were really pointing as they were laughing?

Dr. Katz had said that death was like slapstick, one minute you're alive and the next you're not.

And April could not deny that. She relaxed and let herself freeze. She kept her ear on them and tracked their teensy feet and their sticky hands as they crept around her bedroom. She noted that, though they seemed to think that she or Juan or neither of them were getting up any time soon, they still crept. It was very possible for her to wait for one of them to get close to her, maybe even try that old trick people did before they knew to check for a pulse, to put a mirror under her nose to see if she was breathing.

April did not have a mirror in her bedroom, save for the one over the bureau. She had a lot of porcelain animals as prizes from boxes of tea. She had a sewing kit.

The children noticed the animals. They found the sewing kit.

They threw the animals on the floor. They snapped the dispensable tape measure in and out of its case, thrilling at the zip. They dug out the pinking shears and cut jagged-toothed shreds out of the drapes. The animals burst into rubble, little quick explosions, the eagle, the owl, the turtle, the rabbit.

Now was the time to rise up and scare the ever-loving hell out of them.

She cracked an eye. She could not make out a face or a gender, just small hands that knew exactly what to do with her pins. The child, the creature, was busy sticking pins into Juan's unresponsive arm, and fashioned a trail from elbow to just above the wrist. It had the look of an acupuncture, if the acupuncturist had a driving hand, as this one did. And all the while, the sun outside was bright, the trees nodded passively through the window, Julia Child talked about emulsion sauces, a radio from a car that played a song with lyrics that went "I love your smile" and the car did not stop for a minute. Nor did the sun, nor the trees. Nobody would guess at anything out of order.

As for April, she gathered herself. She filled with excitement because she was going to fly out of this bed with claws and fangs. The children were going to go right for her tit, how could they resist, it was so swollen and round, like a balloon. She was going to empty these kids of their bowels. She was going to send them running. She would wait until she heard the one with the pins come at her, by feeling its foul and candied breath on her, and when she knew that the hand with the pins was about to descend, she would—

"—bake a cat." Pal was imitating Julia Child. "What about baked cat?"

Jenny was snorting. She was also telling her, in breathless intervals, to shush.

"It's very light, lighter than a chicken, believe it or not," Pal went on. "It's very nice with a beurre blanc. It's very economical. And if you happen not to like your cat, this really is the best dish of the day—"

April started.

The Arizona Room was cool and dark and burnished gold from the wallpaper. The television was on, Julia Child and Jacques Pepin roasting a chicken.

Jenny crossed and uncrossed her legs from an armchair by the window. Pal had the spot on the bed where Juan's legs just curled around her, not touching.

And through all that, still he slept.

April sat up, stretched. "How did you get in here?"

Pal told her that they'd used the key.

"I'm the only one with a key to this room," April said.

"They gave us another one," Pal said.

"Well, why didn't they give me a key to you all's room?"

"Because you don't need a key to our room." This from Jenny, who'd gone through her mother's kit bag while she slept and was snipping her too-long toenails with April's clipper.

Juan's arm was bare. That was something.

Her breast did not hurt. That was another.

She righted herself, looked around, blinked. "What are you all dolled up for?"

Jenny, shedding toenails onto her mother's hotel room carpet, sniffing, snorting, and Pal, grinding buds in what resembled a tiny round box for an engagement ring, scattering green crumbs on the bedspread and packing a bowl, looked lovely. They'd discarded their white spa robes and donned loose, sleeveless frocks that could be dressed up or down. Jenny's was peacock green and blue, gracing her ankles like a formal gown. Pal's was a standard little black number with a high, square neck and its own belt. They'd decked themselves in what jewels they could dig up from their luggage, Jenny's jade earrings and Pal's cloisonne bracelet from Mexico. April noted that they must have given up on elegance when it came to shoes, for their sneakers were close at hand.

Jenny spoke. "We thought we'd go down for some mousse. Whenever you're ready."

April grabbed Pal's wrist, pushing aside the cloisonne bracelet. "It's barely five. You all want mousse now?"

Jenny shrugged. "Sure. Why not?"

April reminded them that the way a meal was typically mapped out was by having dinner first, with or without appetizers, then dessert. "If I had vanilla mousse, or whatever it is, without having some kind of real food in me first, I'd be sick as a dog."

"I never get sick." Pal took an enormous hit from the pipe, a dainty little thing of emerald glass, and extended her lips like an ape to try at blowing smoke rings.

"You'll get us thrown out of this hotel," April said.

"No, I won't," Pal said. After issuing a series of hazy swirls, she finally did a perfect circle and cheered. She cleared her throat. "Tommy Chong's here. They're not going to kick him out."

"People will think I'm running a dope den out of my room," April said.

Jenny seemed about to say something and thought the better of it, scoffing instead. She took the pipe from Pal and showed her how a smoke ring was properly done. "More like you're whistling," she said, and moved her lips in a slow purse-and-pucker for demonstration.

"Does your husband know what you're up to?" she asked her eldest.

"Do you want some?" Jenny extended the pipe to her mother.

April primly declined. She declined because she understood that grass would never be what it had been since she first had it. Back then, it was generally much weaker, which made the public service films of the day that much more laughable. Juan had gotten ahold of something good, the stuff that the Woodstock crowd praised, and was ahead of the game by twenty years. Nancy Reagan's Just Say No initiative had backfired, first with the lie that cannabis was the gateway to huffing battery acid. Now everyone and their mother smoked. Willie Nelson had smoked a joint on the White House roof while visiting the then Commander-in-Chief; Jimmy Carter confirmed it. Juan sometimes lamented that he could've made some real money if he'd just stuck with it, as though he were talking about missing out on the real estate boom, but he was at Wells Fargo by then and too old to go back to that life. His daughters need not know about that life, and now they never would.

April watched him sleep, watched him twitch, watched him drool.

I suppose you got away with it, didn't you?

If that was the worst his girls knew of him, they would find it cheeky. Pal would idolize him. Jenny would bring it up at social gatherings, gleeful, breathy: "In the forties, my dad was a pot dealer." Times change.

Of everything else, the old rules of human decency still applied. There would be no idolatry. There would be no gleeful stories. Their parents would not even be able to say that they did it for the money, because it was never about the money. There is never a need so great to warrant the degradation of another body-and-soul.

April would rather die if they knew.

So, she tried to look the part of the woman who had never done anything seedy in her life and ordered Jenny to snuff out the pipe. Jenny obliged, rolling her eyes, blocking bowl and stem and side-hole with her fingers and gave it to Pal, who zipped it into one of her purse's inner pockets.

"Before we stink out this room," April muttered.

She stalked to her bags and pawed for a dress. She found one, rose pink and gold with capped sleeves and a boatneck. It was midi-length (she'd stopped wearing long frocks when she became less steady on her feet) and complemented her hair. It made her look like Jackie Kennedy, if Jackie was a carrot-top. The girls praised it and found a pair of Velcro-strapped sandals in an outer pouch, a turquoise pendant on a silver chain that did not match, but was the easiest to untangle from the rest of their mother's jewelry.

April minced before them, in her old sandals and good frock. She mimicked Jackie, "We have a committee that does all the decoration—" She made an elegant gesture toward the antlers. She looked to Juan, indirect, out of her periphery, making sure he saw the girls laughing and playing with her. He did not. He was asleep. She was almost convinced that he was faking it. She exaggerated her merry-making, namely her own laughter, in the hope that he would wake and think that all the hullaballoo was about him.

But he did not. Only his chest rose and fell, in cadence with even breathing.

They entered the dining room like ladies. You would never know that their footwear was better suited to the outdoors. The seating host asked if they were with the Burnaby-Bravo party.

"The what?" April asked.

The three of them peered around the host's podium. Here was where the flowers and festoonery had come to take shape. The dining room was half-filled, having originally been contained in a private nook off to the side, overlooking the lake, sectioned by a set of French doors from the rest of the space. Now the doors were flung open and the party had tripled, the result of more guests showing up than expected or simple mitosis. It was a queer mix, old and young, not many who were Jenny's or Pal's ages. The young, who were anywhere from fifteen to eighteen, and the old, who were anywhere from sixty to eighty, appeared to have divided themselves naturally, the young talking quickly, softly, excitedly, the old talking slowly, loudly, easily. The smell of wine was thick. Two tables had been put together by one tablecloth to form one large table in order to accommodate a mound of gifts, some already torn into, not for a single recipient. The wrapping paper signaled this, as did the messages on the balloons: OH, THE PLACES YOU'LL GO alongside BETTER WITH AGE. Every now and then, a member of one or the other of the two joined parties would cross into the opposite territory, a granddaughter going to greet a grandmother, a great aunt going to fetch a nephew.

The cake, at the forefront of the gifts, had been cut into, but its icing, even from here, was perfectly legible. MANY HAPPY RETURNS TO ROSWITHA MARIA ENGELS BURNABY. The blue sugar curlicues were melting under the lights, along with the blue sugar flowers, and the M in Many had been halved. Someone had jokingly switched the seven and two shaped candles to make a twenty-seven.

After April turned sixty, she'd referred to herself, privately, as "sixty-something". It was biting to see her real age, albeit in reverse, writ large. It was never out of a need to preserve her youth. It helped to make time a little foggier when you blurred the numbers. One of the young, a granddaughter on her way to greet her grandmother, took the seven shaped candle and sucked the icing from its bottom.

In a ferned and ivied corner of the room, Flora and Milly had thrown off their weekday office wear and put on their casual best, cotton sheaths and heeled sandals and simple gold earrings and chains. They hovered around a lady who was most likely the birthday queen, Roswitha Maria Engels Burnaby herself. She was seated among the ferns, smiling gently, nodding sedately, shaking hands, accepting embraces but not giving them. Her hair was quite white. Her eyes were quite cloudy. She looked older than seventy-two, and she did not appear to understand what all the gaiety was for. She ducked between Flora and Milly, who were quick to point people out. They stood back to make way for another woman, also white-haired, but spry, and an older fellow, who seemed to be taking up their posts after respective trips to the restrooms. She was sharp-eyed, as was the fellow with her.

"Aw. This is sweet—" Pal held up a small booklet, stiff and staple bound. "It's a little biography her sister and brother made for her, and her daughters."

She read. April listened; her breast ached.

Rossi Engels, known at one time as Schnecke, had fled the coop after the war and, through her work as a botanist and a thirty-year marriage, found herself in New Zealand, tromping around primeval forests. There was a picture of her, taken maybe twenty years post-Peralta Farm, her hair in a kerchief, fanning herself with a fern as long as her arm. No biblical digs for her, as it turned out, but she had ferns and fat green kakapo and a Ph.D. and a husband who had passed away eight years ago and four grown children. Her sister, Emma Engels Forrester, who had not taken the vows, died last year from the very cancer Rossi had beaten. Her surviving siblings were Peter Engels (joined by his partner, Anthony Dunne), an editor, and Nikola Engels Bravo (joined by her husband, Dante Bravo), also an editor.

Peter Engels was balding and bespectacled, in linen trousers and a natty bowtie. Nikola Engels Bravo cropped her white hair and wore jazzy earrings that matched her glasses chain.

I remember when you two were very small and stuck feathers all over your passed out mother and called her a bitch.

April wondered if they'd been capable, at that age, of driving pins into their mother's arm.

The host had apparently asked if they wanted to sit at the bar and Jenny or Pal had answered for their trio. In the time that Pal was reading from the booklet, they'd been led to a table with wingback chairs in a room that was wood-paneled and heated delicately by a wide-mouthed fireplace. Glasses of Sauvignon Blanc had been put before them, as well as a saucer of ciabatta cut up into squares, a saucer of fat green olives, and a saucer of olive oil, to dip the bread into, April guessed. Jenny and Pal went to work on the olives, filling their cloth napkins with pits.

"Don't spoil your dinner," April told them. "Remember, vanilla mousse."

"We're not," Pal said, blotting her bread with oil.

"We thought we'd do a sort-of dinner in reverse," Jenny put in. She was stoned and already a bit tipsy on top of it. She kept eyeing Pal, trying to harness her attention for the connection of a shared joke.

That was what it looked like to April.

Pal caught Jen's eye and grinned, her mouth full of bread and olives.

"Well," April breezed, "tell me about that. What's the plan? Are we having mousse first, and then the entrée—"

"We were thinking," Pal began, her voice slow and honeyed, primed for wheedling. When did the girls ever ask anything of her? In spite of herself, April inclined her head. "We were thinking," Pal continued, "that we could have dessert here, and then you could make one of your famous dinner party dishes."

April perked up. Then she asked, "Which one? I have a vast repertoire that they will remember me for when I go." She found a flaw in this scheme. "And how will I prepare this great dish? There's no kitchen for me to cook in."

"Oh, it's nothing that needs cooking," Jenny said. "You know that tomato and cucumber salad with that vinaigrette you do? That's what we mean. And we'll order room service, just appetizers."

That was when a small to-do came up, of the server approaching their table with new glasses of wine, new olives and bread, and their mousses, which were piped in swirls into three margarita glasses. The raspberry cassis at the bottom dripped into hollow of their glasses' stems and bled into the black-speckled mousse on top. A rose of whipped cream crowned the display, with a filing of herbs that April found was chopped rosemary.

"That's very clever," she mused. "I always used mint."

"I always preferred the mint," Pal said.

With a surgeon's eye, she picked the rosemary filings from the whipped cream rose, and when it became too involved to excise every single bit, she scooped the whipped cream from the glass and dropped it into the olive oil plate. Idly, she stirred it with one finger. It looked like a disease in a petri dish.

She knew April hated it when she did that.

She'd done it with ketchup and mustard and mayonnaise and yolks from fried eggs. She mixed mashed potatoes and salad dressing and raspberry jam. It was a sign that she did not approve of what she had in front of her. It was her way of saying that no amount of care or artistry that went into the making of the food on her plate could persuade her to think of it as anything other than fingerpaint. April forbade Pal from eating at the table with her and Juan and banished her to the kitchen, where Pal made do with ham sandwiches or peanut butter on toast. "You creature," April would tell her. "People will think you're feeble in your mind. Lord knows, I do."

Now Pal was twenty-something, a medical student. She was not beyond toying with her mother's nerves, especially now, at this time, in this place.

She used to say, "I didn't even know I was doing it until you pointed it out." But she never asked to regain her place at the table.

April wondered if that had been the plan all along. Not just to eat in the kitchen, it was more calculated than that, a bit too innocent, of the kind of patient thrill you get when you know your prank is due for a big payoff.

You will have me in chains and on the rack. This is what you do to me. This is how you flay me alive. Playing with your food, you creature, you creature. You know that this is a low level of Hades for me.

There was nothing she could do. Nothing for April Nimitz to do but start on her own mousse. She'd only observed it. Her first bite was bliss, thanks to just the right amount of vanilla bean, and a hint of rum, too. The cassis was smooth, tart, not too sweet.

She dug to the center of her mousse. The dull curve at the end of her spoon hit, felt as though it had cracked, solid matter hidden by the cream and cassis. She probed it again, and such a stink rose from it that she put both hands to her nose. In her revulsion, she'd dropped her spoon, and when she bent to pick it up, she found its curved end furred and tarred, as if with animal scat. It might have been then that she knew her daughters were watching her eat. Their mousses, margarita glasses and all, were gone and in their places were Jenny's, then Pal's folded hands.

"It has an under-taste," she recalled Mia Farrow saying in *Rosemary's Baby*. "A chalky under-taste."

The girls watched, sighed, looked around. They were simply waiting for her to finish. Jenny talked about how she'd always expected Meryl Streep's voice, for whatever reason, to sound much smokier than it was in real life. April heard herself telling Jenny that she felt the same way about Sylvia Plath, from the Voices and Visions tapes, whom she'd previously imagined sounding very dour, and was shocked at how much she really sounded like a fifty-year-old woman, though she died at thirty.

It was best to keep an even keel. It was best to continue the conversation, to ignore the animal scat in your dessert. It was possible that April could take up her spoon again and go right for the knotty little turd and, with enough mousse and raspberry around it, to swallow it down, easily, with a sip of water, followed by a generous mouthful of wine. She did these things and did not bring any of it back up.

Though Pal, through all of this, never stopped toying with the whipped cream and olive oil abomination she had made, and just now added her unneeded fork to the procedure. The tines scraped the dish. She made sickly white streaks across the green-gold oil, and this was somehow fouler to April than the shit she had eaten.

She let out one word in a scream, "STOP", meant to freeze the whole room like a punched hole in the atmosphere.

But no heads turned. Not one. She would have to count for a reaction Paloma's jumping eyebrows. She might as well have not said anything.

What she wanted, more than a new vanilla mousse, was for Juan to perch at her side and bark some cutting thing that would make her laugh and make her furious and make her feel that she was part of a set, and not orbiting the gathering of others like a lost cosmonaut around a hostile planet.

If Juan weren't pretending to sleep.

She remembered, again and again, that it was best to keep an even keel. It was no good shouting if everyone chose not to hear you. It made her feel stretched at finger and toenails, her limbs going out of joint, and she stood up with grace, as though nothing at all had happened, and told her daughters that she had to use the ladies' room.

"We'll meet you out front," Pal said. "There's a Stop 'n' Shop we can walk to from here."

It gave April a chance to slink into the Burnaby-Bravo party.

She wanted to get a closer look. She wanted to present herself to the Ogawas and the Burnaby-Bravos, gnashing and wild, like a real criminal. Let them recognize the face behind the creases and the spots, and let them take her apart, starting with a straight incision going from gut to groin and ending with her wrists hand ankles bound to four bucking horses that would make a mad dash the moment someone smacked their rears.

She did not want forgiveness.

She did not want forgiveness because, firstly, it was too late for that and the crime too grim, and secondly, there was no hope for change. That was then, this is now. It was in the past. It was in the past, and all this time April Hesse, also known as April Nimitz, also known as Hassi, also known as Hussy, had been waiting for this moment. Would it be perverse to say that she relished it? Real criminals, who confessed their evils with a small measure of pride, looked forward to their execution day. April imagined the grand, operatic humiliation of what it would mean to look at her old stable in their faces, have them acknowledge her, have them rally one and all, Meryl Streep included, into a mob, to carry her off and burn her alive and feed her charred cinders to the lake.

Then it would be over.

Threading her way through young people and old people, she caught a server by the shoulder and took a glass of champagne from his tray. The stuff pricked the back of her throat and went flat. It would not do for Dutch courage. It was not moxie. Moxie was Hadean ichor, and she hadn't had anything like it since. She accosted another server, who let her have a shot glass full of something brown and sweetish-smelling. It made her wince, and she asked if it was mouthwash.

"Jager," the server told her.

April asked her if she had something called moxie.

The server shook her head.

April pressed, "Haven't you heard of it?"

The server paused, brightened. "It's a soft drink, isn't it? From Maine? Kinda like an off-brand Dr. Pepper?"

April pushed past. She hissed, "Fuck Maine" and hoped the server heard.

And she had, if not the F-bomb. She was helpful, "I can see if we have any in the bar, if you want."

April fixed her with a wide smile, pleasantry outdoing pleasantry, and declined the offer, saying that she would be happy with her Jager and her champagne. She remembered that her champagne glass was half-full, and that she still had it, dangling from her fingertips in her right hand, while her left handled the shot glass. She asked for another Jager and poured it into the champagne, the daffodil color darkening as if with syrup, and gulped it down.

It occurred to her that she might not have to approach anyone at all. April could stand in the square middle of this party as the still point and let it whirl around her. She could pick out who was who, and how they were all related, and how they'd come to be here in this delightful buzz and hum, with its flowers and frosting and DJ that played "Down South

Camp Meetin'", while she felt herself growing transparent.

So, she stood. And she listened. And she watched.

Folks approached her, they were curious, and she knew to ask them, "How do you know Rossi?" before they could ask her. It gave her time to make something up: She was an old college friend, she was a cousin, she was a neighbor. She said her name was May, June. She told one woman that her name was Beverly, and the woman said her name was Beverly, too, and laughed, roaringly, in one ear. April jumped when she heard another laugh, just as sharp, just as much of a roar, in her other ear. "HA HA HA."

The other laughter came from Peter Engels. She felt safe with him, he was sure not to remember. It was through him that she learned of someone from the Ogawa clan marrying someone from the Engels crew, and now, in his words, "We're one great, big family." It was through him that she learned of how Milly Ogawa had gone into interior design and made a killing, and how Flora Ogawa had gone into graphic design in the book world and made a killing, and with their joined fortunes bought this hotel. Meryl Streep was a regular here, often coming for dinner, just to sit in the bar and chat if Milly or Flora happened to be around.

"Actually," Peter said, and he paused to squint into the crowd, "Meryl's here now, if you want me to bring her over. She's got her dog, too, thank God. He tore off into the woods around the lake and just strolled up with some dead thing in his mouth, so pleased with himself, while the rest of us were going crazy trying to find him—"

Sure enough, there that dog was, at Meryl Streep's heels, and being cooed over by Flora Ogawa. April knew that she loved dogs. She knew that Flora Ogawa had been the one at Peralta Farm who'd fed little tidbits to the Rottweilers, who loved her, and said of them that it wasn't their fault, they didn't know why they were there and what they were doing.

April thought of a truth, concerning dogs and children: They watched everything you did, the perfect witnesses because they did not know what they were looking at.

Peter Engels must be at least sixty, as is little Nikki, whom I'd dismissed with Juan as nonpersons.

The dead thing was still in the dog's mouth, a raw pelt that was matted with dirt, with drool. A bone, perhaps a rib, stuck through the fur. It had stopped bleeding, and that was not enough to keep the dog from whipping its head in a blur, to make sure that the thing would not escape. It had long ears and longer hind feet. The cottontail had been wrested from its backside in the chase.

"We could make one of the feet into a good luck charm," someone said, and Flora and Meryl and anyone in their immediate vicinity laughed, including Peter Engels, again right into April's ear.

"Now—" This from Peter after he'd let his merriment draw to a close in a big, dwindling sigh, "—

now, I hear a twang there. You're not from the Bluebonnet State, are you?"

There was no masking it. Texas was the size of the United Kingdom. It was an easy place to come from.

"What did you say your name was? I'm sorry—"

April told him that her name was Beverly Dunne. She'd dug through the recesses of that part of her brain responsible for storing clutter, names and dates and trivia that gathered there, dusty, but not obsolete, ready for use. The two names seemed to go together, and April thought that she might use it as a sort of veil that would enable her to cruise through the party with relative invisibility. It was also possible that she could change her own name, make Beverly Dunne permanent and invent a whole history. Beverly Dunne never stayed in one place for very long, she was a gal who got footy, who hopped from state to state and man to man and made a point of eschewing real attachments, as they slowed her down.

She'd been ready to tell Peter all of that, when his face went somber.

"Oh," he said, "well, we know someone by that name exactly. It's a wild story. My—Anthony, come here, Anthony come here—" He made of his hand a flag to wave down Anthony, who was too amused by the dog and the dead thing to notice. Peter shook his head, continuing, "—well, she's a cousin of Tony's. Well, step-cousin, once removed. Distant. We barely know her. Probably why I can talk so freely about it. But we got a call from our dear friend, Dawna, who lived next door to her for something like forty years. Just the other week, the wildest thing happened, it was the middle of the day, out of a clear blue sky, and she was just coming home, and there was someone—"

What would he do if April decided to play the whole thing off the way Pal did about the bomb scare? If she said, "There was no prowler, it was just me."

Peter spoke of Beverly in the present tense, which did not suggest to April one way or the other the woman's current state. Pal and Jen still talked about Juan as though he were still among them. "Daddy hates that kind of thing," Pal would say. "Daddy loves these," Jenny would say.

It would give April Nimitz away if she asked something as straightforward as, "And how is poor Beverly now?"

It was the woman, whose name April thought was Dawna or Debra, who burst through to pose the question, "Didn't Tony say she was killed?"

This made Peter Engels screw up his face. April recalled an identical expression the day he plastered his mother with feathers and cocoa, making mischief (now gossip) into something that ought to be taken seriously.

Was it wrong to call talk of a relative's demise mischief? Even if it was a step-relative-in-law?

It did not concern Peter. Spurred by getting the facts, getting a story, he tried again to flag down his partner. He had a wineglass in his free hand and managed to slop Chardonnay onto his linen trousers.

Cursing, he kept trying. "Dammit. Tony—Anthony, come over here, I want you to tell us what happened with—"

"It was me," April said, "if you want to know."

But they, Peter and Dawna-Debra, had already moved off.

"It's likely she's dead," April called after them.

Feeling emboldened, she floated around and through and over heads. She saw pocketbooks slumped in chairs unattended, mouths smiling open, and she helped herself to cash and chewing gum. By the time she was bored with it, she made a quick count and had close to three hundred dollars, plus two packs of Juicy Fruit and one Spearmint. These she crammed into her own pocketbook.

Is anybody there?

Does anybody care?

Are they talking about me?

Do they hate me?

She sifted through the flowers, then decided to take a whole bunch. She would pluck the petals from them and shred them, next the stamen, next the carpel, effectively castrating them, as she used to do when she was small and very angry.

The room vibrated and in it was not just one still point, April found, but two. There was herself and there was Rossi. Rossi, whose capabilities appeared reduced to smiling and nodding and looking out onto the festivities with a kind of peaceable calm, as though the party was the seaside and she an observer from a deck chair. Names and dates and where she was now had taken on a lilac tone, a greyish haze that did not upset. If anything, she appeared contented in her senility. The lilac tone and greyish haze had made for her a cocoon, and here she was, safely within it, remembering nothing.

April sat next to her. The attendees were gone and, for the moment, it was just Hasi and Schnecke. Like old times.

She introduced herself to Rossi as Beverly Dunne, and set to work at peeling the flowers apart, starting with a trumpet yellow freesia. Pollen fell onto her dress. Petals and sexual organs scattered over the carpet. Rossi watched with gentle interest; April might have been putting together an arrangement, for all she knew, or April could have been made idiot by the same brain-shrinking affliction and they were keeping each other company in their idiocy.

Rossi extended her hand, thickly veined, brittle boned, dry skinned, and, in her way, asked April if she could join in this bizarre activity. Well, April could not begrudge her that, and she let her take a carnation from the pile, the same yellow as April's freesia, and they made a mess together. April told her a story about how Juan had forgotten her birthday one year and woke her the next morning with a bouquet of carnations, picked up from the florist at HEB. He called them consolation carnations.

This made Rossi laugh. She sounded it out, "Consolation carnations. I like that." She still had a twang. April knew from the booklet and from around the party that she'd lived in New England for four years with one of her sons. She'd lived in New Zealand for over twenty before that.

I watched a man pull your pretty hair out and choke you to the point of near-collapse. I stopped him before you passed out because you had another man coming into the chapel next, and you had to be alert. Or else he would take me, and I'd be the one getting paid to be choked.

April tried to talk at medium speed. She knew that she was rambling. It took a dropped shot glass and a shard of it that she'd scooped up when no one was looking to secret in the built-in brassiere of her dress, and one good squeeze to push the shard halfway into her breast to make her ask if Rossi knew of a place called Peralta Farm.

At this, Rossi blinked.

April pressed her hand to her chest, deeper and deeper, until this shard submerged all the way into her flesh with the others. It was an effort, sounding casual.

Again, her companion only blinked. And then, she smiled.

April nodded, and her other hand poised in the air. It was possible to draw it out, intangible though it was, with April's own hand, if that's how it was to be done—

"Do you know, I used to live on a farm near Kerikeri," Rossi said suddenly. "It was never a big farm, mind you. We had an avocado tree. We made such guacamoles. They say cilantro is the thing that can make or break the perfect guacamole. Well, that's bunk. A fresh avocado, right from the tree. That's the thing. But we got all these rabbits that would come and eat the spoiled avocados that dropped off the tree. And then they'd just go for the rest of the garden like it was a salad bar. Well, you know what we used to do to get rid of them?"

April shook her head.

"My husband has a little pellet gun. He no sharp shooter, so he left most of it to me. I'm the keen eye of the two of us. What we used to do was, we used to set up on the back porch with a pot of tea and some sandwiches and just—" Rossi made a barrel out of her forefinger and aimed at lilac and grey rabbits in the carpet. "Pow, pow, pow. Goll, but they would make an awful sound. It wasn't always enough to kill them outright. Poor lil things. But. We saved the avocados. And they should've known better than to play with old Ready Steady Rossi. That's what my husband calls me."

The flowers and their parts spilled to the floor. April brushed the pollen from her thighs and excused herself. "My girls are waiting on me."

"Do you know what the motto of Kerikeri is?" Rossi asked. "*It's so nice, they named it twice.*"

For whatever reason, this made her laugh so much that her eyes squeezed shut. When Rossi opened her eyes, tears had gathered on her lashes and dripped down her nose. They seemed to have come from another place entirely. She dabbed at the curve of her cheek, surprised to find it wet.

April bent. She put her mouth to the hollow of Rossi's ear. Her mind was gone, but she was not hard of hearing. Surely, she could hear April's pleading whisper now, "Just tell me you hate me. Say you hate me. I know you do. I know you hate me. You just have to say it."

Now she had Rossi's full attention. Now Rossi was meeting her eye-to-eye. Now old Schnecke was going to drop the act of senility, for her eyes had cleared and her face was that much sharper, and she had stripped away the years and saw April as Hasi, after all this time, sitting right there, and she would say—

And she would say, "Why would I say such a thing? Why, I don't hardly know you."

People were singing, almost in unison, if mumbled, because they all knew the song and all liked the song, and they all liked Frank Sinatra, even the young ones.

Just a jackknife has MacHeath, dear
And he keeps it, way outta sight

The bathroom mirror revealed her breast swollen and red and the skin was hot to the touch. The nipple was erect with infection. It would not be long before the whole mammary turned gangrenous and spread to its twin.

And her dress.

She remembered being seduced by it five years ago on the sale rack at Neiman Marcus and whistling at the price. She could not summon the figure, only that she recalled thinking it high, despite its forty percent discount, thinking Fuck it, and buying it anyway. It had a designer's signature sewn into the tags, so it had to be nice. Had she even liked it? Had it even really suited her? It did not matter because she had a number of dresses picked up in the same manner, swinging like skin bags from the hangers whenever she opened the closet, worn once, maybe twice.

And now look at it, the stain having progressed down the bodice as though she'd been bleeding out for hours. Rossi had said nothing of it, as had everyone else.

Dampening a towel in cold water would do no good. It was not wine. And it would stay.

She had to make peace with it. She had to brush and re-fasten her hair into its tortoiseshell clips. She had to make the pendant that did not match prominent. Let them think that she was a woman who did not know how to put colors together.

Jenny and Pal were lounging in the lobby. They were chatting with Milly Ogawa, who'd peeled away from the party for a bit of air. Jenny was telling her about her conversion process and, in turn, Milly

Ogawa told her about having picked up some Yiddish when she lived in Crown Heights. Pal was saying, "Now, that's German in Hebrew characters, right?" and commenting on how neat the development of languages was. Milly regaled them with a story about being invited to a Lubavitch wedding, receiving a blessing from the bride and playing keep away with balloons on the women's side of the mechitza.

"See, I barely know where my folks come from," Milly Ogawa was saying. "We never spoke Japanese, we never learned about any customs or anything like that. We knew some stories, fairy tales and myths, things like that, but that was pretty much it. I mean, Chanie, the gal who invited me, she said that the Lubavitchers come from this little po-dunk village in Russia, and—"

April strode up and scared Milly off, just as she'd meant to, with her horror of a frock and her one inflated tit.

To her, her younger daughter said, either miffed or impatient, said, "Well. What happened to you?"

She was not speaking of April's dress.

The walk to the Stop 'n' Shop was over grit and a highway bridge. The girls were in sneakers, which made their excursion easy. Ahead, they rolled, and together they whispered, heads inclined, giggling. Behind, the third wheel to this tricycle, April limped. Teva sandals were good for a stroll around the lake, but unwise when you set out to walk two miles to the nearest grocery store. By the time they crossed the parking lot, her ankles were rubbed raw and a blister, popped as soon as it filled to capacity, oozed down her heel.

"We should've made a list," Jenny said.

They were in the produce aisle, hovering over the avocados. April checked the high corners of the store for pellet guns and stepped away.

"I've made that dressing so many times, I practically have it memorized," she boasted, and dispensed orders for the girls to stay where they were, and to pick up two cucumbers and four Roma tomatoes, one lemon, one sachet of fresh basil, another of oregano, another of rosemary, plus one garlic bulb. "If you get the pre-diced stuff in a tube, I'll disinherit the both of you."

It was a sin, she felt, to use anything pre-diced, pre-crushed, pre-seasoned, out of a tube, out of a can, out of a mix. It was what her mother did, and filled their pantry with vegetables that tasted more of their containers than the garden. It made their food feel sterile, and April imagined that it was how people must eat in prison or a lunatic asylum or some other liminal place that was untethered from the rest of the world. When she became the mistress of their house, she banned her mother from the kitchen and resolved to make everything from scratch.

She even made her own dressing. No one else she knew did that.

Scoffing, she passed the displays of Ken's and Wishbone and Hidden Valley, pausing to put out her tongue at Paul Newman's charitable face illustrated on everything that was Newman's Own, and moved to the aisle next door, where there were golden rows of olive and canola and grapeseed oil encased in glass. Beside them were vials of vinegar and flagons of extractions and floating peppers like jewels.

Her particular recipe called for canola and olive oils, balsamic vinegar and apple vinegar (not apple cider vinegar, for she was firm in her stance that the two were very different things, apple vinegar being a hint sweeter), onion powder and dried mustard.

For all her carping over the freshness of her ingredients, April was not about to stomp her own apples just to wrest from them a few lousy ounces of vinegar.

One consolation of truth: If she could not bring herself to touch her children, she could, at least, feed them.

(And what a thing to look in the mirror every morning and feel proud over, covering what is now thought of as so basic it was ludicrous to think otherwise: Of never having hit her kids.)

Did she absolutely have to go back to them? Not indefinitely, just not immediately.

When April felt a bit down, or angry but not terribly angry, or a particular shade of suicidal, she would get in her car and drive to the nearest grocery store, park, and just walk around inside. She toured the aisles as she would a museum exhibition. The first gallery was Produce, where she always made a beeline for the fruit section. It was her favorite. The fruit displays often varied, according to sales and seasons, and there would be a new formation of them every three weeks or so. Summer brought berries and peaches, winter brought pears and citrus, and the management at every outfit seemed to hire their stockers with artistic aptitude in mind. They were usually about late high school, just graduated or about to. They were eager, this perhaps being their first job, and made geometric abstracts out of nectarines, persimmons, pomegranates, and clusters of green and blue grapes.

At first, she was wary of being noticed, but in time she recognized that no one was going to bother her about drifting through the aisles without buying anything. No one saw her at all. She used her invisibility to her advantage, nothing major, simply helping herself to little things that could fit in the sleeve of her coat, dental floss, a package of walnuts, Tic Tacs, a roll of Scotch tape. Once, after the Walmart where she lived installed detectors at the exit doors, she got caught with a bag of Goldfish crackers. She'd been stupid that time, and stuck it in her coat's outer pocket instead of the sleeve. She managed to convince the young man who stopped her that they were on her person before she entered the store. The young man believed her, apologized, and it was over in all of three minutes. At home, she made a pot of tomato soup and had a bowl of it for lunch with the orange little fish bobbing on top.

Not that April really wanted anything today.

She took her usual route, following her visit to the produce section, for most grocery stores had the same layout. It took ages to perfect it: One loop around the perimeter, a zig zag through the more obscure areas, such as Diapers or Meal Replacements, a survey of the yogurts in Dairy, a stroll through Coffee to smell the dark roast, up and over and a peek into the Baked Goods, and there she was back at the fruit.

Another thing she liked: You never had to listen to a song in its entirety. From a grocery store speaker, all you can make out is one line, maybe two.

I love your smile—

You didn't even have to know who the singer was either.

She'd never timed it, but she estimated that the path she cut took about twenty minutes. This store was on the small side, certainly a third of what her HEB was back home. She found herself back at the avocados in half the time and at twice the speed.

That was another thing she disliked about this Stop 'n' Shop. Their fruits and vegetables were lumped into bins on slanted racks, and there was no thrill of picking one orange, or whatever it happened to be, from the bottom of a pyramid.

Around corners, she glanced. Over bananas, she peered.

No Pal and no Jenny. No Pal and no Jenny, when she knew she'd told the pair of them to stay where they were.

I recall it clearly. I noted that the time was 6:34 PM, on this date. I could call the little lady piling bell peppers for my witness, so they know and I know that I am not a dingbat.

She made one loop of the perimeter, then two. Of her fellow customers, there appeared to be only one, a little lady who tended to hover around the section dedicated to Pets.

Back at the avocado bin, April brainstormed what she ought to do, in the event of her abandonment by her daughters. This leap came as logically to her as anything. There had been no interval in which she examined the What Ifs in their cosmic many. Her brain, quite against her will sometimes, shut against all in-betweens. There was this and there was that. There was never and there was always. And here the hour had come in which it finally happened. The apocalypse did not come with horsemen and trumpets and the gnashing of teeth. It heralded the end (of April Nimitz, anyway) in a Stop 'n' Shop, enshrouded somewhere far, far within the Connecticut ether. No operatic, infernal descent, just a halting of progress, leaving her trapped to weave through the aisles of this grocery store like a wormy, white laboratory rat.

She supposed she would have to resort to self-cannibalism, when she ran out of food.

But all plans changed when April heard herself called Mom for the third time. She turned, and there in the parking lot were Miss Jenny and Miss Pal. They waved and beckoned, they smiled, on the impatient end of affability. Jenny had a plastic bag twisting and untwisting around her wrist.

April had been about to rush out when a girl from the register called her back. She paid for her potions and stalked to one of the land islands out in the lot, full of mulchy plants, where Jen and Pal waited.

"You make me run around the place, when I said for you to stay where you were." It made April so angry she huffed like an animal.

At this, Jenny's face split in a grin, and Pal's did, too. They hovered and mirrored each other for a moment, and when April was really about to lose her cool, Jenny lowered her eyes in an imitation of the honorable, elliptic beauty she had been at fifteen or sixteen, and asked her to guess who she and Pal had seen at the sushi bar, and subsequently trailed through the rest of Stop 'n' Shop, all the way out to his car?

April gawped. "Who?"

As if she should care, she stood, feeling blistered all over and rooted to the spot, having to hear the two of them go on about how they saw Sting, with someone who may or may not have been Trudie

Styler, and just had to follow to make sure they weren't crazy.

"You slunk around after them like a couple of ghouls to make sure you weren't crazy?"

"Well. Come on, wouldn't you have?" Jenny scowled. "Nothing have better happened to my shirt."

April wanted to know why her shirt mattered.

"He could be staying out here." Her eldest's tone was aghast, as one civilized person to one who willfully lives under a rock. "I could get it signed."

Pal broke in, not to make peace, but to point. "Your bag there is leaking." She sounded vaguely disgusted.

Down April's leg and into her sandal, oil dripped from a bottle with a hairline crack in one of its bottom corners. Judging by its faint green, it was the olive oil, extra virgin, so it caused April's feet to slip in her sandals whenever she took a step.

She did not like her daughters. It might have taken April long enough, just their whole lives, to have admitted it. The vaults of her skull echoed with such give to it, she was tempted to believe that she'd said the words aloud. She had not, of course. She did not think that she needed to. It was a common enough dislike, the kind built on a benign sort of resentment, not quite jealousy, that parents harbor. It was not jealousy because it did not psyche itself out with notions of possibility in the envious one, of the old sour-grapes variety, which insists (too much) that you could have done this or that, you just chose not to. It was not jealousy because she did not really want whatever Jen and Pal had.

April just wanted to know how they did it.

She did not want their education or their intellect or their youth. She did not want elasticity, energy, or estrogen. She did not want to relive it at all. Sometimes, you had to acknowledge the lateness of the hour. You had to be resigned to the fact of your one chance. At some point, your capacity for change is over.

She just wanted to know how they did it.

It was definite and also very vague. April thought of this word, It, in no exact terms, maybe related, in essence, to the phrase It Girl. An It Girl had grace and style and charm, was good-hearted and good-humored and good fun, a little mischievous, a little dapper. She always seemed to know what to do. She did not fly into rages. She was not arrogant. She had intuition.

April thought of a time when Pal came home from school, a winter day in her youngest's sophomore year. It was an unusual day, April remembered, because it had actually looked like winter when she left the courthouse at noon and found the parking lot covered in frost. It was a bit anticlimactic, just being this close to real snow, and no one was prepared for it. The schools let out by lunchtime, as did many businesses. Somewhere in the confusion of April leaving the courthouse and school letting out, Pal had called to get a ride home. She called the courthouse, the house phone three times, and twice called Beverly Across-the-way. Her next step, when it fell into place, was to accept a ride from a boy she knew in her class. His truck skidded into a culvert, a mile on foot from the Nimitz house if they were going to take the roads. But Pal knew a shortcut through the woods that would lead them right into her yard.

April knew as well as Pal that sometimes men appreciate being the one who is made to blush. It must have been, for the boy, something out of a fairy tale, he, a traveler, following an imp of a girl through bramble and briar. Everyone said of the day that the ice made for a spectacular picture. In the woods, the trees must have been knitted together in crystal. This was a memory that April predicted was stored in a vault within the boy's head to pit against dark times. He will have always had that walk through the icy woods with Paloma Nimitz. Even if that were it. Even if nothing ever came of it.

And April will always have had that, coming in through the front at the same time that they were coming through the back, hearing Pal huff and laugh and say, "Here we are." It was not a grand adventure. There were no dangers in these woods, nor anything wonderful. Pal had conjured in that boy these things, and it was a story he would always re-tell himself, of that time his car broke down.

It was a type of magic.

Some call it proof of God.

In April, it was not so much a feeling of "Here is what you could be" or "Here is what you should aspire to be", as "Here is what you ought to have been". As per the predestination of some divine, breathing intelligence, of whom you had nothing to do. And there was nothing you could do. This was how you were formed, wrongly, intentionally.

It made sense to dislike the thing you are meant to be but cannot.

Pal, the weirdo, the one who called a bomb threat when she was in seventh grade, made someone look fondly on her. She was a good dream to that boy then, and to no doubt a number of people since.

Should April hold Jenny responsible for the rough charm that endeared the world to both of her daughters, and not to her? No one would miss her, at the end of the day, and she was to be cremated, as per her own living will, so that there would be no place for anyone to make obligatory, mopey visits to. She, for one, had no intention of going back to Himmel Creek for a peek at Juan's headstone. She had asked him, flat out, "What is the point?"

He had said, "I want to be resurrected."

She had asked, "Since when?" It was firmly understood, up to then, that Juan was what they called a cafeteria Catholic; like someone who chooses lentil soup over chili, there were items of belief that he did not care to ingest, and he left them where they were under the hot lights. An afterlife was impossible, he'd said. It was the melancholic's relief, that you would never have to do it all over again.

And at that hour, on that day, he wanted to be resurrected.

They'd gone off the highway some minutes ago, and they had all come to a silent understanding that Pal was the leader. So, they followed, off the road and into one of those ovals of soft dirt that folks can pull their cars into and disembark at once for a walking trail. The trails themselves were marked on various tree trunks with a swatch of colored paint. Here, there were only two, the Blue Trail and the Yellow Trail. You took the Blue Trail around the lake, while the Yellow veered along one of the smaller streams dammed by a colony of beavers.

If the boys had been there, April could have persuaded them all to have a look down the Yellow Trail. Maybe they could catch sight of a mother beaver braving the channel on her way back to the dam.

As it was, Jenny wanted to get away from the bugs, and Pal surmised that the beavers wouldn't be out at this hour, anyway. Just as well April hadn't made the suggestion.

It was just as well, because they came down the path right onto a beach where folks who had summer cottages liked to picnic. The sand was empty, as were the tables, save for one of them, occupied by a bowl of tomatoes. Next to a bowl of tomatoes, you might find in its company a heap of forks, or a knife, or salt and pepper, and they sat here alone in what could have been a patch of their own sunlight. They were perfect, misshapen, with green at the top grading into red, from somebody's backyard vines. The misshapen ones, everyone knew, were the best of all, almost savory and not too juicy. It made April remember to ask her girls what they'd managed to get at the Stop 'n' Shop.

The girls seemed as transfixed by the tomatoes on the table as April. They snapped out of it when April brought her hands together, sharply, twice in both their right ears. Jenny, still as a dunce, handed her the bag without comment or turning her head. All along the walk, Jenny had been twisting the bag ends, so it now unfurled, wide open, at the stuff inside, which were two tomatoes, Beefsteaks, not Romas, and swollen all the way around in a malignant sphere, and the light which hit them faded their already horrible, measly pink to fleshy, white man color. The lemon took its form in that of a lemon juice carton, and the herbs that should have been fresh had been long, long ago dried, shredded, distributed and sealed into these two little red-lidded bottles that cost fifty cents more than the real thing.

How angry she would have been if only she had an audience. Jenny had her head cocked one way, Pal the other. Meanwhile, the bowl and its six tomatoes stared back. They might have been having a conversation; who knew if tomatoes were telepathic?

To be upstaged by the beauty of malformed fruit. It was enough to silence her.

So, she simply went to the table and tipped the bowl into the Stop 'n' Shop bag. Let them hide the hard, pink ones.

And the truly ludicrous thing about it was that her girls were appalled at her. Here they were, flailing and shouting and gasping, as though it were the most sacred of all decencies broken. "How could you?" they howled, like a lot of pansy-ish ghouls that would be insulted at your style of breathing. How could you, how could you, how could you. There are a great many horrible things you can do, and tomato snatching, April thought, were among the least of them.

They hadn't even bothered to pick up cucumbers.

That was when she noticed a third party. The shouting was not her daughters' duet but a trio, and this third marched from an azalea bush that was just outside April's periphery. A woman about her own age, white hair braided and bunned, turquoise jewelry clicking, brown eyes flashing, waved her freckled arm at the now empty picnic table. Her denim dress was dotted up and down in reds and greens and yellows and browns, and still April Nimitz did not put it together until the woman in the denim dress shrieked, "THAT WAS MY STILL-LIFE."

April hadn't seen it. Jenny had and Pal had, and it was all they could talk about on the walk around the lake and up to the garden behind the hotel's outdoor pool. They'd never chanced a painting like it, not in a museum, certainly not as a work-in-progress. It was a visual miracle. It was an abstract and a photographic reproduction at the same time. It was a Monet, an O'Keeffe, a Flemish master. It was plain and real and otherworldly. You almost didn't want to eat any fruit again.

"Who talks like that?" April barked at them.

Gushing, verbose. As if either of them knew anything about art.

Jenny stared. "You saw it, didn't you?"

"Oh," April huffed. "That masterpiece back there?"

Pal glared, the one who dragged her feet when April took her at seven or eight on a tour of the Blanton Museum in Austin. "Yes," she hissed now, "that one." She cocked her head. "What did you think of it?" Her voice was so newly low that even Jenny drew herself up.

What did April think of it? April, who hadn't seen it? Had very nearly put the very vision asunder by grabbing up the still life like a greedy little animal? Why should she develop a thesis now, let alone have to defend herself? Likely, it was a sub-par watercolor, or a mediocre oil. She knew ladies like the one in denim who trolled the galleries up here and flocked to the basements for the classes they offered, life drawing, studio portraits, charcoals and pastels, issuing semi-competent reproductions of apples and pears that would end up alongside their grandchildren's crayon doodles. Still, these gals fancied themselves artists. It made April sick.

So, she told Jenny and Pal that it wasn't anything she would call a national treasure. To herself, she held her glee as she'd held the shards to her breast. It was not a lie. How could she call the painting anything if she hadn't seen it?

April had always thought that if a great parting were to occur among the four Nimitzes, each of them conceding that this was it, they were done, and going their own ways, it would not be the cause of anything catastrophic. The girls would visit April in jail, if it ever came to that. They would surely have visited their father, were Juan in April's place. No, it would be an argument over nothing. You wanted to put it writ large, make it epic, An Argument Over Nothing. April had once wanted to kill Juan for getting a line in a song wrong. He had wanted to kill her because she had misplaced a pack of batteries. They had wanted to kill Jenny and Pal for doing something, being told to stop, and doing it again.

Now Pal wanted to kill April over a still-life of a bowl of tomatoes, and Jenny would not move to stop her.

So be it. I will take execution over abandonment any day.

April braced herself, and the knives did not come. Instead, her daughters shared a look, one look on top of another that had its own language, scoffed, turned and went up to join the party that everyone but April, it seemed, had been invited to.

"HERE WE ARE," she hooted, and no one heard.

The garlic was the one thing they got right. In the Arizona Room, April found an old Swiss army knife of Juan's and used the large blade to dice it as evenly as she could. The room stunk and her hands were sticky with the stuff. It was no easier trying to slice the tomatoes. April had never liked tomatoes in chunks, but, after a few ragged attempts, making slices that looked like beached pink jellyfish, she scored the blade into the tomato's pointed end to cut it into wedges. She told herself, the part of her that was forever the optimist, the perverted Girl Scout who issued such palsy encouragements as, "You got away with it", that this was an exercise in improvisation. April Hesse ought to know as well as anyone that you could make do with what you had and still produce a delightful meal.

The cups here were glass and she used them to mix the dressing. The wooden bowl that had been heaped with the courtesy gift of a fruit basket April dumped out on the bed and filled with the half-mooned tomatoes. If she'd had basil, she would have rolled the leaves into cigars and shredded them into the salad with her fingers. She had dried herbs and lemon juice in a squat, fruit-shaped jug. No cucumbers for added crunch. Not even the proper kind of tomato.

The oils made the wedges look greasy. The dried herbs were like specks of dirt. It was not the salad that the girls had enjoyed by any stretch of the imagination. It was a half-assed. It was less-than. It was certainly edible, if you did not care what your food looked like, if you did not care how it tasted.

Meanwhile, room service showed up with all the dainties and delicacies that the girls had ordered from downstairs, and they ringed the room on their steaming dishes, sucking the life out of her already limp tomato salad. There were fried portobello mushrooms accompanied by a high-end dill sauce that looked to April like ranch. There were grilled shrimp and pineapple kebabs. There was a cheese plate and a charcuterie plate. There were dark chocolates in delicate, molded swirls. There was a bowl of local berries, raspberries and blackberries, dusted with powdered sugar. There were maki rolls filled with salmon and topped with avocado. There were warm, covered bowls that held a better French onion soup than April had ever in her life produced.

Did they know what they were doing?

They must know.

Only Jenny and only Pal would know. And now they had roped Milly and Flora and Rossi and even Meryl Streep into it. They had set her up to fail.

Through all of this, Juan did not stir. And it was just as well. Were he animate, he might have been as oblivious as he was now, asleep. He would have helped himself to the treats brought up by room service. He would have asked what she was in such a funk about. He would have overlooked the tomato salad and gone right for the shrimp and pineapple kebabs.

"I am working under a great handicap," April would have told him.

As an experiment, she repeated it to the room in a voice of capital letters, to see if the volume would startle him. Juan could sleep through anything; he'd slept through thunderstorms and hail and the town siren issuing a tornado warning. Juan slept through a burglar stepping into the house (Pal, sadly, not yet born) and woke only when he heard April's shriek at running into the burglar as he was going out the front door.

Now, nothing.

April stood over him. His face was pink and swollen, full fathom five in deep sleep. The shape of him rose with each breath that was more of an emission, token air that escaped between his teeth and through his narrow, whisker-dotted nostrils. She picked up his arm by the wrist, watched the hand dangle. It reminded her of handling an overgrown Dammit Doll. The devil of it was that Juan was too heavy to hoist around the room by the ankles, into walls, onto tabletops.

She tried something that she used to do with Jenny when she was young and picky about what April put on her plate. If Jenny did not eat it, she would wear it. How many overturned dishes upon that sacred crown, the fruit of April's loins, how often

Jenny sat in shellshocked silence, her hair clumped with hot tetrazzini or whatever it was, her face blank, before April brought her to the sink to scrub the mess out. Usually, because the water at their house in Himmel Creek burst through the taps boiling or freezing, that snapped Jenny out of it.

April had the tomato salad in one hand, the plate flat on the palm like a waitress would do. She did not tip it or dump it. She simply let it fall in a graceful cascade, pushed by a breath of air, sending tomatoes, olive oil, and vinegar, plus the plate, down onto Juan's body in a beautiful splash.

She had never thought of Juan as a body until now.

When she woke that last morning and he did not, she had tried to affect the routine of a normal day. She'd showered, made coffee. She picked a few ripe tomatoes from the vines in the garden and talked awhile with Mrs. Glau. Juan was stiff and cool and, though ichor still circulated in her, April, too was stiff and cold. Was it only her heart that had died with him? It sounded mawkish, but it was fitting. Her heart had died, and the rest of her was still going, punishment for not having joined him.

Or try this: In the time it took for April Nimitz to shower, make coffee, pick tomatoes, and chat with Mrs. Glau, it was very possible that Juan had not yet died. It was very possible for April to have begun chest compressions. She might have stuck her finger down his throat to bring the poison up.

Mounting him, shifting him on the bed from his side to his back, April knotted her fists together and brought them down, bouncing them, looking silly, looking half-assed, not knowing, really, what a chest compression was. She imagined the same scenario, but on Juan's side, where he could just as easily be straddling her and bouncing his fists up and down on her chest, just as silly, just as half-assed. The Juan of the cross-country sojourn by Astro might not have been Juan at all. Might that have been, instead, a phantom? Might the girls have been ghouls, the very same ones who had delivered her here and were now playing a straddling game of their own, in which they delighted in quiet torment, the secret smiles, the deliberate failure to hear her?

In the old dream, creatures came wearing the skins of people she knew. They mostly favored her mother. They sat at her kitchen table, smiling. They said, "I'll pull out her eyes, and I'll pull out her teeth" before telling April what they would then do with her. It would have struck less terror, had the creatures appeared with fangs and claws.

The pounding exhausted her and her wrists were bruised. For all her labor, Juan snored once and went quiet. She doused him with ice from the bucket in the minibar. She smeared the upscale ranch and tomato oil into his face and hair. Making a prong of two fingers with her hand, she forked them into his eyes until they were red and puffed around and, very quickly, darkened to proper shiners. She scratched around his nose, caught one nostril with the diamond of her ring, and tore it with one quick jerk, and by the time she was done, there was little of Juan Nimitz to recognize.

Now she could begin to think of him as a body.

As for the appetizers, it had been hours, they were cold and would be unpleasant to eat. April herself could not stomach them, and did not trust them. She considered taking the old practice of Eat It or Wear It down into the Burnaby-Bravo party, showing her impious daughters what she was made of, for an audience that included Meryl Streep.

As it was, the food surrounded her on their varied plates and trays, placed haphazardly around the room on the dresser, the corner desk, on top of the television. Some were under the cover of fancy, heat-containing bell jars that now sweated what moisture the dish had left, the steam having evaporated and thinned to little runners that crept down the glass and leaked onto the plates. It had the look of a funeral feast. No, no, that was incorrect. It had the look of a party, one that you had built your life up to, one in which you had consented to every detail, down to your clothes, only to be stood up by your many (or in this case two) esteemed guests. You sat in your party frock and your finery, in the middle of a banquet that no one showed up to, and what was worse, you knew that every one of your guests had instead gone off to make a party of their own, where they could laugh at you with abandon. Its violence would be in its exclusion, its suggestion, its constant needling of her insides, squeezing them, twisting them, making them into pretzels. She would be left to her own devices while they all caroused in the ballroom.

That, to April, was Pandemonium. Such things are Pandemonium when all that remains is your pride.

"You lump," she spat at Juan. "I'll show you. And them."

The sun had set. The hour was dark. They were miles from anywhere.

Now, April Nimitz would go downstairs.

She stepped into the hallway barefoot. All suggestion that there had been or ever were any other guests, trays for room service, Do Not Disturb signs, were gone. April heard her small movements magnified in the vaults and corners, the walls around her having grown as they do when a place is empty, save for you. One light blinked and went out, then another, then the one farthest down, closest to the elevators. The dingy light, doing at last what day and full-powered fluorescents had been able to mask, summoned every peck of dirt, every stain, every strange smell in their corporeal nastiness out from wherever they'd hid during the sunny hours. It was not that April could see the filth; she could feel it. She rolled grime between her fingers and found that her nails were gritty and black underneath. Her feet crunched along the carpet, which was either sticky and dried into stiff, shaggy patches or foully damp, and she winced at the squish between her toes. Had they all purged themselves on this carpet? For the filth had an oiliness to it, a hormonal stink that did not come from spilled Pepsi-Cola. It filled April with visions of every guest in the hotel's history voiding themselves, bowels, bladder, stomach, testes, having abandoned any idea of shame the moment the fluids hit the floor. No one to scrub it out, no one to burn it away with bleach.

Imagine the night that Juan shat himself at the Fielding's dinner table. Had he abandoned shame when he saw in the bathroom what he had done to his clothes, and after, when he saw what he'd done to Simon Fielding's deerskin chair? There had been a moment, perhaps a full minute, wherein Juan's face became a perfect blank. Chaos ensued, especially with Val Fielding, who was a self-proclaimed alarmist, who had acted the part like a virtuoso when she jumped to get cleaning supplies, then dropped them when she bleated her conviction that they ought to call an ambulance. Juan had not blinked. He did not move, had stood straighter than usual, barely breathing. In that moment or minute, he seemed to have given up the ghost. April stepped in to say that calling an ambulance for a man who hadn't made it to the bathroom in time was overkill. She had been prepared that night to hoist him up, tuck him under her arm like a mannequin and march home across the street that way.

Evil will out, she thought then, and thought it now.

There were two windows at either end of the hall, and April looked out into one to find the parking lot deserted, the lights out, the sky clouded, the moon snuffed.

Finally, it's happened. Finally, they've done it. Clever girls are Jenny and Pal, to have conducted this whole scheme in the way they had. Finally, a trembling April thought, they've gone. This is where they meant to leave me all along. A clever scheme.

The last knocked itself between her hemispheres in the elevator riding down, and continued when she reached the lobby, when she began to repeat it aloud. A clever scheme, a clever scheme, a clever scheme. It became entwined with the other phrase, the first one, until it fell into a singsong pattern.

A clever scheme, a clever scheme. Finally, it's happened. Finally, it's happened. A clever scheme, a clever scheme.

She descended to waterlogged magazines and vegetation growing in the cushions. A hole eaten by rot into the wood paneling. The translated Bible whose pages looked grey and furred—that is, what April could see of it through the scum over its glass case. The plants had dried out long ago. The bell at the reception desk was flaky with rust. A dog, perhaps Meryl Streep's, left a pile of turds that crumbled when April stepped into it.

A clever scheme, to do it this way. To lure me, then laugh into the ether when my back is turned. Finally, it's happened.

She gathered her breath with every intention of shrieking until her she wore herself out. She'd been about to release a good, blood-curdling one when, in that brief stillness, she thought, then knew what she heard to be music. With the music came singing, and she followed it through the corridors, through the smells, into the ballroom where the Burnaby-Bravo party continued, now in full swing, on the other side of the closed doors.

April peeked.

Here they were, the Burnabys and the Bravos and the Ogawas, and there in a spot-lit corner which drew all attention like a spell where Jenny and Pal, yowling into the tinny microphones that came with the karaoke machine. They were hamming it up, free arms flung out operatically, free hands playing with the audience in a series of stage-sensual gestures, fingers curling, beckoning, spreading, stroking the mic heads. They were sozzled. They were stoned. They had nearly forgotten where they were and as for what purpose, it had slipped their minds completely, as far as April could see.

They had talked about Daddy. Had they, on Juan's side of the veil, talked about April? In their respect for the dead, their father had become a pseudo saint. Had they at least bestowed that status upon April, that she'd had her troubles, but did her best? It was the phrase they used about Juan. "He did his best." He had not, and neither had she, but would it be too much to allow her that, in respect for the dead?

They were singing an R&B version of a Disney song, the version that was performed by pop stars. This was from *Pocahontas*, it was meant to be a duet between the Powhatan princess and John Smith that had not made it into the movie itself, but was gussied up for the end credits so as to keep audiences in their seats that much longer, but to April, really only ever served to evacuate people from the theater before the lights came on. Raffi and Gabe went to just about every Disney movie, and they had all the Happy Meal toys. The Ben Ami family stereo was usually on a cycle beginning with the *Aladdin* soundtrack and ending with *Hercules*. There was always a duet, Sting and Sade or Mariah Carey and a one-hit wonder.

Jenny was John Smith, Pal was Pocahontas. The ballroom was Broadway. The karaoke screen corrected them when they stumbled, which they often did. When they could not make out the lyrics on the small screen, they just repeated the song's chorus and title, "If I Never Knew You", until it finished. They collapsed into each other, giggling, snorting. Pal threw up when they stumbled away from the machine.

It made April burn, for her daughters were shameless. She had often told her girls how embarrassed she was for them, but never before had she really felt it.

Not that it mattered. Their performance, sloppy and inept as it was, had won Jenny and Pal a standing ovation. Milly Ogawa embraced Pal, Flora Ogawa Jenny. Someone had red roses. Someone had yellow roses. Someone had a day lily. They threw them, laurels for Mesdames Jenny and Pal Nimitz.

Jenny, who embraced perfect strangers, her bad breath.

Pal, who had puke down her t-shirt.

April, who howled, "HAVE SOME POISE, YOU CREATURES", loud and clear, all capitals.

This to a fair little mob, to which her voice might have been as a mouse's or a snail's or a sparrow's or a rabbit's, softer than an unfurling blossom. They called for an encore, and the girls ate it up with spoons. Tinny mics in hand, they did "If I Never Knew You" once more, and maybe this time they had sobered up, and they would remember their mother, their only mother, who might, as they collect their laurels, be turning down a dark corridor where the floorboards were like paper and where one false step could be the end of her.

They found her, Pal first, then Jenny, and they looked away from April, shedding the years and becoming slouchy teens before her very eyes. They held off connecting again over the crowd, just as they had done when April had to pick one of them up somewhere. Sometimes they introduced her with pride. Others, they were too ashamed. Had it been like it was with most pubescent pupae, who are embarrassed by the idea of having been birthed at all, let alone having parents? Was this Their Moment? Would they just rather that April wasn't there?

That woman Dawna knocked her, shoulder-to-shoulder, and had the nerve to take April in, head-to-toe, and had the greater nerve to frown at HER.

While her girls made a conjoined mess of themselves.

They sang "Ladies Who Lunch", and their voices were the right amount of rough for it. Pal looped her ankle around Jen's in an attempt to do a jazzy little dance, where she and Jen were meant to put one leg in front of the other or some such thing, instead causing both to fall, cackling, to the floor. Jenny knocked into the mic stand and sent a staticky shriek across the ballroom. It took two tries for Pal to get to her feet, and it was one of the Ogawa sisters who pulled Jenny up. The mic picked up every little dust mite, and Jenny's voice was magnified as she fell into Milly Ogawa's shoulder, sobbing, "You're a real mother to me, you know that? A real mother, you really are. A real mother to me."

Finally, April could bear no more of it. Had they been children, she might have been able to threaten them with excommunication. As children, the horror of it would have made them love her. Jenny was thirty-eight. Pal was twenty-six. They supported themselves. They had been worn thin. What did they need April Nimitz for? What a relief it might be to them, to have it in writing that their responsibilities, of the continued stewardship, housing, and affection for their mother until her death, were now null in void.

So, she shouted for the pair of them to get off the stage.

To think, this could have all gone perfectly. If April had to think about it, there was chance upon chance.

She lay in the bed she shared with her husband, in their house in Himmel Creek. It was one of those moments in which they both woke at the same time before going back to sleep a little while later. A little while could be as long as an hour. They would watch Julia Child make Queen of Sheba cake. They would chat. Juan might doodle, April might read. They might make love or masturbate together. And, just as they had woken, just as inexplicably, they would be out cold and snoring until the real hour, the true wake-up hour. Neither of them had ever mentioned what was said or done in these lapses, no reason, other than the fact that April and Juan did not count them the same way as if they had happened in the daytime. Not like the old saying, "Whatever happens in Vegas stays in Vegas." It was like a dream.

Juan was there and he was awake. April was awake, too. They did not move to look at the other. They did not move at all, save for their eyes, which noted the pattern of light and shadows, leaves and veiny branches, making stars, making a marching line of bears, cubs following the leader.

She was asking Juan, "What'll happen if it's me who's gone first?"

He told her, "Then I guess I'll have to be the responsible one. Get the body people here, whoever handles the remains. Get the house in order."

"Would you stay on here?"

"Maybe."

April pressed. "Because it's too big, if it's just going to be you living here."

"Well." Juan mused. "I don't suppose the girls would mind coming out for a couple of weeks."

April could imagine that. The days would be held up by a bolster of jokes and excursions, a drive to Fredericksburg, a segue from funeral expenses to something Juan heard in a dog food ad. It might be fun. Nothing would get done. The fuel would run out and the humor would dry up and Juan would be reduced, more or less, to the way he was right here, right now, straight as a log in his bed, his toes pointed up.

April sighed. "I'm so tired."

"Then go back to sleep," Juan told her.

"Are you getting up?" April asked.

"Not decided yet."

"I'm so tired."

"Then go back to sleep."

She ran out of the ballroom and bolted the doors behind her. Just beyond their reach, she waited. April Nimitz had the impression that she'd just now managed to contain a whole disaster in one room.

Her memory of it, removed though she was from the event by mere moments, was hazy. Hazy, that is, as a whole. There were pieces that came forward and froze, and these she lined up in her mind like triptychs. Here, for one, was an altarpiece dedicated to the moment in which Jenny and Pal sang, under the influence of divine inspiration, to the masses. They were haloed in gold leaf. Their voices were lettered scrolls. And in a side-panel was April, a scowling devil under a bush. And another, in which Jenny and Pal receive the Annunciation. This one was terrible to behold: the Annunciation itself, delivered by a servile Peter Engels, also wreathed in gold leaf, is so awful that, upon hearing it, Jenny and Pal were poised to attack. April, again in a side-panel, again a devil, again scowling, cowered from her place under the bush. Here, as in Bosch, the side-panels showed a place that could have been feet away from the action in the center or in another dimension. April could have been in their face. April could have been across the room, which was miles away.

But all was said and done.

Now they knew.

The triptychs were in chronological order. It took April less time to view them all than if she'd been let to dawdle in a supermarket. She was proud of the fact that her mind worked the way it did, for as long as it had. The thing about that, though, was the effect it had of making the ugliest recollections stand out in sharp, gorgeous relief, like the art on the elevator doors. Jenny's eyes, the moldy yellow and red of them, the hot tears, the black, spidery lashes running into mucous trails. Pal's mouth, pink and wide, the outrage, the undulating tongue, the rows of teeth, the lips cracked and papery. Indeed, they were creatures.

April had to think about that, being their creator. Not that she would ever claim to have molded them like clay from her own two hands. Could she prostrate herself forever for the unluckiness of time and place, of Jenny seeing this, Pal hearing that, just because they happened to be in the same house when this happened, when April said that? A lot of your growing up is circumstance, simple as that.

You weren't knocked up. You wanted to be a mother.

Nix that last.

You wanted to be an anchor. Otherwise, who else would keep you out of their own volition?

April Hesse Nimitz permitted herself to wail. The sound bounced off the vaulted lobby and broke into shards. There was no one else to hear.

There was no one else to hear, unless April wanted to open the ballroom doors.

She approached it. She touched it. She even gave the handles a tug. And yet, she knew that if she were to take both handles in order to fling the doors wide, and the snarling, the howling, the nails and teeth that were Jenny and Pal would come at her with a force that would tear her to shreds and leave only a stain. As she felt she deserved. As she needed. After decades like centuries of coaxing, then pleading, then demanding for her daughters to tell her that they hated her, now they would do it. At last.

What April prepared for, what she had been practically chomping at the bit for, was not silence. She'd flung the doors wide. She'd stood, not prostrate because that was not how you showed yourself before a fight. She'd stood tensed and fists balled, and did not know what to do when she saw that the ballroom was deserted. It had been minutes, ten at most. And the whole bawdy affair, with its bouquets and balloons and shrimp cocktails and melting birthday cake and karaoke machine and its guests, seemed never to have happened. Yes, there remained bits and bobs, a sagging streamer, a few balled napkins, the flowers themselves dried into twigs, a staleness in the air, as though this was all the room had ever contained.

April fled from it.

Better she'd opened the doors and released a whole demonic legion. Better she'd stepped through and found herself trapped there and made to listen to a litany of her faults, read by her daughters, by Juan, across eternity. Virgil showed Dante the Infernal circles, in which the worst of the worst became a sort of punitive snack enjoyed by Lucifer, who worked a sinner in his jaws until the end of time like a piece of bubble gum.

Better any and all of that than a void.

Her girls should want to kill her.

Beverly was like a mother to them, after all.

J uan was gone, too.

April could not bring herself to take the elevator, for reasons that were practical. It might get stuck. April would be trapped. She did not worry for food or water, only the narrow dimensions, and the fact that all she would have to look at was a scene of cunnilingus between a maiden and an octopus.

There were worse fates, she knew.

It occurred to her that any number of similar things could happen in a hotel as big as this, an empty one. Doors blew shut and locked. Beams fell. Floorboards rotted, and with one misstep you descended into another small space, a leg broken, an internal bleed, and no one to hear you.

At one of the Holiday Inns, she'd watched that movie *Alien* on TV with Pal while they waited for Jenny to get done blow-drying her hair. The tagline was, to April, more terrifying than the whole movie: "In space, no one can hear you scream." It was something that Juan used to say to her, too, when they were prostrate on the screened porch in the Himmel Creek house, too heavy to move, too drunk to reason, and the sparks overhead that were planes in the sky had the look of flying saucers. April asked Juan if Neil Armstrong said that.

No lack of food, water, even air could outweigh the awfulness of being trapped in your own stink, having to hear only your voice, to touch only yourself, and no one to touch you.

So, she took the stairs. They creaked underfoot, and shortly after she began bounding up them, her foot caught the edge of one step halfway, slipped, and while she did not feel her knee crack, she had to contend with its consequences. The rest of the climb was slow, one foot at a time until her knee went out from under her and she crept on all fours, like an animal, favoring her injury down the hall, the Kansas Room, the Alaska Room, the Rhode Island Room, craning her head to read the plaques until she came to her own, the Arizona Room.

She brushed the fug and hair and crap, what Juan called dust bunnies, from her dress. The carpets were thick with it, as though ages had passed since they last saw a vacuum. She waited, one leg lifted, ears alert.

Is anybody there? Does anybody care?

Am I pretty? Do I party?

What pit have I dug for myself?

She faced the door and turned the handle. It was unlocked. It was bright and clean, waiting for her. It smelled of bouquets, consolation carnations. The bed was empty. Juan was not there. There was no indentation in the mattress. The covers had been pulled tight. The pillows were plump. She would be warm. She could bathe and get into bed. Lay head to pillow, put out the light, close her eyes, bid farewell. She could say now that she got away with it.

"Fear no more the heat o' the sun," as Shakespeare had said, "nor the furious winter's rages."

And how tired she was. Her organs were as an anchor. Her bones, her cracked knee whose hurt she could not feel. She swayed on her feet. Here was the edge, the edge of a bed that seemed to have grown from a queen to a king. Her jaw slacked and there was drool on her chin. Her eyes clouded. She ran a hand over her red hair and looked at the fistful that fell to the floor.

What was her name?

That bothered her.

What was her name?

That perked her up. She nearly fell asleep on her feet. Her balance was poor, from exhaustion or otherwise, and the sight of the bed made her stagger into the clothes horse. There were her blouses, still stained. Here was her breast, a throbbing balloon. Here was infection, already crusting, already yellow and salty around the nipple. She would sooner look at these things, she knew, than to have to glimpse the bed again.

Not that there was anything terrible about it. The pillows were plumped and the covers were neat, tucked with hospital corners. The only thing that had changed in this minute or hour, however long she'd been swaying at its edge, was the mattress, just a hollow space fitted to her limbs and weight, a divot in the pillow where her head would rest.

If I lie down, I'll never get up.

She'd said that before, on lazy weekends, on days when her bones felt the years or a rainy day.

No one will wake me this time.

And she hid her face from it because there was nowhere she could go to escape a sight so coolly grotesque. She wept. She swayed. Her tears were sticky and hot and alive. Her fingers burned with them, and she let them run over her palms, erasing the dirt and dust bunnies, emptying her, making her clean.

What is my name?

What is my name?

It was not a prayer, not her notion of one. She was only doing what she had seen her daughters do in a Holliday Inn parking lot. Her daughters were Jenny and Pal. They had it in them to crack open the heavens.

She almost had it. Her chest heaved and took some of the ache from her breast. My name is. My name is. My name is. My name is.

"Aaaaa-prilll."

It was a small noise, and it brought her to the window. She parted the drapes and cranked the handle that wound the panes out, and was halfway over the edge when she heard it again.

"Aaaa-prilll."

She called, "Jen?"

She called, "Pal?"

She looked up. The sky was dark, save for one line down the middle of them that could split the heavens and flood the parking lot with silver light, like morning.

"AAAA-PRIL."

That was Jen.

"AAAA-PRIL."

That was Pal.

"AAAA-PRIL."

They were in the parking lot. They were at the lake, in the woods.

Her leg was over the window ledge, the good one, let herself drop into the hydrangea bush below.

"AAAA-PRILLL."

Louder now. She crunched and crashed her way out of the bush, trailing blue petals, leaves in her hair. She wept freely. If she were to look into a mirror or into the lake, might her face be round and red, the way her eyes felt? No matter, for it lifted her from the ground—or made her light on her feet, at the very least.

I am April.

I am not April Hesse.

I am not April Nimitz.

I am not Hasi.

I am all of those things, which, in conglomeration, make April.

I can walk. I can see and hear. I can run.

Toward the crack, which beamed and widened, and trickled dawn's silver light like good oil.

"AAAA-PRILLLL."

She did not sprint, not at first, going on hesitant, feeble tiptoes, mindful of her knee. There was nothing to run from, only toward, and this thought spurred her in picking up the pace, a brisk walk, still hobbling, then a trot, then a gallop.

"AAAAP-PRILLL."

That was Juan. Juan, who was a creature like her.

April howled for them to stay where they were, for them not to leave her. If she could reach the crack, she would find them. If she could split the sky, she would wake. She would wake and do what? Apologize? Prostrate herself? Go across the street and embrace Beverly, who was like a mother to her children?

She ran and grasped, fell, ran and grasped again, ran and fell, in case the fissure narrowed and the sky closed, in case she grasped and fell again and changed her mind about waking, just to spite them.

Acknowledgements

To my family, who are loving and supportive, unlike the Nimitz clan.

To my husband, Michael.

About the Author

Pam Jones was born in 1989 and raised on the East Coast. She now lives in Austin, Texas with her husband. She studied creative writing at Hampshire College and is at work on her next book. She released *The Biggest Little Bird* with Black Hill Press/1888 Center, and *Andermatt County: Two Parables* with The April Gloaming. Her short fiction has appeared in *The Cost of Paper* and *Boned: A Collection of Skeletal Fiction*.

About the Publishing Team

Nate Ragolia is a lifelong lover of science fiction and its power to imagine worlds more hopeful and inclusive than the real one. His first book, *There You Feel Free*, was published by 1888's Black Hill Press in 2015. Spaceboy Books reissued it in 2021. He's also the author of *The Retroactivist*, published by Spaceboy Books. He founded and edited *BONED*, a literary magazine, has created webcomics, currently hosts a podcast, and pets dogs.

Shaunn Grulkowski has been compared to Warren Ellis and Phillip K. Dick and was once described as what a baby conceived by Kurt Vonnegut and Margaret Atwood would turn out to be. He's at least the fifth best Slavic-Latino-American sci-fi writer in the Baltimore metro area. He's the author *Retcontinuum*, and the editor of *A Stalled Ox* and *The Goldfish* for 1888/Black Hill Press.